The Classic Rockers Reunion with Death

By

RJ McDonnell

© 2012

Killeena Publishing
PO Box 3611
Scranton, PA 18505

First edition
This book is a work of fiction. Any similarity to real people, alive or
dead, is purely coincidental and not intended by the author.

Printed in the United States

ISBN: 978-0-9814914-7-9

www.rjmcdonnell.com

rj@rjmcdonnell.com

Chapter 1

Louie Amanesco was a creature of habit. In spite of the fact that a light snow was falling when he left work, he still drove six miles up Route 307 to his favorite watering hole for a couple of beers with the regulars. Upon exiting the bar an hour later, flakes were still falling at a steady pace. He used his combination brush and scraper to dust snow off of his windows.

Another of his habits included driving 10 miles an hour over the posted speed limit, even on snowy January evenings. His workday as superintendent for the family's construction business had been as uneventful as every other one since the housing bubble burst. His wife of 25 years had left him as soon as his income could no longer support her shopping addiction.

There were no pressing matters awaiting him at home. He had no children or grandchildren to check on. Sure there was a 12-pack of beer in the refrigerator, although a hot toddy seemed more attractive at the moment. But Louie couldn't bring himself to ease off of the accelerator as snowflakes blew through the barren trees of Northeastern Pennsylvania. He wondered if maybe he would be considered a thrill seeker or just a guy in his late 50s who was set in his ways.

Cresting a rise by Lake Scranton, Louie spotted three deer crossing the road at the bottom of the hill 200 yards ahead, making their way toward the lake. Slamming on the brakes would have sent his SUV out of control. Louie laid on his horn while flashing his high beams on and off as fast as possible. The two larger deer showed Louie why they managed to survive hunting season, which had just ended a few weeks earlier, by trotting out of harm's way. But a yearling doe froze in her tracks and stared directly at him.

The outside lanes of the four lane highway displayed uncovered paths where tire friction had left a final modicum of safety for stragglers still making their way home. The yearling straddled the uncovered paths. Louie tapped the brakes lightly and felt the rear end slide a few inches to the right. The passing lane was covered by about two inches of powder. If he changed lanes he would not only have to deal with the traction issue, but also hope that the deer remained perfectly still because he would be passing directly in front of her.

The pitch of the hill was more severe as he was now about 80 yards from impact. He tapped his brakes again and slid once more. The instant he regained traction he steered into the passing lane. At 40 yards he refocused on the yearling in time to see a large buck leap over a rock and onto the highway. Louie knew that the brakes were no longer an option. Whatever was going to happen was out of his control.

The buck smashed hard into the yearling's butt, propelling her all the way across the highway. The buck lost his balance and skidded forward. Louie turned the steering wheel a couple of inches toward the far right lane, just in time to avoid the back legs of the buck. When his tires found purchase on the blacktop tire paths he cut the wheel back and regained control. He stroked his salt & pepper goatee and let out a deep breath as the SUV decelerated on the flat stretch at the bottom of the hill.

Louie made a right at the light onto Lake Scranton Road, and a left onto the Elmhurst Boulevard. His family earned huge profits prior to the housing market crash, transforming the more remote sections of the winding Elmhurst Boulevard from a deathtrap for young drivers with more balls than brains, into an upscale custom home paradise for those who valued huge lots and much privacy. The close call with the deer had his heart racing and his mind on doubling the liquor in his hot toddy.

Louie's house wasn't immediately visible from the road. Two

three-foot stone pillars, topped with ornate light fixtures, marked the entrance to his driveway. The lights were on a timer, so he had no trouble emptying his mailbox to the right of the driver's side pillar. He then dropped the SUV into 4-wheel drive and climbed the hill to his beautiful Tudor home. It was one of his few possessions that survived the messy divorce with Rose.

After parking in the garage and entering the house through the kitchen door, Louie placed his briefcase on the kitchen table and hung up his coat. He considered departing from his routine of immediately checking email, but decided it would be best to take care of that before erasing his close call with Bambi & friends with a double shot of Wild Turkey. So he put on a heavy green sweater, unlocked the French doors to the backyard, walked around his covered pool, and unlocked the door to his home office.

Turning on the lights, Louie was startled to see a familiar face in his favorite wing chair. "What the hell are you doing here?"

Louie's guest removed a Sig Sauer P220 Compact. "Open up the wall safe, Louie, and you won't get hurt."

"The wall safe? Are you kidding me? You're not going to fire that thing."

At the flick of a finger the intruder turned on the pistol's tactical light and laser option, illuminating a red dot on Louie's green sweater.

"It's beginning to look a lot like Christmas all over again, Louie. Now, unless you want me to add a whole lot more red to that sweater I suggest you open the wall safe."

"There's nothing of value in there. You should know that."

The intruder stood up. "I didn't ask for an inventory or an argument. Either open the safe right now or I'll blow a hole through your kneecap. If that's what it takes to show you I'm serious, then so be it."

Louie had nothing to hide in the safe, so he opened it up. The intruder walked behind Louie and nestled the gun into the soft spot at the base of his skull.

"Take a close look out the back window."

Louie turned to his right and felt the gun remain pressed against the back of his head. He tried to think of what could possibly be in the safe to warrant this behavior. It was the last thought to ever cross his mind.

Chapter 2

Returning to work after a two week Christmas vacation was very difficult this year. I usually only take off for one week, but after four months of grueling work on my first serial murder case, my psyche and my girlfriend both needed more time. Watching Kelly get ready to greet her second graders put my funk on hold for a few minutes. But once she departed it dawned on me that I had no active cases waiting for me at the office, and I would probably have to stalk a cheating spouse or pour over the financial records of a businessman suspected of embezzlement. It reminded me of the time my old club band warmed up a headliner for the first time. Playing in front of a Saturday night audience of over 10,000 people was a tremendous rush. Playing in front of 12 drunks and two hookers the following Tuesday night captured my current state of mind.

The cloud lifted briefly when I walked into my office and was greeted by my administrative assistant, Jeannine Joshlin. She spent the holidays with her boyfriend (and my former band mate) who had been on the road touring for five months before returning in mid-December. Her enthusiasm was not contagious.

Once the formalities were out of the way I asked, "Any messages on the machine?"

"Just one - from a Mrs. Vincigura. She said something about her husband's behavior at his company Christmas party."

"Damn!" I shouted, and Jeannine's seven-month-old German shepherd barked from under her desk.

"Maybe you can talk with her and let Cory do the field work if she wants a full investigation," she said.

Cory is my part-time photographer and stakeout specialist who suffers from Tourette's syndrome and, along with Jeannine, used to be clients of mine when I worked as a counselor at an outpatient mental health center for two years before starting my private investigator's training. He was originally hired specifically for this type of assignment.

I reached out and Jeannine handed me the pink message slip. "Let's hope she got tired of waiting for me to call her back."

"The call came in yesterday, on New Year's morning," she said.

"Wonderful. A cheating husband and a New Year's resolution rolled into one. Was she bitching about him watching football games, too?"

"Aren't you Mr. Grumpypuss this morning?"

Wishing I had sworn off divorce cases as my New Year's resolution, I reluctantly called Mrs. Vincigura. She turned out to be a sixty-something know-it-all who interrupted me incessantly. I tried explaining the changes in California divorce law that took place since her days as a legal secretary in the 1970s. But Mrs. V. insisted that she was the expert on the subject, and that my job was to shut up and help "take her husband to the cleaners" in divorce court. Since arguing with her simply invited more interruptions, I quoted her a rate that was quadruple my usual charge, and I asked for a $10,000 retainer, fully expecting her to insult me and hang up.

Instead she said, "You better be worth it, hot shot. I'll be there with a check at 2:30."

She hung up before I could think of another way to keep her retched demeanor out of my life.

I received a call from my mother at 11:00 AM. "How about ringing in the New Year by having lunch with me?"

"Don't you mean *lunch with us*?"

"Now that the holidays are over, your father has been making up for lost time mourning O'Malley's death at Casey's Bar."

"Will that be our luncheon conversation?" I asked.

"I do have a special reason for inviting you today, but it has nothing to do with your father's tradition of grieving with Guinness."

"I'll head over now. I have a 2:30 appointment coming in."

My parents live on the outskirts of the Little Italy section of San Diego. If America's Finest City had a Little Ireland section I have no doubt that I'd be heading in that direction. My father is a retired San Diego Police Detective, and affiliates himself almost exclusively with the law enforcement branch of the Friendly Sons of St. Patrick. My mother was cutting hard rolls when I entered the kitchen.

"You sounded a little stressed on the phone, Mom. What's going on?"

"I'm using leftover turkey from Christmas. I hope you don't mind."

Mom's not one to jump right into the main topic. I gave her a kiss on the cheek.

"It looks delicious. Does Dad know I'm here?"

"Bob Kerrigan picked him up before I called you."

"I know how he gets after a cop buddy dies. I'd offer to have a talk with him, but I think we both know it wouldn't do any good."

"That's not why I asked you to come over today, Jason. Have a seat and get started on your sandwich. Would you like a cup of tea?"

"Tea sounds great, Mom. It's barely into the 50s out there. I hate the winter."

"I know, son. Can you imagine how difficult it is for your poor Uncle Patrick in Northeastern Pennsylvania? I spoke with him last night and his porch thermometer read 14 degrees."

"He stuck a check for $20 in my Christmas card again this year. I thought you were going to tell him that I'm fully grown and gainfully employed."

"It's Patrick's way of telling you that he loves you, in spite

7

of the fact that he hasn't gotten along with his brother since the 60s."

"How is he doing?"

"Not well, Jason. Not well at all."

"Is he still grieving for Aunt Megan?"

The tea kettle whistled and Mom held the string on an Irish Breakfast tea bag while pouring. She wrapped the string around the cup handle and tucked the green paper label underneath before adding a dollop of milk.

"I'm sure that five years seems like a very long time to you, but Patrick and Megan were closer than any couple I've ever known. He'll grieve until he meets up with her in heaven. But that's not the source of his pain right now."

"What's going on?" I asked.

"Patrick's best friend was murdered last Thursday night," she said, and blessed herself.

"That's terrible, Mom. Do the police have any leads?"

"Patrick said that he was found in his home office under an empty wall safe. Apparently the Scranton Police have assigned a rookie detective to head up the investigation."

"I don't see Uncle Patrick being best friends with a bum. Why the low priority?"

"There's a serial killer running around the area and their Homicide Division is focused on catching him," she said.

"What makes them think he wasn't murdered by the serial killer?"

"He's called the Society Page Slasher. All of his victims have been women who have appeared on the Society Page of the local paper within a month of their deaths. All of them had their throats slashed. Patrick's friend was shot in the back of the head."

"I imagine Uncle Patrick will be running his own investigation," I said.

"Patrick is an insurance investigator. His specialty is the recovery of stolen property. He's never worked a homicide investigation in his life. When he called last night he asked if I thought your father might be willing to bury the hatchet and help him out."

"What did you tell him?"

"I told him about O'Malley, and how he wasn't able to help you with your last case because he was beside himself with grief. I didn't want to tell him that his brother hasn't uttered a kind word about him in our 34 years of marriage."

"I'm surprised Dad didn't give you a hard time about keeping in touch."

"I didn't really have much contact with Patrick until Megan died. She was one of the kindest, most generous women I've ever known. She and I made a few attempts over the years to try to get those two to reconcile. Megan once told me that the biggest arguments they ever had involved those reconciliation talks. We finally gave up on them, but kept our friendship very much alive."

"What would you like me to do?"

"I know you have clients here, son. Maybe you could give Patrick a call and be a sounding board. Offer him some advice on how you would proceed with the investigation. If you think your father could lend a hand, ask him as if you were asking about one of your own cases."

"I'll be glad to do that, Mom."

She wrote down Patrick's home and cell phone numbers on a slip of paper. "Please remind Kelly that I was sincere when I offered to help chaperone her second graders field trip to the Wild Animal Park."

"I will, Mom. And, I'll let you know how it goes with Uncle Patrick."

Mrs. Vincigura looked every bit as formidable in person as she sounded on the phone. She was built like a 50s Buick with a black helmet of hair, and enough platinum around her neck to plate a front bumper. I stood and extended my hand.

"Sit down and listen up, young man. I'm going to tell you

all about that no good philandering husband of mine, so pay attention."

Instead of arguing with the woman I reminded myself that I had priced in a huge asshole tax. So I folded my hands on the desk in front of me and assumed a state of mind that my college friends and I called AEM. It stands for Automated Educational Mode. We used it when we were stuck listening to lectures by boring professors who considered their every word a priceless commodity. On the outside we appeared interested and even jotted the occasional note. On the inside we were somewhere between daydreaming and recovering from the previous night's revelry.

Mrs. Vincigura was quite content to drone on for a half hour without a break. At long last she asked, "What do you think?"

"The man sounds insufferable. I don't know how you put up with him."

Satisfied that I was appropriately sympathetic, she forked over the hefty retainer. "How do you propose we catch him in the act?"

"Before we get into specifics let me ask you a question. Why now? He's obviously been carrying on behind your back for years."

"It was that horrible Christmas party. Right after the formal dinner his boss led him into a conference room, gave him a big bonus and told him he'd be sorely missed on the sales staff when he reached mandatory retirement age at the end of the month. Vinnie gave me the news and the check right away. Before my purse was snapped shut he was making eyes at Doris Dyer, who was the event coordinator and a member of our country club. I don't care what he did out on the road, but I'll be damned if he's going to make a fool out of me in front of my friends at our country club."

"Do you really want the photos to use at a divorce action, or are you thinking of blackmailing him into behaving at the club?"

"I don't feel the need to explain myself to the help, Mr. Duffy. Do what I tell you and we'll get along just fine. If not, I'll find someone else who will."

I spent the next half hour hammering out the details of our contract. It was worded so that I could technically have Cory do most of the surveillance work, and to minimize future contact with Mrs. V. By the time she departed I was drained.

I called Cory and explained his assignment. You'll rarely hear me recount Cory's exact words because his Tourette's syndrome makes it difficult for the uninitiated to focus on anything but the obscenities. Cory is a bright guy in his early 40s whose photography skills are astounding. I once saw him capture the image of a perp in the back seat of a car that was flying past us at 70 mph. Usually Cory has to limit his field work to the back of his van, which is why he will be spending several evenings in the parking lot of Vinnie's country club.

Chapter 3

I decided not to call Uncle Patrick last night after getting home from the Belvedere Heritage Country Club at 7:00 PM. It was 10:00 PM on the East Coast, and if Uncle Patrick handled his grief anything like my father he would be well into his cups by that hour. Shortly after Kelly departed I made the call.

"Uncle Patrick, this is your nephew, Jason. I'm very sorry to hear about your loss."

"Thanks for calling, Jason. I haven't heard from you since Megan died. I appreciated the sympathy card."

"I wish I could have been there for her funeral, but it happened during finals week when I was finishing college."

"I know, Jason. Don't worry about it."

"My mother said you could use some help investigating your friend's murder. Did she tell you that I've been a private investigator for the past two years?"

"She did indeed. Congratulations on continuing the Duffy career path, such as it is."

"Uncle Patrick, I–"

"Jason, call me Patrick. You're 28 years old. It's not like we have a longstanding tradition to uphold. When you call me uncle it just reminds me of all of the family gatherings that we missed out on."

"OK, Patrick. Mom tells me that you're a wiz at finding stolen property, but are a bit out of your element on a murder investigation and could use some help."

"I was hoping your father might be willing to set aside our differences after all of these years, and come out here to give me a hand," he said.

"There are two things that Dad is not particularly good at: dealing with the death of a friend, and letting go of a grudge. Mom said she told you about his friend passing recently."

"She did. I hope your generation breaks the tradition of 100 proof mourning, as well as never ending grudges."

"I understand you did your fair share of breaking with tradition in your day," I said.

"Too much for your father's liking, I'm afraid."

"Why don't you tell me about what happened to your friend and I'll see if I can offer any suggestions?"

Over the next twenty minutes Patrick gave me the long version of what my mother told me over lunch. He felt he owed it to his friend to find the killer and see that he's brought to justice.

"Louie and I were in a band together back in the day. We almost broke out of Scranton and hit the big time. But a couple of bad breaks shot us down and eventually broke up the band. After about seven years of sulking, we started getting together once a month to relive the glory days."

"What instrument do you play, Patrick?"

"I play lead guitar and Louie played rhythm."

"I play rhythm myself."

"Your mother told Megan about your career for years. She shared every detail with me. It was my only connection to your family. When Megan died, so did my lifeline to California. The last I heard, you had just graduated, were getting a job as a mental health counselor, and still playing in Tsunami Rush."

I said, "The counseling gig lasted for two years. I couldn't take the political bullshit that went with the job. I kept playing with the band until I left the counseling job to start my apprenticeship with a local PI."

"Do you still play at all?"

"Our lead guitarist is now with Doberman's Stub. But I get together with the other guys about once every couple of months."

"Your mother tells me you just finished a big case. I'll bet you've got a lot stacked up on your plate now that it's over."

"Nothing terribly important."

"Jason, can I hire you to come out here to Scranton and help me find out who killed Louie?"

Uh-oh! I didn't see that one coming. Unpaid phone consultant – fine. Spending January in the great northeast made Mrs. Vincigura decidedly more appealing. My pregnant pause must have hit 10 centimeters.

Patrick said, "I know what you're thinking. If you come out here to help me it will put you in the doghouse with your father. I don't want to be responsible for getting another family grudge going. Forget I asked."

"My grudge with Dad started the day I got my first guitar. If Aunt Megan was really keeping you up on things, you should have known that."

"It's been a tough five years since I lost her, Jason. You're right; she did mention it, but only once. After she saw how it got me riled up she must have filtered the news. I'm sorry. I got the impression from your mother that Jim helped out on your cases once in a while."

"The Cold War started winding down when I left Tsunami Rush. Dad was a big help on a couple of my cases. But I certainly don't feel obligated to carry his grudge into the next generation. Let me see how soon I can get a flight out of here and I'll get back to you."

Chapter 4

My girlfriend, Kelly Kennedy, was more than a bit distraught at the conclusion of my last case a mere three weeks ago. Then came the usual pressures of Christmas, coupled with my father's expectation that I would be buying her an engagement ring. He believes we're living in sin, and has never been one to keep his opinions to himself. Fortunately, his only reference to our current status came during Christmas dinner when Kelly asked how he was doing. He told her he had been busy reading a mystery novel. When she asked which one he replied, "The Case of the Missing Diamond."

I was not looking forward to telling her about my upcoming trip to Scranton. She comes from a family of alcoholics who have a history of violence. During my last case her older brother, Danny, got into a bar fight with their father and was charged with attempted murder. I met them for the first time just before Christmas and introduced them to a friend who has been a longtime member of Alcoholics Anonymous. Although they haven't actually attended a meeting yet, Kelly says their booze consumption was cut in half over the holidays, and she attributes my getting involved as playing a significant role. I tell you this not for self-aggrandizement, but to prepare you for why this otherwise selfless and wonderful woman is likely to show a wee bit of her Irish temper.

"Hi, Jason. You're home early today."

"Jeannine's working undercover tonight as a cocktail waitress. I'll need to go check on her in a couple of hours."

"Is it dangerous?"

"I'll know more after I see her uniform."

Kelly bunched her long chestnut hair on top of her head and turned around. "Will you unzip me?"

"It's funny how four little words can turn my whole day around."

I briefly weighed the ethics of making love to her before delivering my news about the trip. Thirty seconds later I carried her into the bedroom. I was going to be in dire need of some warm memories where I was headed. Besides, it wouldn't be fair to have her last memory of our love be a vague recollection from 2:30 AM on New Year's morning. Not exactly one to lock away in the memory treasure trove. I should have majored in moral justifications at UCSD. My GPA would have earned me a full scholarship to grad school.

I met Justin Emerson in front of the Belvedere Heritage Country Club at 7:30 PM. He's my favorite night club manager and also a golfing buddy. Through his expansive network of contacts, he arranged for Jeannine to be immediately hired as a cocktail waitress without the formality of a job interview. I'm sure he could have gotten me into the country club without making a personal appearance, but as my confidant in matters of the heart, I was glad he agreed to meet with me.

The bar at the country club was upscale and had the look of a fresh remodel. Beveled copper and black lacquer was the dominant theme. We grabbed a table near the entrance where I had a good view of the bar and most of the other tables. Jeannine spotted us and took a direct route to our table. Her shoulder-length blond hair and pretty face couldn't compete with her waitress uniform, which made Hooters-wear appear conservative.

"Jason, I can't be seen in public wearing this!" Her excited whisper drew a leer from an old duffer, who rallied from a near stupor now that her frilly panties were in his sightline.

"It's really not that bad, Jeannine. If you wore that outfit to any beach in the county you'd be the most conservatively dressed woman on the sand," I said.

Looking down she said, "I can see my navel from here, and I know that dirty old man behind me is looking at my underpants."

Justin put his hand on top of hers. "Those aren't underpants, they're just part of a costume; like a cheerleader's outfit. The waitresses dress like that to cheer up the old golfers who can't play as well as they used to. I'm sure your legs are the best thing that old guy's seen all day."

She smiled. "You're the guy who helps Jason get out of the doghouse with Kelly, aren't you?" Without waiting for an answer, she turned to me and asked, "What did you do now?"

"I have to go to Scranton for a couple of weeks to help my uncle with a murder case. I'll need you to hold down the fort while I'm gone. Can you handle it?"

"You shouldn't expect me to cover your backside when I can't even cover my own." She then turned around, yanked down the hem of her skirt, took two steps toward the bar, and returned.

"I better not go back to the bar without your drink orders."

I said, "Why don't you bring us a couple of Hei-"

Justin interrupted. "We'd really appreciate if you could bring us two Coronas, Jeannine."

Once she departed I asked, "Why did you stop me?"

Holding his index finger an inch from his thumb he said, "She sounded this close to bailing on you. I think if you asked for a couple of Heinnies she would have been out the door."

"Animal Planet has the Dog Whisperer, I have the Woman Whisperer. Let me tell you how Kelly reacted to my news."

We spent the next half hour talking about how to undo the damage from my *sex before the storm* approach. He also offered some suggestions on ways to keep Jeannine from walking out on her not-so-undercover operation. I didn't tell him about how her Obsessive Compulsive Disorder would complicate matters.

At 8:15 he stood up and said, "I have to make sure the club is set up before tonight's band hits the stage."

I dropped $20 on the table. "I'll walk out with you. I want to see how Cory is doing in the parking lot."

"I don't suppose you have any recommendations on how to get two brothers back together who haven't exchanged a civil word in over 40 years?" I asked.

"Not a clue, Jason. You're on your own with that one."

"Let's play some golf when I get back from Scranton. I'm going to need a huge dose of sunshine."

"Give me a call," he said, ducking into his bronze Porsche 911 Turbo S.

Justin's manager friend at the country club had informed Security that Cory worked for a foreign diplomat who would be playing golf at the course sometime in the next two weeks, and to stay away from his van at all times. He was parked in front of a maintenance building facing away from the bar entrance. The van had what appeared to be a roof mount light bar, but actually was a set of four telescopic lens video cameras. When I opened the rear door, Cory used all of his 140 lbs. to keep Jeannine's giant puppy from exiting to do the dance of euphoria at my feet. After all, it had been four hours since I'd seen him at the office. There was no sense in starting a conversation until Hoover's cheek-slurping greeting was out of the way while Cory tried to keep his tail from resetting the surveillance control panel.

I broke the news about my trip to Scranton, and worked out the logistics on how to keep tabs on Mr. V. Cory's Tourette's only manifests itself when he would normally feel compelled to speak. Hoover has the uncanny gift of knowing when Cory is about to cut loose with one, or a whole string of obscenities, and provides bark-over censorship. The news of my impending departure caused a *Who Let the Dogs Out* fiasco in the back of the van. I kept my visit brief, lest a departing diner call the pound.

I phoned a former coworker from my days as a counselor while I drove to the Kennedy clan household in Lakeside. He confirmed that if Kelly's parents and brothers got into family counseling immediately it would go a long way toward keeping

Danny out of jail.

The family lived in a rundown clapboard house on the rugged outskirts of the city. I never actually set foot in the house, but let Kelly direct me to it one Sunday afternoon when she was into swapping stories about our upbringing.

All four of them were at home watching television and drinking beer. They were enthusiastic in welcoming me until I told them the purpose of my visit. All of the men hated the idea of getting into counseling.

"As I see it you have two choices," I said. "You can either spend an hour a week for the next year going to family counseling, or you can spend an hour a week for the next five years visiting Danny in jail."

Kelly was in bed when I got home. She showed me her back, but I knew she was awake because of the illuminated lamp on her nightstand. She never fell asleep with that light on.

"I just came from your parents' house."

This got an immediate turnaround, but no reply.

"They all start into family therapy with my old boss, Andy Stelzner, on Monday."

I could tell that she was still upset, but couldn't hold back her smile. "Are they being treated for twisted arms, or having sneakers removed from their backsides?"

"I didn't lay a hand on them. I simply pointed out that it would make you very proud if they would commit to a year of counseling."

"And, that it might keep Danny out of jail," she said.

"That, too."

Chapter 5

Flying into the Scranton/Wilkes-Barre Airport provided me with one of those life experiences I would have preferred to skip. It was nearly dusk, but just bright enough to notice snow falling as we approached the runway. I briefly considered asking my flight attendant if our plane was equipped with snow tires, but decided I'd rather not know the answer. When we touched down without incident I wanted to kiss the tarmac.

Like at many small airports, the ground crew rolled a set of stairs up to the plane. Rather than easing into the climate change gradually, I was smacked in the face by single digit temperatures and a breeze that blasted down the neck of my Chargers jacket. I tried concentrating on the L.L. Bean arctic wear I would be welcoming at the luggage carousel as I jogged past fellow travelers.

Mom had provided me a relatively recent picture of Patrick. I had no trouble spotting him on the main concourse with his thick white hair combed straight back, matching mustache, and soul patch. A strained smile broke across his face as he saw me approach.

"Jason, you have no idea how much I appreciate you coming here."

The first thing I learned about Patrick is that he's a hugger – not a common practice in the criminal justice community.

"I see my mother gave you a picture of me."

"Actually, it was the autumn wear Chargers jacket that was my first clue. I hope you have some warmer clothes." Patrick looked down at my Nike Cross Trainers.

"It took two suitcases to cram in all of my Nanook of the North wear. I used to snowboard at Big Bear all of the time when my band was still together."

We kept the conversation light while we waited for my luggage. One-by-one, my travelling companions rolled their bags away from the carousel. When the conveyor shut down it became apparent that my luggage opted for an alternate destination. A half hour later we left the Baggage Claims office with a receipt and the sincere apology of a man who knew his lines a bit too well.

"At least the heater in my Prius is working like a politician on election eve," Patrick said.

"Which way to the rental car counter?"

"If you need a vehicle, you'll use Megan's. I couldn't bear to part with it."

"Thanks, Patrick. That works for me."

My hands clinched into fists as we emerged from the elevator and walked away from the covered parking structure. Patrick looked like he wanted to start telling me about his friend. But his investigative prowess picked up on the fact I was striding into the lead despite the fact that I had no idea where the car was parked.

"Hang a right, Jason," he called from five paces behind me.

I stopped in front of the first Prius I encountered, and bounced up and down with my hands in my jeans pockets.

"End of the row," he said as he strode past me.

True to his word, the car heater took the chatter out of my teeth before Patrick finished paying the lot attendant.

"I was going to drive you by the scene of the crime. But considering your wardrobe situation, I think it's best we wait until tomorrow."

"We can drive by if you like. You were right about this heater," I said.

"You can't see anything from the road, and the cops have crime scene tape across the entrance to the driveway."

"Tomorrow it is. You can show me some pictures tonight if you think the layout is important."

Patrick nodded and drove on. The snow was coming down harder now, so I let him focus on the road. He took the freeway (aka the Interstate) to Scranton, and quickly turned onto Route 307 South. We immediately left the metro area behind us and eased up a steep hill.

"This is Moosic Street. Did you ever hear of Harry Chapin?" he asked.

"Absolutely. He's the guy who did *Taxi* and *Cat's in the Cradle*."

"He also did one called *Thirty Thousand Pounds of Bananas*."

"I heard that one a couple of times. It's about a truck that loses its brakes going down a hill into Scranton."

"This is the street," he said as we crested the knoll and coasted down the other side to a stoplight. "We'll turn here when we go to Louie's house tomorrow."

"That's a pretty flat field of snow over there on the right."

"You're looking at Lake Scranton. Megan and I must have walked around it a thousand times."

We rode in silence for about five miles then turned onto a paved road which quickly became snow on dirt.

"Are we still in Scranton?"

"We're in Roaring Brook Township. This is my place," he said.

We navigated the ups and downs of Patrick's quarter-mile-long driveway at a cautious pace. A natural wood two story home with a snow covered roof glowed in the floodlights. Huge piles of snow bookended the house where the plow had cleared prior accumulations. Patrick drove 40 feet past the house to a huge garage. He backed into a combination garage and band practice area, which took up half of the floor space. A custom quilted cover blanketed another vehicle the size of a van. My eyes were drawn to a couple of Marshal Amps, and a Peavey P.A. system.

"Do you have all of your band practices here?"

"Four of us have similar set-ups." His face changed as he corrected himself. "Make that three of us."

He gave me an animated tour of the house, placing a strong emphasis on Megan's contributions to the layout and décor.

"You've kept it in great shape, Patrick."

"She'd come back and haunt me if I let it go to the dogs. Have a seat in the living room and I'll grab us a couple of beers."

I sat down opposite the fireplace, and Patrick took the hint. Five minutes later he struck a wooden match and newspapers and kindling blazed.

"You're probably tired from the flight. Why don't you catch me up on what's happening in your life while I make dinner. We can talk about the case tomorrow."

"It's only 3:00 PM in San Diego. I'd like to dive right in if you don't mind. Tell me about Louie's background tonight and we can talk specifics tomorrow after you show me the crime scene."

He walked into the adjacent galley kitchen while I remained in front of the fire. "Louie was the creative guy in our band. He wrote most of our original songs."

"Was he the band leader?"

"From a musical arrangements standpoint, he was our leader. Russell Shapiro was our manager and made all of the business decisions for the band."

"I read a few online newspaper articles about the murder. One said the police suspect a business connection," I said.

"Bullshit! Louie's last name is Amanesco. They think that because he's Italian and works in construction management he must have been connected with the mob."

I heard a couple of dishes rattle and the refrigerator slammed shut. "Are you ready for another beer, Jason?"

"I'm good for now. What kind of construction projects did he manage?"

"Mainly high end residential new homes."

23

"I imagine he'd been having a tough time since the housing bubble burst," I said.

A wooden spoon clanged in a metal pan. "It definitely went to shit around here. If you think San Diego is bad, think of the old real estate mantra – location, location, location. He would have been better off going into the foreclosure business. Wait till you see all of the *For Sale* signs in his neighborhood. It's a shame."

I walked into the kitchen. "It doesn't sound like there were big piles of money in the wall safe."

Patrick pulled a couple of placemats and two heavily used cloth napkins from a drawer. "I was surprised that the cops jumped to that conclusion. Anybody who knows business would know that. Anybody who knows his ex-wife would figure she bled him dry in the divorce."

Before I could respond, he flipped a boiling pot of tortellini into a colander and gave a final stir to his sauce. The timer beeped and he removed warm garlic bread from the oven. Two minutes later we were seated at the dining room table in front of steaming plates.

"Maybe we should hold off on talking about Louie's ex- until after dinner," I said.

"She isn't any easier to swallow with dessert. What do you want to know?"

"Do the police consider her a person of interest?"

"If you mean the Hardy Boy they put in charge of the case, I wouldn't know."

"Would that be Detective Flannery?" I asked.

"I found out he just made detective in September."

"I hope you don't feel that way about all detectives in their 20s."

"Jason, you have no idea how much it means to me that you're here to help. I just meant that I know how much experience has helped me as an investigator, and I resent how Louie's murder immediately hit the back burner as soon as they found out he hasn't been on the Society Page for several years."

"I have a pretty good understanding of how a serial killer can dominate police resources."

"Your mother tells me it's been less than a month since you closed the Concert Killer case. I didn't even know to look for you when it was on the national news," he said.

"What do you say we combine your investigative experience with my homicide skills to help Flannery get his man?"

"Or woman. Don't forget about Rose."

I laid my fork across my empty plate. "Tell me about her."

"Louie met Rose after our band broke up and before we started playing together for fun seven years later. His parents were thrilled when they began dating. Rose's father was the biggest real estate developer in the area. At first, the Amanesco family thought it was a match made in heaven. Unfortunately, Rose turned out to be a bitch made in hell."

"How long had they been divorced?"

"Rose filed right after the housing bubble derailed her gravy train. She goes through money faster than you went through that garlic bread. Louie told me she took four vacations their last year together. He was in on just one of them."

"But Rose knew Louie was broke. It couldn't have been money she was looking for in that wall safe," I said.

Patrick led us back into the living room after retrieving two more beers from the fridge. He added a log to the fireplace and pulled a matching three volume set of books from a shelf next to his chair.

"What are you reading?" I asked.

Without answering, he pushed on the spine of the middle volume and revealed his pot stash. He removed a small glass bong, added some water from a plastic bottle, and packed the bowl.

"Time to relax a little bit," he said, and lit the bowl.

Chapter 6

I woke up at 9:00 on Saturday morning to the smell of eggs and the sound of Sheryl Crow floating through the house. The instant my feet hit the cold hardwood floor they instinctively jumped back on the mattress and under the covers. I inverted yesterday's cotton socks and made a mental note to purchase a half dozen pair of the woolen variety regardless of the status of my luggage.

"Are you ready for some breakfast?" Patrick called.

"I'll be there in a minute."

I was surprised that I fell asleep right away when we turned in around midnight. It must have been the contact high that put me out.

I sat at the dining room table, and Patrick removed pan lids from our plates.

"Sheryl Crow? I was expecting the Rolling Stones," I said.

"Megan had all of her CDs. Waking up to Sheryl reminds me of waking up with Megan."

"Did Baggage Claims happen to call yet?"

"No, but I did manage to find you a warm down coat and a pair of boots. That should hold you until your luggage gets here."

The breakfast conversation centered on my sister and her family.

"When Megan was alive, she and your mother would talk at least once a week. I remember her telling me about how Lisa used to torment you as a teenager."

"Some family dynamics never change."

"Really? After all these years?"

"Patrick, I was a teenager nine years ago. How long have you and my father been holding that grudge?"

"Good point. Enough said. Let's hit the road while the sun is shining. Another storm will be blowing in this afternoon."

I noticed that the driveway had been plowed as we pulled out of the garage. "How much snow did we get last night?"

"It must have been at least four inches or Bongo wouldn't have plowed."

"Who's that?"

"He's the drummer from our band. We have a deal that he plows whenever we get four inches or more."

"You have a drummer named Bongo?"

"Not Bongo, like the bongo drum; Bong-o, like what I was smoking last night, with an *o* at the end."

"Oh," I replied. "Is driveway plowing his full-time job?"

"He works for Amanesco Construction as a laborer until the snow flies. Then he gets laid off and plows driveways under the table for beer money."

"How did he get along with Louie?"

"Bongo is an alcoholic and a drug addict. When he gets behind his drum kit, if he isn't already loaded, he's brilliant. He definitely had the chops to be a rock star. But once his blood alcohol level gets to a certain point, his personality does a Dr. Jekyll and Mr. Hyde. Louie had to deal with Mr. Hyde on the job at least once a year since the early 80s. He also had to bail Bongo out of jail after a few DUIs. It was a strained relationship, but I'm sure he's devastated over Louie's murder."

We turned onto the road across from Lake Scranton, and turned left a minute later.

"This is the Elmhurst Boulevard. Louie's house is on the Scranton side. If we wanted to see the custom homes that he built we would have turned right at the stop sign. When I was a kid it was notorious for car racing and horrible accidents. There were only a couple of houses for several miles. Louie saw its potential for luxury home development and made a fortune for Amanesco Construction for about 25 years."

Just as we crested a hill, Patrick swerved to avoid an SUV that was cruising down the middle of the snow-packed road. Following the swerve, our car fishtailed a couple of times before he regained control. I had both of my arms extended straight out, bracing for impact against the dashboard.

"Settle down, Jason. This happens all of the time."

"Not to me," I said, putting my hands in my coat pockets.

"This is Louie's entrance coming up on your side. I'm gonna pull into a neighbor's driveway over here and we'll walk in.

I tried taking a shortcut around the crime scene tape tied to the ornate lamps that sat on three-foot pillars on either side of the driveway. My left leg sank into the snow until I was up to mid-thigh.

Patrick pulled me out. "I forgot to tell you about the drainage ditch. You better let me lead."

"Good idea," I said, brushing myself off. The toes on my left foot tried pulling back like a turtle into its shell.

Louie's home was spectacular. "Is that Tudor architecture?" I asked.

"Good eye, Mr. Duffy. I thought your experience was limited to Spanish arches and tile roofs."

"And I thought your selection of footwear would be limited to the waterproof variety, Mr. Duffy," I replied.

Patrick smiled. "Let's see if you can hobble on back to Louie's office before frostbite sets in."

More crime scene tape made a big X across the doorway. Patrick used a key to retract the deadbolt and unlock the knob.

Louie's office was an 800-square-foot one-room building that was definitely not a multi-purpose facility. Bay windows faced east and west in the front and rear walls. His walnut desk was large and functional; not built to impress. It sat two-thirds of the way back from the entrance on the left side of the room, with enough space from the wall to allow access to his chair from either side. The safe was in the near wall at a right angle to his desk chair. It sat open.

"Was this Louie's only office, or did he also have one at Amanesco Construction's headquarters?"

"He had a desk at their building on Lackawanna Avenue in Scranton, but did almost all of his work here."

"What's the first name of the lead detective?" I asked.

"You mean lead and only detective? That would be Colin Flannery."

"An Irishman. Did that score you any points in finding out what's happening with the investigation?"

"I guess it's true when they say *the apple doesn't fall far from the tree*. No, we haven't shared any secrets over pints of Guinness Stout."

"For a guy who hasn't talked to his brother in over 40 years, and lives 3000 miles away, you sure have a good idea of how he operates."

"Like I said yesterday, your mother and Megan were very close."

I stood over the outline of the body. "How do you see it going down, Patrick?"

"I think he either knew the killer, or the killer posed as a new customer."

"Why?"

"The coroner figured the time of death around the hour he usually gets home from work. His mail was on the kitchen table. I know his routine. He stops at the mailbox out front, drops it on the table, then goes to the office to check his answering machine and email. There was no sign of forced entry, so he either let the killer in or his murderer was waiting for him here in the office."

"I imagine the police have the computer."

"You are correct."

"How many people had keys?"

"I don't know. I have a key. Rose definitely had a key – he never changed the locks after the divorce. I'm sure there was at least one key at Amanesco Construction. I really don't have any idea."

"I imagine he made a few enemies running construction crews for most of his life. Did he mention any specific problems in the last few months?"

"I'd say he had to fire about one guy a year for drinking on the job or pilfering. He talked about that kind of stuff before Megan died. But since then he was always moving the conversation onto a positive track. He knew how much her death tore me up. We talked a lot about music and sports until we got loaded. Then I'd talk about Megan and he'd listen.

"Did you do the same for him when his marriage fell apart?"

Patrick sunk into one of the wing chairs in front of the desk. "I'm sorry to say, no. I'm sure it was tough on him, but all of his friends saw it coming years before it happened. On some level I'm sure I avoided the subject to keep Louie from seeing how happy I was that the bitch was out of his life."

I eased into the matching wing chair. "So, how are you going to get me a sit down with her?"

"I suggest you work through the Hardy Boy on that one. She's probably looking to shoot me next."

"First of all, let's stop calling Flannery the Hardy Boy. If that gets back to him you'll totally screw up an important source of information."

"OK, what else?"

I removed my boot and wet sock. "I need you to call Rose and pave the way for me to stop by her house."

"Not a chance. If I tell her you're my nephew she'll immediately assume I told you she was the number one suspect. I'll ask Flannery if you can tag along next time he talks to her."

"Couldn't you tell her we need to pull together to find the killer since the cops are so preoccupied with the Society Page Slasher?"

"All she cares about is the six million dollars she'll be getting from the insurance company."

"What six million?"

"The divorce settlement stipulated that Louie had to keep paying premiums on an existing policy without changing the beneficiary. She knows that I'm aware of it."

"Alright, nix the intro. But I need your help on something else, and I'm not taking *no* for an answer."

"What?"

"I need wool socks and I need them now."

"Stay here," he said.

Five minutes later he came out of Louie's house with a pair of woolies in hand. "Put these on. We'll stop by a sporting goods store where you can stock up."

Colin Flannery met us at Chick's Diner on Moosic Street. The instant I saw him I understood Patrick's Hardy Boys reference.

"Is that a baby face or what?" Patrick whispered as he walked in.

"More of a toddler face," I replied. "Now let it go."

"Flannery, over here," Patrick called, and slid into the booth next to me.

He peeled off a navy blue stocking hat, revealing dark red hair, and stuck it in one pocket of his black leather jacket while tucking his gloves into the other pocket.

Patrick waved to our waitress, pointing at his coffee, then at Flannery.

"This is my nephew, Jason Duffy. Jason, Colin Flannery." We shook hands. "Jason's come out from California to help with the investigation."

"Are you a sworn officer out there?" he asked, sliding into the booth opposite us.

"Private investigator."

"I take it you're not licensed in Pennsylvania."

"I'm not looking to step on your toes, detective."

He said, "I don't think this is a very good idea."

31

"Did you see the national news story about the Concert Killer in California last month?" Patrick asked.

"Of course I ... That was you?"

Patrick started to talk, but Flannery raised his hand while he found the story and pictures on his phone.

"Son of a bitch."

"I know how a serial case can eat up manpower. I'm here to help however I can," I said.

"Without a license there's not much you can do."

"Oh for God's sake, deputize him if you wanna cover your ass. The case is getting colder by the day and you're worried about how this will look on your performance evaluation," Patrick said.

"Patrick, take it easy. Detective Flannery strikes me as a bright guy who's perfectly capable of figuring out a work-around."

Flannery asked, "Were you ever deputized, Patrick?"

"Three times. Once in New York and twice in Jersey. When you get back to your precinct house make a copy of what you saw on your phone, show it to your captain, and tell him you got a nationally acclaimed PI willing to work the case at no cost to the department. All he needs is to be deputized. Unless your boss is a complete idiot, you'll be handing Jason a badge the next time we get together."

"I sure could use some help."

I said, "Detective Flannery—"

"Just Flannery."

"What did forensics turn up at the crime scene?"

He pursed his lips and shook his head. "I'm gonna take your uncle's advice and have that conversation with my captain before I start disclosing any details on the investigation."

I glanced at Patrick and saw the muscles in his neck tighten. I quickly clapped my hand on his knee before he could explode.

"Good idea, Flannery. I'm sure that Patrick and everybody else with a key to that office is on your suspects list. If you start forging alliances without your boss's OK, you could end up back in a squad car," I said.

I gave him my card so he'd have my cell number, and he departed.

"We're wasting valuable time," Patrick said.

"That badge could open a lot of doors for me. Great idea. But if we force a rookie detective to go out on a limb without permission, I might never see it."

"I'm too close to this case to be objective. I was the same way when Megan was killed. All of my instincts as an insurance investigator went out the window when my emotions took over."

I spent all day on Sunday talking with Kelly, Jeannine, and Cory. Kelly was concerned that her family was going to back out of the therapy session scheduled for tomorrow. I coached her on talking points and attitude. She didn't complain about me being in Scranton, although I got the impression she took a bit of perverse pleasure from me freezing while waiting for my luggage.

Jeannine was much more of a project. I had four separate conversations with her. The main topic in all of them involved getting her butt pinched twice on Saturday night. Vinnie behaved himself in the lounge by staying close to his golfing buddies.

Cory had a long evening, as the foursome went to a hotel room for an all night poker game. Two of the foursome staggered out around 3:00 AM, but Vinnie and one of the others had the good sense to keep off of the roads. Cory sent me a video highlight reel that covered the past two days and three nights. I called Mrs. Vincigura to give her an update and was chastised for interrupting the Lord's day.

Chapter 7

Patrick and I were shown into the conference room of Attorney Edward C. Pohanick at 9:30 on Monday morning.

"How come you won't tell me why we're here, Patrick?" I asked, after an attractive receptionist closed the door.

"I want you to form your own impression of this guy. Just follow my lead."

We sat in silence for five minutes. Floor to ceiling bookshelves held law books rendered obsolete by software and computer search engines. The lawyer certainly knew how to make an entrance. He extended his arms toward Patrick, expecting a hug, and got one.

"You did a wonderful job on the eulogy, Patrick. I was moved to tears."

Pohanick appeared to be about seven years younger than my uncle. On closer inspection I confirmed that his hair was dyed black, and strongly suspected that plastic surgery had contributed to the younger image. His waistline left little doubt that exercise was a priority.

"This is my nephew, Jason. Jason, Eddie Pohanick, bass player for the Luna Parkers."

"I'm glad you have family here to help you through the sorrow," Eddie said.

"Eddie, I know you probably don't have much time so I'm going to get right to it. You handled Louie's divorce and drew up all of his financial disclosure documents. What do you think was in his wall safe?" Patrick asked.

Eddie was obviously a muller. Straight answers did not come

naturally to him. "It definitely wasn't piles of money."

"I didn't ask what wasn't there."

"Then how should I know? I helped to negotiate his master settlement agreement two and a half years ago."

"Can I take a look at his assets?"

Eddie mulled some more. He poured a glass of water from a pitcher on the conference table.

"Patrick, I know you need to use your investigative skills to help the police. Lord knows they need all the help they can get with that Society Page Slasher running around. But I also know Rose is a litigious bitch who'd love to get my nuts in a vise grip."

"You'd have to grow a pair first, Eddie."

"That isn't fair, buddy. I've put my rep out there for you and the rest of the band for years. I make almost all of the practice sessions. I try to be a good friend. But I also have a fiduciary responsibility to this firm, and jumping into Rose Amanesco's crosshairs would put the firm at risk."

"Is that why you rolled over and played dead at the negotiating table when Louie was trying to secure his future?"

"We've been down this road too many times, Patrick. I've got to go prep for a deposition."

"Before you leave I have a question," I said.

"Go ahead," he replied.

"I've been thinking of installing a wall safe at my house, but I'm not quite sure what it's big enough to hold. Do you think you could give me an idea?"

Once again, Eddie mulled. "They're not very practical for things like architectural plans or works of art. They're OK for things like jewelry if you're married, but if you aren't you probably wouldn't keep anything like that in there. But they are a great place for documents, especially ones with sentimental value."

"Like what?" I asked.

"I'm a musician. If I had one I'd probably include cover art from our album, sheet music, maybe a playbill or two from big shows, a picture or two from the old days – things like that."

"Thanks, Eddie. It was nice meeting you," I said, standing up to shake hands.

Patrick remained seated with a pensive look on his face.

"Let's go," I said.

Patrick stood up. "Eddie, did Louie mention any arguments or problems he was having that I might not know about?"

Eddie adjusted his royal blue tie while he mulled. "Did you hear about Bongo's big win at Mohegan Sun?"

"Not a word," Patrick said.

"He won ten grand at the slots the week before Christmas."

"No shit!" It was Patrick's turn to mull.

Eddie looked at his watch. "I'm in a hurry, so I'll fit the pieces together for you. Bongo has been borrowing money from Louie for years. Louie was in a financial bind since the real estate market nose dived, and Christmas expenses were probably maxing out his cards. The last time I saw Louie I told him about Bongo's win. What he did with that information, I can't say. Now if you'll excuse me I need to get to the dep."

Patrick followed me to his car without speaking. "Would you like me to drive?"

"I've got it," he said.

When we crossed the Spruce Street Bridge and turned onto Moosic Street, Patrick broke his silence. "I know you think Eddie just told you what was in that safe, but I'm not so sure."

"I gave him plausible deniability. Even if Rose was in the room she couldn't sue him over his answer."

"Louie once told me that Eddie's been a lawyer for so long that lying is as automatic as breathing for him."

"He couldn't stand the idea that you thought of him as a eunuch. He just needed the guise of the hypothetical to cover his ass."

"I'm not saying it was a pack of lies; just not the whole truth and nothing but the truth."

"Point taken, Patrick. What do you think about Bongo's win?"

"Bongo's not a killer. But the subject needs to be discussed."

Right after we passed Lake Scranton I asked, "Where did you get the band name, Luna Parkers?"

"Luna Park was one of the biggest things to ever happen to Scranton. It was part of the first amusement park chain in the world during its 10 years of existence, from 1906 to 1916. When we were teenagers we used to hang out near the old west entrance to the park. By that point there was hardly anything left to see. But all of our grandparents talked about it like it was Scranton's entertainment pinnacle. We hoped that our band could bring back that feeling."

"Why did they tear it down?"

"It was built almost entirely out of wood, and burned to the ground."

I was out of Patrick's twenty-degree wear all of about two minutes when the airport baggage claim rep called to say my luggage had just arrived. Patrick had changed into his log chopping apparel, so I borrowed his car and made the run myself. My cell phone rang on the return trip.

"Hello."

"What the hell do you think you're doing in Pennsylvania with my brother?"

"Exactly what you should be doing, Dad."

The next five minutes involved my father going into a curse-laden rant about sheltering me from his pinko hippie brother.

"I'm not a little kid, Dad. You don't get to decide who I associate with anymore."

"You're certainly not showing any loyalty to your old man."

"Dad, you're always trying to get Kelly and me to go to church with you and Mom. Isn't the Catholic Church all about forgiving sins?"

"The church is also about the Ten Commandments, and the first one is: Honor thy father and thy mother. You just blew that one big-time, buddy-boy!"

I cut loose for a couple of minutes in spite of the fact that he was no longer on the line. He hung up because he had an indefensible position and we both knew it.

Darkness had fallen, but Patrick's porch light illuminated my way. Before entering the house I glanced at the clock-sized wall thermometer – 15 degrees. My breath looked like a ghost escaping through my mouth.

Patrick sat by the fire reading a newspaper. "While you were gone I got the word that I'm corrupting your morals by turning you into a vegetarian, tree-hugging commie pinko."

"You actually spoke to Dad?"

"He left a message on the machine while I was cutting wood. I've gotten three or four of them over the years, usually after he's had a snoot full."

"He called me on the way back here. I want to hear the long version of what happened to the two of you."

"I have vegetable stew on the stove. Let's grab a bowl and I'll tell you over dinner."

Five minutes later Patrick savored a spoonful at the dining room table. I held my spoon at the ready, waiting for the story to begin. My uncle didn't need any further prompts.

"Your father is five years older than me. Jim was my hero when we were kids. He was a starter on the high school baseball and football teams, which helped my status in junior high. He also helped me with homework and scout projects. When our father told me I was too young to attend night football games, Jim talked him into letting me go."

"It sounds like a pretty good relationship, so far," I said, to give Patrick a chance to slurp a couple of spoonfuls.

"It started unraveling as soon as he graduated from high school. He broke up with his girlfriend right after the senior prom. He never told any of us why, but he was in a very surly mood from that point on. Our mother wanted to throw him a graduation party but he refused. The day after the ceremony he enlisted in the Navy."

"I didn't realize it was that soon," I said.

"Back then, the first fifteen minutes of every national newscast was about the war in Vietnam. When I thought of the war I always pictured caskets draped in flags. I was sure it was only a matter of time before he'd be killed."

"So you were 13 when he enlisted."

"I was, and it seemed to me that he was throwing his life away because things didn't work out with his girlfriend. Did you ever hear the Country Joe & the Fish song, *Feel Like I'm Fixin' to Die Rag*?"

"Many times," I said. "Are you thinking of the line: *Be the first one on your block to have your boy come home in a box*?"

He nodded. "Jim was in Vietnam the first time I heard it. There were thousands of kids protesting the war. Some thought it was immoral, some thought we were there to protect corporate interests, some protested because it was the cool thing to do. I got into it because I wanted my brother to come home alive and well."

"When did the blow-up happen?"

"He came home on leave in the summer of '68. The minute he saw my hair and found out I had been protesting he treated me like an enemy combatant."

"Did you tell him why you were protesting?"

"I tried to, but he wouldn't listen. In his eyes I was one of those ingrates who didn't recognize the sacrifice that true patriots were making to keep the world free from communism."

"What did your parents think about the war?"

"Publically, they were proud of Jim. Privately, they were worried sick. TV coverage was a lot different then. Every night we got the sights and sounds of war. VC bodies would be lined up for the cameras. Stories about news being slanted to paint a rosy picture were rampant. Free press newspapers were springing up all over the country and an *us versus them* mentality became the norm."

"Did Grandma and Grandpa give you a hard time for being a protester?"

"At first they did. But after the Tet Offensive started getting analyzed by trusted broadcasters, they came to realize that the public had been misled about the size of the Viet Cong Army."

"Did they let you travel to protests?"

"To be perfectly honest, by the time I was a sophomore in high school my band was my top priority. We formed a year after Jim joined the Navy, and we were playing high school dances about a year later. While most protesters were trying to get to a rally, I was trying to get a PA system for our next gig."

"It sounds like we have a lot in common," I said.

"You have no idea. Megan's reports from your mother were a real shocker for me, and I'm sure even more so for your father."

"It helps to explain why he was so down on me playing in bands."

Patrick finished his stew.

"Do you think you two will ever patch things up?" I asked.

"The closer we get to meeting our maker, the more likely we'll feel compelled to abide by His rules."

Chapter 8

We got on the road early Tuesday morning. Patrick arranged a meeting with Louie's uncle, Constantine "Connie" Amanesco, president of Amanesco Construction.

As we turned onto the highway I asked, "What's the agenda with Connie?"

"I figure we'll start with the easy stuff, like old clients who might have wanted Louie dead. Then we go for current clients, employees, and coworkers."

"How well do you know this guy?"

"He knows Louie and I were best friends and that I work as an investigator, but Connie was never a fan of the Luna Parkers."

"Does that mean he's giving you an audience because of your relationship with Louie, but might cut it off if you ask the wrong question?"

"That's about the size of it. But I have a fallback position if it gets too tense," he said.

"What's that?"

"I'll change the subject to Rose. I'm sure Connie would like nothing better than to see her in an orange jumpsuit."

"I thought her developer daddy was the best dowry ever for Amanesco Construction."

"The honeymoon ended for both Louie and the company about two years after the wedding. Rose's father pulled out of a development deal at the 11th hour, leaving Amanesco with a huge stack of bills. The families battled in court for years and the only ones who made out were the shysters," he said.

Amanesco Construction occupied the second floor of a

building that was renovated to look like it did in the early 1900s. In fact, the whole block had that retro look. I was hoping for a throw-back elevator, complete with an operator wearing an organ grinder monkey hat, but it was not to be. Instead we knocked a couple of inches of snow off of our boots trudging up the stairs.

The receptionist looked like she was born around the time the building's architecture was considered Nuevo. Eight other desks in the large room sat empty.

"Patrick Duffy to see Connie."

"I remember you from the funeral. You did the eulogy," she said.

"Louie was my best friend."

"I'm sorry. Every so often he would come in and sit at that desk, right over there," she said, pointing to her left.

"That looks exactly like my father's old desk. Do you mind if I have a look at it?" I asked.

"Who are you?"

"This is my nephew, Jason," he said. "He's visiting from California."

"I'll bet you're freezing your little tukas off," she said.

I smiled and asked, "May I?"

"Go ahead. Louie did all of his work out of his home office. So I'm sure Connie won't mind."

Patrick schmoozed her while I looked through the drawers. It was apparent that the receptionist was a people person who was used to being around men all day. My uncle put his gift of gab to work while he directed her attention away from me. When I finished I gave him the OK sign.

"I suppose we better get in there and meet with Connie. Louie said he's a stickler for punctuality," Patrick said.

"It's his way of letting the subcontractors know he won't put up with missed deadlines."

Connie's office spanned the entire front of the building, providing an excellent view of Lackawanna Avenue. He was in his early 70s with thin gray hair combed back at an angle. He wore a starched white shirt and red print tie, loosened to accommodate an open top button.

"I s'pose you're lookin' for Louie's killer," he said.

"Do you mind if we sit down?" Patrick asked.

"Who's da kid?"

"This is my nephew, Jason Duffy. He's a private investigator from California. Jason, Constantine Amanesco."

I stuck out my hand and he shook it. "Call me Connie. Go ahead and take a load off."

When we were seated Patrick said, "I'm surprised you haven't pulled some strings to get more police manpower on Louie's case."

"Business has been in the shitter since the subprime mess. Once I stopped greasin' the palms of the local politicos I've been treated like a turd in a punchbowl," Connie said.

"I thought you would have banked a few favors over the years."

"I'm afraid my chits are being held down by gravestones."

"Did Louie make any business enemies who might have done this?"

"I been wracking my brain since it happened, askin' that same question. The answer is that I really don't know. People get pissed off at their contractors all the time in dis business. We do quality work and usually meet our schedules. But sometimes we're at the mercy of a sub who gets behind, or a supplier that don't come true. Shit happens and we get blamed. Ya gotta have a tick skin ta survive in dis line of work."

"Did he get any threats from guys he fired, or subs that got dropped?"

"Prob'ly all of 'em. But with business down, there's been a lot less of that stuff over da past couple two, tree years."

"Do you have any idea who killed him, Connie?" I asked.

"That bitch, cunt, no good ex-wife, Rose, prob'ly done it!"

He opened his mouth as if to elaborate, then closed it and crossed his arms.

"What was in the wall safe?" I asked.

"Fuckifiknow."

"What was he working on when he died?" Patrick asked.

"He had a retail tenant improvement over the Steamtown Mall, and a couple, two, tree foreclosure fix-ups for one a da banks. No problems with any of them."

Patrick stood and I followed suit.

"Thanks for your time, Connie," he said.

"I appreciate what youze two are doin' with yours."

As I shook hands I said, "One last question. Do you know if Rose has a gun?"

"Fuckifiknow."

We power walked into a headwind back to Patrick's car as snow flurries washed our faces. How do people live like this?

Once the heater thawed his lips, Patrick asked, "What do you feel like eating for lunch?"

"Did you ever hear of a place called Thar Saile's Lounge?" I asked.

"Don't tell me the snow put you in the mood for a Hibernian burger?"

"While you were scoring points with the secretary, I found Louie's Christmas card from Connie in his desk. On the back was a note that said: Thar Saile's Lounge, 4:00."

Patrick turned off the radio and made a U turn at the end of the block. "That's one of Bongo's seedier hangouts over in South Side. I wouldn't be surprised if he's over there right now."

We cruised to a section that was untouched by urban redevelopment. It sat in the middle of a large lot. An abandoned factory was across the street, and condemned buildings appeared to bookend the parking lot. By the time we arrived the snow squall had ended.

"Thar must value his privacy," I said.

I reached for the front door and Patrick stopped me. "I'm surprised you don't recognize the name from your Terry Tucker case research. Thar Saile is an organization that advocates for allowing former IRA prisoners to immigrate to the United States."

"Have they been successful?"

"I'll let you tell me after you check out the clientele over lunch."

Every day was St. Patrick's Day at Thar Saile's Lounge. Green lights and shamrocks were everywhere.

"I expect to hear Dennis Day bust out his rendition of *Clancy Lowered the Boom* any minute now," I said.

"You're more apt to hear him sing *Finnegan's Wake* if you stay until the wee hours."

Patrick strode toward the bar. A large man in his early 50s stopped pouring in mid-draft. "Patrick Duffy, top 'o the mornin' to ya."

The fact that it was nearly 1:00 PM was irrelevant. "And the rest of the day to yourself, Liam."

"What brings you to our humble establishment on this miserable day?"

"I can't start band practice without my drummer," Patrick said.

"I assume Bongo owes you a wee bit of coin."

"Not me. I leave the lending to the banks and that part of your clientele that specializes in high finance."

"Bongo just ran out to the cheap smokes place on South Washington. He'll be back soon. What can I get for you and your friend?" Liam asked.

"This is my nephew, Jason. We'll have a couple of Harps and menus."

Liam extended me a hand across the bar. "How is it that a Duffy in his late 20s never graced my fine establishment before this?"

"Just visiting," I said, and shook his hand.

We took our drinks and menus to a booth that gave Patrick a view of the door. Most of the patrons at the bar were smoking cigarettes, something I'd never seen in California. Patrick explained that bars that earned less than a certain percentage of its revenue from food could still allow smoking. Immediately after placing our lunch orders, Bongo walked through the door.

He grabbed a chair, spun it around so that he could rest his arms on its back, and threw his coat on the adjacent table. His dark brown pony tail whipped across his red flannel shirt.

"I'm really sorry about the scrape at the funeral party," he said.

"It's called a bereavement luncheon," Patrick said.

"Call it what you want, it was a bad scene, man."

"That's no excuse for getting plastered and screaming obscenities."

"Fuck that! How could you stand watching Rose cry into her $50 hankie after she bled Louie dry for the last two years?"

"Let's not talk about the funeral now. I want you to meet my nephew, Jason."

"Far out. Good meetin' ya, man." Bongo gave me an arm wrestler-style handshake.

"I understand congratulations are in order," said Patrick.

Bongo stroked his brown and white beard. "Oh shit! Don't tell me I owe you money, too."

"Not a dime. Relax. Jason's giving me a hand looking into Louie's murder and we were hoping you could help us out."

"I don't know anything about it. You can't think I had anything to do with it."

"The thought never crossed my mind. But we do need to talk with everybody that Louie met with during the week before he was murdered."

"Louie laid me off at the beginning of December. I shouldn't be on that list."

"I just saw the Christmas card he got from Connie. Louie made a note on the back that said he was meeting you here at four o'clock," I said.

"Oh yeah. I forgot about that. I suffer from a bad case of

CRS."

"What's CRS?" I asked.

"Can't remember shit," Bongo said with a laugh. Patrick and I were not amused.

"Seriously guys, I did meet with him a few days before it happened. I just don't have much of a short term memory left. Ask me about what Diane Tannamack wore on our first date and I can give you all the details. But quiz me about what I ate for dinner two nights ago and I'm shit out of luck."

Patrick said, "I always told you that better living through chemistry would have its downside."

"That you did, Patrick. That you did."

"We need to know what you two talked about in that meeting, Bongo. And, don't give me any of that CRS bullshit. I know you can pull that one out of your ass," said Patrick.

"Can we talk privately?" Bongo nodded at me.

"No. My nephew is here to help me with the investigation. Whatever you have to say you can say it in front of him."

"Are you some kind of cop?"

"I'm a private investigator from San Diego."

"No offense, but I don't talk in front of anybody remotely related to the pigs."

"Would it help if you knew that Jason played rhythm guitar and did lead vocals for a rock band for 10 years?" Patrick asked.

"It would help. But I don't get that modern alternative rock shit. It's not my scene."

"The last song I played before coming out here was *Badge*," I said.

"Do you know why Clapton called it *Badge*?" Bongo asked.

"Because the chords are B,A,D,G, and E," I said.

"That's what most people think. The real reason is that it was a mistake. He was working on it in the studio, but hadn't finished the bridge yet. He wrote *bridge* on the tape to remind himself to finish it. When the recording engineer saw Clapton's bad handwriting he thought it said Badge, and assumed that was the name of the song."

"Great story, Bongo. Now let's hear the one that tells us what you and Louie talked about," Patrick said.

Bongo ignored him and looked at me. "I'll tell you what you want to know if you agree to fill in on rhythm guitar with the Luna Parkers. We were putting a reunion show together, and I think it would be a good way to send our musician brother off into the hereafter if we make his dream come true."

I looked at Patrick. "This is bullshit, Bongo." Patrick was angry. "We have more important things to do than teach Jason our songs. I thought you'd want to help find Louie's killer."

"Maybe filling in for Louie isn't such a bad idea," I said.

Patrick gave me a curious look.

"How about this?" I asked. "If you answer our questions today, I'll go to band practice and give it my best shot. If the band wants me to stay on for the reunion show, I'll do it."

"We'll probably get between 1000 and 2000 people for the show. Did you ever play in front of that many people?"

"Last month he played in front of 14,000 people at the new arena in San Diego," Patrick said.

"What do you want to know?"

"Tell us everything you remember from that conversation with Louie," said Patrick.

"I need a drink."

Before Patrick could reply, our waitress came to the table and took Bongo's drink order. He lit a cigarette, but kept it in an ashtray on the table that held his coat.

"Louie heard about my win at Mohegan Sun. I owed him a shitload of money from over the years, and it was pretty clear that Rose had turned his pockets out. I told him I'd split it with him, but he said three grand would get him through."

"So, did you go and get him the money?" Patrick asked.

"It was almost 5:00 on the Friday before Christmas. People were rolling into this place already drunk from parties at work.

Louie didn't expect me to jump in my car while I was half in the bag and make a bank run. He told me he needed the money to cover his bills. That's first of the month stuff."

Patrick was about to tear into his drummer when our food arrived. The chatty waitress took the steam out of his temper.

"I don't want to be blowing smoke on you guys while you're eating, so I'm heading up to the bar."

Bongo grabbed his coat and walked to the far end, out of sight. A group of four men who looked like mug shots personified, took the table next to our booth and one immediately lit up. My Hibernian burger was surprisingly tasty in spite of the unusual cigarette smell, which Patrick identified as an Indian bidi.

We joined Bongo at the bar before departing, and Patrick paid him for plowing his driveway. Bongo recommended a few songs that Patrick should teach me before band practice, which he asked Patrick to schedule.

Driving home Patrick asked, "Why did you agree to play with the band?"

"Louie got killed after opening his wall safe. Eddie all but told us that he kept band-related materials in the safe. I need to spend more time with the band."

Chapter 9

"I've got bacon and eggs ready in the kitchen," Patrick said from the entrance to his guest bedroom.

The bedside clock read 8:00 AM. Patrick and I put in a four hour practice session last night, and the chords to the new songs floated around my head until after 2:30. I wasn't quite awake, and definitely not asleep. Hangover best described my state of mind. The four beers during practice didn't help. At least I managed to fend off Patrick's insistence that I join him in smoking some pot.

I was in no mood for a chat. "Do you mind if I turn on the morning news?"

"Start on your eggs, I'll get the TV."

One bite into breakfast I put down my fork and joined Patrick in the living room.

The newscaster said, *"I'm standing outside the home of Annabelle Grainger. The police have confirmed that she appears to be the fourth victim of the Society Page Slasher."*

"Did you know her, Patrick?"

"We travelled in different circles, but I certainly knew of her. When I was in my 30s and 40s it seemed like she was in the paper every month for one function or another."

"I heard Aunt Megan was involved in a lot of charity work. I'm surprised your paths didn't cross."

"Megan worked with the needy. Annabelle always kept her distance from the little people."

"As you can see, the Grainger trash cans are out here at the curb. I'm talking with Green Ridge resident Rachel Young.

Rachel, why did the police ask you about the trash cans?"

"I took my dog out for a walk last night at 11:30. When we walked past here I noticed that Annabelle hadn't put her trash out yet."

"Is that unusual?" asked the newscaster.

"Most of the people in our neighborhood put their trash out just before going to bed to maintain an aesthetically pleasing ambience."

"That means Mrs. Grainger was killed after 11:30."

"Or, the Slasher took out the trash after he killed her," said Rachel.

The phone rang and Patrick turned off the television. "Just a minute," he said to the caller, and handed me the phone.

"Jason Duffy."

"It's Flannery. I got authorization to deputize you last night before all hell broke loose down here. Can you make it over to HQ at 11:00?"

"Sure. Where are you at?"

"Next to the Steamtown Mall on South Washington. Your uncle knows where it is."

The media had HQ staked out when we arrived. Patrick spoke with the officer guarding the front door and we were shown to an interview room. Flannery walked in promptly at 11:00. He made me swear my allegiance to God, country, the Commonwealth of Pennsylvania, Scranton, and probably threw in something about Dunder Mifflin just to make sure I was fully aware of my obligations.

"Patrick, can you give us a few minutes alone?" Flannery said.

"I'll be in the donut room," he replied with a wink.

Flannery sat in the chair Patrick had just vacated and placed a huge Dunkin Donuts cup on the table. He looked like he had pulled an all-nighter.

"I thought you were working Louie's murder full-time," I

said.

"I got an *all hands on deck* call at 2:30 AM. I should be home sleeping right now, but I needed to get you sworn in before the bosses that opposed it could muster political sway."

"Why would anyone oppose it?"

"You know that family members are always the top suspects. Your uncle and Louie were like brothers. He has a key to Louie's place and there was no sign of a break in."

"Do you think Patrick had anything to do with it?"

"My gut says no, but my lieutenant says to investigate by the book. That means I'll need to talk with you privately from time to time. If that doesn't work for you then I'll be doing a repo on that badge. Do we understand each other?"

"Got it. Now let me ask you this: How soon can you get me a meeting with Rose Amanesco?"

"What's the rush?" Flannery asked.

"The people I've met describe her as cold and calculating. I'm thinking she might be a little less guarded in her answers today since she's a Society Page regular. If you could get us together this afternoon I could probably learn a lot more than when she's in a more composed state of mind."

"Give me a minute." Flannery left his vase of coffee on the table and departed. Five minutes later he returned.

"What's the word?" I asked.

"She'll meet you at her home at four o'clock." Flannery put a pocket-sized recorder on the table. "I need you to record it."

"The purpose of the meeting is to get her to tell us something she hasn't already disclosed. The minute she sees the recorder she's going to shut down."

"How do I know you'll tell me if she says anything important; especially if it's about your uncle?"

"Do you honestly think my uncle would be calling in extra help if he was the perp?"

"It's not unheard of, but no, I think he's too smart to bring in a guy with a national rep if he was in on it."

"Then trust me to do this my way. Rose is going to be feeling vulnerable today. I plan to become her confidant. By the way, what did she say when you told her my last name?"

"I kind of coughed through your last name. She didn't ask me to repeat myself."

"Way to go, Flannery. We're going to make a good team." I stood up.

"Don't make me regret this, Jason."

My uncle and I walked next door to the mall where I upgraded my winter wardrobe. Patrick filled me in on Rose's excessive spending to make herself look young. He said she's had more tucks than an origami dragon.

Unlike the Rose Amanescos of the world, I don't care for the notion of using my looks to get my way. However my Behavioral Psychology coursework gave me an appreciation for the effectiveness of modeling other people's behaviors in gaining trust. If I look like I value the same things that Rose values, she should be much more likely to confide in me.

"Why don't you just buy an Armani suit today and return it tomorrow?" Patrick asked.

"You don't buy Armani off of the rack without tailoring, and I don't have time for that. Besides, cops can't afford Armani. I need to be credible. A good knock-off tells her I'm willing to accept a reasonable facsimile of true elegance."

"So you think Rose's affinity for plastic puts her in the same boat?"

"That's the plan."

"You're not going to actually try to seduce her, I hope," Patrick said.

"Emotionally, but not sexually." I inspected a pair of black fur-lined leather men's gloves to replace my Nordic ski model.

"I'm reverting to the military's old *don't ask, don't tell* policy on this one. Feel free to filter out the details," Patrick said.

Patrick laid out his case for why he thought Rose was a viable suspect over lunch at the food court. He described several instances where she hit Louie, threw plates and expensive vases, and threatened to destroy him. He said she loves all of the mafia films and books, and brags about having watched *Scarface* over 100 times. Louie said she quoted lines from the movie on a daily basis; usually ones with threatening connotations.

"I know a lot of people who quote *Star Trek* on a daily basis, but have no illusions about actually beaming up," I said.

"The expression *where there's smoke there's fire* has been around for a long time for a very good reason. In their final year of marriage Rose hounded Louie to build a target practice range in their basement. She has at least four handguns that I know about. Megan gave up on trying to bring her back from the dark side when she found out about the guns and the fascination with gratuitous violence."

"How long will it take me to get to her house?"

"Since you'll be dropping me off back at my house, we better get going now."

Rose Amanesco lived in a beautiful villa at the base of a hill on the outskirts of Clark Summit, which is located a few miles northeast of Scranton. Her alimony checks from Louie couldn't possibly be financing this grand estate. Daddy must have done very well for himself and Rose must be an only child.

I expected a servant to answer the door in tux and tails. Instead, Rose appeared in an outfit that could finance a European vacation for a family of five. As a connoisseur of quality reproductions, Kelly keeps me up on some of the fashion trends. Rose wore a Dolce & Gabbana silk crepe top, a Juicy Couture pink floral skirt, and Manolo Blahnik pearl heels. She appeared to be in her mid-40s, although Patrick said she's well over 50. Her perfectly coiffed panther-black hair fell in ringlets below her shoulders.

Before she could ask to have a look at my credentials, I held up my badge and said, "Thanks for agreeing to meet with me today, Mrs. Amanesco. I know the Society Page Slasher has everyone on edge."

"This is a dreadful way to start the year. I didn't get your name."

I took off my coat to reveal the new wardrobe. "Dreadful is the perfect word to describe it." I flashed my most charming smile. "Although I'm a deputy, I usually work in more of a police consultant role. Why don't you call me Jason?"

Rose returned the volley with teeth so white they'd require shades if viewed in the California sunshine. "And you can call me Rose." She offered me her hand in a manner that called for a kiss. Instead I took it with both of my hands.

"What exquisite nails you have, Rose."

"Thank you, Jason. I do my best."

"May we sit down for a few moments?"

"Follow me," she said, crooking her bejeweled talon under my nose.

We entered a sitting room with a ceiling that had to be at least 25 feet high. The trappings of wealth were as apparent as the trappings of Irish in Thar Saile's Lounge. Through the rear window I saw a tinted glass pyramid that reminded me of the one outside the entrance to The Louvre.

"Why do you have a pyramid in your back yard?"

"That's just the pool cover. I couldn't stand looking at vinyl all winter. Would you like a drink?"

"Coffee would be nice."

"It's nearly cocktail hour, Jason. Are you sure I can't interest you in something a little more daring?"

"I'm on duty, Rose. But I must tell you I have a hard time distinguishing between flavored coffee and Irish coffee."

"Say no more, detective. I have some of the most powerfully flavored coffee in town."

"I'll bet you do."

When she left the room I did my best to ignore King Solomon's treasures and looked for anything related to Louie or the Luna Parkers. The only thing that contrasted with the opulence collection was a wall photo of Al Pacino as Tony Montana in

Scarface. The inscription read: *I always tell the truth. Even when I lie.*

I was about to open a few drawers when Rose walked back into the room with a steaming cup in one hand and a martini glass in the other.

"That was quick," I remarked.

"Those single cup coffee makers are a godsend, especially the morning after big parties."

I sniffed, "Wow, what flavor is that?"

"Irish."

"Rose, how often did you talk with Louie during the month before his murder?"

"About once a week. Do we have to talk about this before we have our drinks?"

"By the smell of this coffee, if I don't ask my questions now I might forget to do it later."

"Well I certainly wouldn't want you to forget how to do it." Rose actually batted her eyelashes at me. I gave her the low-beam smile.

"Did he mention anything that was unusual or hinted that something out of the ordinary happened in his life?" I asked.

"During Christmas week we asked about each other's relatives, or at least those family members that we could stand." Rose put her drink down and folded her hands in her lap. When she did this her skirt rode up a few inches. I loosened my tie just a bit.

"Did Louie owe money to anyone besides you?"

"Louie owed everybody. I don't know why he felt he could keep that house, pay alimony, and afford a social life on top of that. Most of our conversations involved him telling me why the alimony check was short – again. But, as far as I know, he never borrowed from wiseguys, if that's what you're thinking."

"So who did he owe?"

"Mainly credit card companies and personal friends. You might want to talk with the members of his old band, the Luna

Parkers; except for that horrible drummer, of course."

"What about the drummer?"

"Were you planning on staying for dinner? I could tell you stories about him all night long." Rose crossed her legs in a manner that told me *Basic Instinct* was in her video collection.

I said, "How about just giving me the highlight reel."

"Is that like a teaser?" Rose's flashed the 100 watt smile.

"I think we've seen the teaser. What can you tell me about Bongo?"

"He's a very crude man who's been attached to Louie like a leech since we first started dating. As if it wasn't bad enough that they associated with one another through that horrible band, Louie carried that loser on his company payroll for over 35 years. If you're looking for a suspect with a sleazy background and no morals, Bongo Bexton is your man."

"Wouldn't Bongo be cutting off his main source of income by killing Louie?"

Rose finished her martini and stood up. "Bongo Bexton surrounds himself with the scum of the earth. If he didn't kill Louie himself, he probably introduced him to his murderer."

"Anyone in particular?" I asked.

"We don't travel in the same circles. But when I was married to Louie there was many a night when he would show up uninvited and ask Louie for an advance on his salary. His companions always looked like they just walked out of a methadone clinic. I never asked to be introduced."

Rose's temper was starting to show and I needed to keep the momentum going. "Was Louie dating anyone?"

"I need another drink – come," she said, once again crooking the fabulous fingernail of fate. I followed her into the barroom and watched her fly through the mixology ritual at a speed that could knock a club manager's socks off. After her first sip she asked, "Do we really need to talk about that?"

"Jealous girlfriends usually rank pretty high on the suspect list, so yes we do, Rose. I'm sorry if it's still painful to think of

Louie with another woman."

"I was over him before the divorce." She drained half of her new drink in one gulp.

"Was there more than one woman?"

"Louie couldn't afford to keep up with our social circle after the divorce. I'm sure he never lowered himself to Bongo Bexton's level, but I imagine he did well for himself at the clubs that cater to the over 40 crowd."

"Are you telling me you don't know of any girlfriends by name?"

"I heard the occasional rumor that he was seen dancing with a blonde half his age, or a redhead with the rack of a pole dancer, but I never heard any names or ran into him at any of the decent night spots." Rose looked seriously stressed.

"I imagine those decent spots are nearly vacant these days, with the Society Page Slasher still on the loose," I said.

"Oh my God." Rose's voice jumped an octave. "If you people don't find that monster soon I'm going to take a stroke." She reached for a shelf behind her and placed a new martini glass on the bar that held twice the volume. The slight trembling in her hands impeded her quick mix skills. When she finished we returned to the living room. She carefully set her drink on a tray built into the arm of a bottle green leather couch.

I sat in a designer chair adjacent to her. "What did Louie keep in the office safe?"

"He used to keep contracts, petty cash, and his stupid rock band crap."

"Why would he keep his music in the safe?"

"Apparently it has some value. Russell Shapiro once told me that he offered Louie a pretty penny for the copyrights to the old songs, but Louie turned him down," she said.

"I'll bet that offer came up a few times when Louie was late with the alimony."

"You better believe it, Buster." Rose was looking a little tipsy for the first time.

"Is Russell part of your social circle?"

"At first I thought he was just another one of Louie's loser musician friends. When I met him he was a car salesman. Please! But that man showed some real ambition and now owns a chain of dealerships. I see him and his wife at social functions on a fairly regular basis."

I hoped she would elaborate, but her chin rested on her chest and it appeared she was about to lapse into sleep.

"Rose?"

"Jus a minute," she slurred. She then pushed her breasts closer together to achieve a more pronounced cleavage.

Before she could ask me for an opinion I asked, "Why did Louie keep paying on a six million dollar insurance policy, naming you as the beneficiary?"

"Shtaying beautiful isn't cheap." She placed her empty glass on a coffee table in front of us.

"I'm sure it isn't. But if Louie was so strapped for cash why would he keep up those payments?"

"Because he loved me. And, it was in the MSA."

"MSA?"

"Master settlement agreement. The court said he had to."

"Did you talk to the insurance company since Louie died?"

"They're gonna wait till you cops find the rat bastard that killed my Louie," Rose wailed. "He better not come here or I'll let him have it."

In an instant, the tray built into the arm of her couch flew open and an Uzi Model A submachine gun popped up on a gun turret. Rose grabbed the gun and took aim at an imaginary target in the backyard.

I glanced at my watchless wrist. "Look at the time. I had better be on my way. Don't get up. I'll show myself out."

When I returned to Patrick's house I found a note on the kitchen counter that said he was going out for the evening and not to wait up.

Chapter 10

Thursday morning it was my turn to be the early bird. I checked Patrick's room to make sure he made it home safely last night. Most people's snoring sounds like wood being sawed. Patrick sounded like a leaf blower. I decided to let him finish the job before starting breakfast.

Comments from the police commissioner in The *Scranton Times* told me that the new crime scene revealed no new clues. Of course, that's not what the commissioner said. But evasive language doesn't vary much from one coast to the other. The reader comments on the Editorial Page led me to believe the Society Page Slasher would continue to dominate the attention of the entire regional law enforcement community.

My phone rang. It was too early for a call from San Diego. "Jason Duffy."

"It's Flannery. How did your talk with Rose go?"

"She was in training for a martini-athalon, so the lucid portion of the evening was a bit fleeting."

"None of the people I interviewed described her as a lush. Do you think she was drowning her guilt?" he asked.

"It was either guilt, fear of the Slasher, or she was still in love with Louie."

"It could be all of the above."

"Did ballistics match the caliber of the bullet to anything in her gun collection?" I asked.

"They did, but it's a Glock."

"So?"

"Markings on a Glock 9mm bullet are rarely identifiable.

Cartridges, yes; bullets, no. It's not a well known fact outside of the law enforcement community. Since the cartridge wasn't found in Louie's office, we won't be doing a ballistics test on her gun."

"What's next on your agenda?" I asked.

"I have a meeting with my lieutenant in ten minutes. Give me something that will justify your deputy status."

"The fact that there was no sign of forced entry means the killer could have had a key. I'm in the process of meeting the key holders through my uncle."

"Keep me apprised of any new developments. In fact, I expect a daily progress report. I'm getting the feeling that no progress will mean getting reassigned to the Slasher case."

"I understand," I said, and hung up.

I gave Patrick a more complete rundown on my meeting with Rose, although I did tone down the flirting aspects of our conversation. He told me that he met with the Luna Parkers last night and it was agreed that I could audition as Louie's temporary replacement this evening.

It's entirely possible that the item Louie's killer wanted out of the safe had nothing to do with music or the Luna Parkers. He could have been holding evidence on an embezzler from his company's accounting department. He may have had a document implicating a crooked building inspector. Numerous possibilities existed. But at the moment, the only thing I had to go on was Eddie Pohanick's veiled reference to a music connection. Considering that all of the band members, with the possible exception of Bongo, were probably key holders, since Louie's office doubled as a band practice site, I decided to spend most of my day learning the Luna Parkers catalogue.

It was a pleasure playing with Patrick. I don't know if genetics played a part in our ability to mesh rhythm and lead guitar so quickly. I'll have to check the Internet for twin studies if I ever get some downtime at the office. Over lunch I asked Patrick how long his band had been getting ready for the reunion show.

"We started prepping over five years ago. Megan got talking to a local record store owner about how we still got together for jam sessions every month. He told her that a lot of his customers still brought up the band when talking about the old days, and he was sure we could draw a decent crowd."

"Was everybody onboard with the idea right away?" I asked.

"I think Bongo was the only one who was ecstatic. Megan made sure the profits would go to her favorite charity, and that meant I had to sell the other guys on the idea."

"Did they give much resistance?"

"We all had reservations about bald spots, pot bellies, and arthritis limiting the stage moves that helped to define our stage persona. But Megan convinced us to put our vanity aside for the sake of the charity."

"You said this happened around five years ago?" I asked.

"Megan died about a month before the show was slated to happen. The police said that one of her group therapy patients ran her over after a session then killed himself a few days later."

I opted not to ask for details in the middle of the day with the audition yet to come. I had the distinct feeling that Patrick would go straight for his bong if I asked him to elaborate on the circumstances of her death.

"Did Aunt Megan volunteer for any official role with the show?"

"She was the publicity coordinator. Megan found lots of pictures of babies with cleft palates, and toddlers who benefited greatly from the surgery. I'm sure her file folder on the event is still in her desk. You're welcome to look it over when we finish practicing."

Patrick stepped up the intensity level in the afternoon session. I think the talk of Megan brought his blood pressure up. It reminded me of playing the final set at weekend club dates. Whenever the crowd got drunker and rowdier, the band played faster and louder. This struck me as unusual since my band mates always drank very moderately before and during our gigs. But the transference of energy from the crowd to the band never failed to affect our pace after midnight.

We finished practicing around 4:00 PM. "I'm going for a nap before dinner," Patrick said. "It'll only take a few minutes to prepare. Wake me up at 5:30 if I'm still snoozing."

"Is the band coming here?"

"We're going over to Eddie's house. Grab a beer if you want." Patrick closed his bedroom door.

I waited until the leaf blower was back in action before I walked into Megan's sewing room. It was obvious that Patrick hadn't made any changes since her death. He also kept the room cleaner than the rest of the house.

Megan's desk had a file drawer that was well organized and indexed in folders written in perfect penmanship. I plucked one out labeled: LP Benefit Show.

Over the next half hour I sorted through the photos Patrick mentioned, along with individual and group band shots. I also read background info on the charity, and a collection of media sound bites relating to their good works. In addition, I read several pages of minutes from Megan's meetings with the event coordinator, record store owner Dylan Conway. Two items struck me as notable. First, in a brainstorming session about possible newspaper story angles, they talked about misconstrued lyrics in the band's big hit song. I once read a book on this topic entitled: *'Scuse Me While I Kiss This Guy.* Apparently it was a fairly common occurrence back in the day when writing sessions coincided with drinking binges and drug experimentation. A San Diego DJ told me that was how *In the Garden of Eden* turned into *In-A-Gadda-Da-Vida.*

The second notable item was that band manager Russell Shapiro, owner of Superior Motors, offered to finance a rather substantial radio ad campaign for the event. Russell's brother, Eli, is the lead singer for the band. I wasn't sure if Russell was supporting his brother or hoped his dealership would benefit from the charity and local band tie-ins.

Chapter 11

Patrick and I arrived at Eddie Pohanick's abode a few minutes after 8:00 PM. He lived in a split-level stone house in a gated community in Covington Township. We entered through an enclosed back porch, where we changed out of our boots and into sneakers. Eddie greeted us at the door in a black Procol Harem long-sleeved T-shirt and matching black jeans. After a brief exchange he showed us down a flight of stairs to a huge finished basement. We walked through a large sitting room that featured a beautiful stone hearth. The next room held a six-seater bar and cocktail tables that would accommodate another 24.

"I played gigs in smaller bars than this," I said.

"We all have," Eddie noted.

The far wall of the barroom extended nearly the width of the house. A series of plate glass and vented windows spanned the wall. Through the glass I could see a bandstand and dance floor.

"Why the vented widows?" I asked

"Volume control," Eddie said. "Some of my parties are business oriented and some are just for fun."

Patrick added, "Our older relatives tend to stay in the sitting room, which has a sliding door to the bar made especially for noise reduction."

Bongo sat behind his drum kit and gave me a wave as we walked in. Two men in their fifties were hunched over the PA system board.

Patrick said, "Let's do introductions." The Shapiro brothers had some similar facial features, but very different body shapes. "Russell, Eli, this is my nephew, Jason. Jason, Russell and Eli."

We all shook hands. Eli could have been an aerobics instructor at a gym. Russell could have been a *before* picture in a Jenny Craig ad.

"We heard that you played a couple of gigs with Doberman's Stub. I hope you don't mind that we're asking you to audition," Russell said.

"Not a problem," I said. "I know what it's like when a musician doesn't gel with the rest of the band. It can be painful."

"I assume your uncle's Stratocaster is in that case. Are you going to be able to play rhythm on it?" Eddie asked.

"I was given one that's very similar over a year ago. This will work just fine."

"Let's rock & roll," Bongo screamed, and crashed his cymbals.

"Settle down, Bongo, the PA isn't even up yet," Russell said.

Over the next 15 minutes the guitars were tuned and PA levels were checked. Eli asked me if my spot on the bandstand was OK, but was otherwise silent. I'm sure that auditioning a replacement for Louie was tough on everyone, even Bongo.

Patrick took charge of the practice session set list. We started off with cover tunes I had been playing for years. We transitioned into ones Patrick showed me this afternoon and played the Luna Parkers big hit just before taking a break at 10:00. Someone had laid out a nice spread in the bar and we all helped ourselves to beers and hors d'oeuvres before gathering around a pair of cocktail tables.

"Jason, how about if my daughter gives you a tour of the house while we talk," Eddie said.

"Are you kidding me! He was great!" Bongo shouted.

"We're sticking to the plan," Patrick said, and Eddie made a phone call. After a few sips of beer and some discussion about a cover song we hadn't played, an attractive blonde in her early twenties entered the room wearing a mid-thigh black skirt and a shiny emerald green top that led Bongo's eyes into the Valley of the Damned.

"You weren't wearing that when you put out the snacks," Eddie commented, before snapping his fingers next to Bongo's head.

"I might be going out later, Daddy."

"Kristen, this is Patrick's nephew, Jason. Jason, I'd like you to meet my daughter, Kristen." We exchanged hi's, nods, and smiles. "How about giving Jason a little tour of the upstairs?"

"Gladly," she said, and angled her head toward the doorway.

The moment we left the room Kristen went into full fledged flirtation mode. I always considered flirting to be a harmless activity that made the *getting to know you phase* rather fun. However, my girlfriend Kelly has a very different take on this rather innocuous tool in my skill set. In fact, I sometimes get the impression she'd like to beat me over the head with this innocuous tool. I've been doing my best to phase it out of my automatic response system, and felt it would be an ideal time to be diligent. Past experience taught me that flirting with a band mate's sister can get me punched. I would imagine that flirting with a band mate's daughter could have more dire consequences, especially considering that the band members were topping the charts on my current suspect list.

The interior of the Pohanick home was made almost entirely out of polished cherry wood. The living room featured a large fireplace with a two-foot by three-foot faux-stone panel. Behind the panel was a small conveyor belt that brought logs up from the furnace room in the basement.

"Did you ever take a ride on it when you were a kid?" I asked.

"I didn't, but my little brother did it until the day Daddy gave him a spanking. It was the only time he ever spanked either of us."

"I'm sure he was worried that your brother would get hurt."

"That wasn't it. He was talking to somebody about the guy in his band that died, and my brother just got caught at the wrong time."

"Did this happen recently? Are we talking about Louie Amanesco?" I asked.

"It happened over ten years ago. Louie was the second of Daddy's band mates to die. I don't even know the other guy's name. It happened way before I was born. Now let me ask you a question."

"Sure."

"I love how that thick dark brown hair of yours is combed back, and how those tresses sweep over the corners of your forehead and back just above your ears. Where do you get it cut?"

"In San Diego. I'm just visiting."

Except for an uncomfortable moment when Kristen closed the door to her bedroom after showing me inside, the rest of the tour was uneventful. When we reached the basement Eddie thanked his daughter, sent her on her way, and directed me to a chair at the head of the two-cocktail table configuration they were occupying.

"The guys have one final question," Patrick said.

"Fire away."

Russell asked, "Now that you and your uncle have reconnected, is there a chance you'll be coming to Scranton on any kind of regular basis?"

"You should think of me like a studio musician that's contracted to play on your album. You tell me what you need, and I'll do my best to make it work. If I come back it will probably be to introduce Patrick to my girlfriend, who will have to advance to fiancé status for that to happen."

"In that case, you're in," said Eddie.

"No offense, but if we replace Louie it will be with someone closer to our own age," said Russell.

"We appreciate you helping us out for this one show," said Eli. "You certainly have the talent to play with us."

"There's only one more little matter to take care of before we

68

can make you an honorary Luna Parker. You have to survive the initiation" Bongo said.

My first thought was to wonder if that's what happened to the band member who preceded Louie in death. "What do I have to do?"

Bongo reached under the black cocktail table and produced an ornate bong with inlays of colored glass. I had smoked pot in the past, but wasn't a big fan. Truth be told, I went on a two week binge the first time my heart was broken. But eventually it dawned on me that my problems weren't going away, and I was just creating more problems. I know several musicians who swear pot makes them better at their craft. I sound terrible. I won't play in front of anyone if I even catch a contact high.

"Let's wait until after practice. I can't play when I'm high."

"In that case I suggest we adjourn practice, fire this puppy up, and run over to the Ranger Room where we can get to know Louie's sub," Bongo said.

Eddie looked at his watch.

"C'mon counselor, two beers," said Patrick. "You'll be in bed by 12:30."

Eddie looked at Russell, who said, "Now that the bong's out of the bag I'd just as soon do the *partners in crime* ritual."

Bongo immediately flicked his lighter.

From that point forward I'm going to give you my impaired recollection of the remainder of the evening. Pot doesn't make me hallucinate, but I believe my IQ drops by about 25 points while I'm high.

I did my best to take in as little smoke as possible, but with a two-foot bong you can't hold a little puff in your mouth like you can with a joint. When I get high I get quiet, and tonight was no exception. Patrick, Russell, Eddie and Bongo each drove their own cars. Eli rode with Russell. The bar was only about five minutes from Eddie's house. It looked like a hunter's lodge, with stone walls, a vaulted ceiling, and enough buck racks on the walls to hang laundry for a hunting party. There were about ten people at the bar and a table of four over by a jukebox. We sat at a table for six near the bar serving station. No waitress was in sight. The Shapiros had beers on the table by the time we arrived.

I sat at the far end of the table, directly across from Bongo. Patrick sat to my left and Eddie sat between Russell and Bongo. I felt that my diminished capacity would be least noticeable talking with Bongo. Russell and Eli were debating possible dates for the reunion show. Eli wanted to keep the originally scheduled date of two weeks from tomorrow. Russell wanted to postpone in deference to Louie, and to give me more time to practice with the band. Patrick informed them that I wouldn't be around indefinitely, and that sooner would be better. To avoid being sucked into the debate I struck up a conversation with Bongo.

"What do you think I need to work on to be ready in two weeks?"

"Louie did all of our backup vocals. He sang on more than half of our original songs. Patrick said you sang lead for your band."

"I'll be glad to sing backup. Do you have sheet music with the lyrics?"

"I have copies of everything this band ever did, all the way back to the Buzzy West days."

Everyone at the table was suddenly silent and staring at Bongo.

"Was Buzzy the band member who died back in the 70s?" I asked.

"Buzzy made Bongo look like a saint. He was our lead singer until his OD," Eddie said.

"He was a big draw at the box office back when we were just getting started. Russell can tell you, that made a big difference to the powers that be at the major local venues," Patrick said.

"Our lead singer doubled as our school's drug dealer. Back in the era of *tune in, turn on, and drop out* that made Buzzy a very popular guy," Russell said.

"Too bad he couldn't sing for shit," Bongo said.

"Let's not speak ill of the dead," said Eli.

I wanted to ask a probing question, but my brain was wheezing just trying to keep up in its addled state.

"Jason told me he'll sing backup and needs the lyrics. Which version of *Parkers Luna Sea* should I give him?" Bongo asked.

"The one that everybody in the crowd is going to be singing along to," said Eddie.

"I heard you sang lead for Doberman's Stub at a club date after Terry Tucker died," Russell said.

"They wanted to test out their new material before wrapping things up at the recording studio," I said.

"That must have been a thrill for a career club musician," Eli stated.

Russell's phone rang. After a brief conversation he said, "My wife just reminded me that I have to be up at 5:30 tomorrow morning." He stood up. "Eli, are you coming?"

"He can catch a ride with us," Patrick said.

Eli stood up. "I better go with my brother. The older I get, the harder it is to operate on less sleep."

"Don't worry, Eli. We won't give Jason more than half of your songs to sing," Bongo said.

Eli smiled, flipped Bongo off, and departed with his brother.

"My turn," Eddie said, and carried the empty beer bottles to the bar.

"Tell me about how Buzzy died," I said to Bongo. I could always get Patrick's version later.

"We were all at our favorite spot at Nay Aug Park. It's pretty close to the old ruins from Luna Park, just a few feet away from Roaring Brook. We played a gig at St. Bart's that night, but the chaperones pulled the plug on us at ten o'clock after two girls were found passed out in the bathroom, and a bunch of other students were all over the place whacked out on ludes."

"We figured Buzzy worked the room pretty hard before the gig that night," Patrick said.

"Buzzy had both ludes and PCP that night. I don't think he was selling the PCP at St. Bart's. I think he picked it up after the show because it was in a baggie and not broken down into anything sellable," Bongo said.

"Is that what killed him, a combination of Quaaludes and PCP?" I asked. Glancing up, I saw Eddie chatting with an attractive red-haired bartender.

"That's what it said in the toxicology report," Patrick said.

"That didn't seem right to me," Bongo said.

"Why?" I asked.

"I was with Buzzy a couple of times when he was selling both drugs. He'd never sell both to any one person. When anybody would ask for both, Buzzy would tell them that the combination of the two would kill them. I can't see him going against his own advice," Bongo said.

Eddie returned with the beers.

Patrick said, "Thanks, Eddie. Bongo was just telling Jason about the night Buzzy died. Do you want to put your two cents in?"

"Damn it, Patrick! It was hard enough getting through our first practice minus Louie, without bringing up Buzzy's death, too." We all took a slug of beer and sat in silence for a couple of minutes. Eddie broke the silence. "I realize that you two are detectives and need to ask questions, but I can't possibly see the relevance of talking about Buzzy."

"Eddie, when two guys in the same band both die unnatural deaths we have to at least consider the possibility that there could be a connection," Patrick said.

"When it comes to drugs, I've always been the lightweight in the band," Eddie said.

"You got that right," said Bongo.

"But that night I tried a Quaalude for my first and only time. Since the show was over an hour and a half early, I figured I'd come down before it was time to go home. So I took one of Buzzy's ludes on the way to Nay Aug. I started getting off on the way down the hill from the parking lot, and it hit me like a ton of bricks. I fell three times crossing Roaring Brook." Eddie looked at Patrick.

"Eli and I carried him over to our rock. He was mildly incoherent for about a half hour. Then he rallied long enough to take a hit on a joint, and passed out."

"I thought Eli didn't come along until after Buzzy died," I said.

"Eli was our sound tech back then," Bongo said.

Eddie said, "To finish what happened; the next morning I woke up with everyone passed out around me. I knew I was in big trouble with my father for being out all night. In a panic, I started waking everybody up. Buzzy was in his usual place on the rock, but he didn't move."

"I shoved him really hard, and he rolled off of the rock. That's when I knew he was dead," said Bongo.

"I'm going home now," Eddie said, and walked out.

I tried getting Bongo to talk about Louie's post-divorce relationship with Rose. But Bongo was locked in on his former band mate and nothing was going to deter him from his trip back to drugging with his bud. We left Bongo at the bar after finishing our beers.

A blast of snow and wind hit me in the face the instant I opened the door. At least an inch had fallen in the time it took us to drink two beers. Looking up at the lone streetlight illuminating the parking lot, Patrick shook his head.

"It looks like a Nor'easter."

"What's that?"

"It happens when Arctic winds from the north slam into a warm air storm coming up the coast from the south. We could end up with a couple of feet of snow."

The ride back to Patrick's house brought out a paranoid streak in me that I had never experienced in my life. Visibility looked to be about ten feet. I pulled off my stocking cap after a bead of sweat rolled into my eye.

"Why don't you use your high beams, Uncle Patrick?"

"The reflected glare off of the snow makes it even harder to see." Patrick looked over at me, and I was sure we'd be careening over an embankment at any moment. "Don't worry kid, I've done this before. We'll get home just fine."

I looked out the side window for the next couple of minutes. If Jeannine was here I would have hit her up for a Xanax. I tried modulating my breathing by counting to 20 on the inhale, then 20 on the exhale. It helped to calm me down, although those last five seconds of each exhale seemed to last forever. I was exhausted by the time Patrick pulled into his garage.

When we got inside Patrick said, "You look like you could use a brandy."

"I'm beat, Patrick. I'm just gonna go to bed."

"Suit yourself."

Chapter 12

When I woke up on Friday morning it was apparent that I had overslept. The clock radio confirmed my suspicion – 10:35. I had expected a montage of spectacular car crashes to haunt my dreams. Instead I felt well rested.

"Why didn't you wake me up?" I asked Patrick, who was reading a magazine in front of the fireplace.

"Bongo hasn't come by to plow us out yet. I suspect that he tied one on after all that talk about Buzzy last night."

Thankfully, he wasn't busting my stones about my near anxiety attack last night. I took a coffee mug out of the cupboard.

"Don't worry about freaking out on the ride home last night. I know you don't get high very often. If I had to battle my first Nor'easter right after smoking some primo chronic I probably would have shit snowballs."

"It looks like it's still coming down," I said.

"We're at the tail end. Most of what you see is just powder being blown around. We have about 21 inches."

"I should have brought my snowboard."

"What did you think of the band?" he asked.

"You were really tight. I wish I could have seen you when you were playing full time. I'm not surprised that a music store owner wants you to do the reunion. You probably still have a ton of fans."

"Thanks for the pep talk. Now give me the working musician critique. What can we do to improve before the show?" Patrick asked.

"First of all, I haven't been a working musician for three

years. Tsunami Rush broke up when I started my PI internship.

"C'mon Jason, you know what I'm fishing for. Let the fans do the back slapping. Make a contribution that will help us take our game up a notch."

"Those guys are barely accepting me as it is. If I go to the next practice and try to run the show –"

"I don't expect you to do that. Tell me. I'm a master of discretion. I'll filter out anything that I think can't happen in the next two weeks, and implement anything with short term potential."

"OK, I know I'm going to regret this, but here goes. Eddie looks at his fingers almost all of the time. It seemed like he was playing his bass from memory instead of feeling it. Eli has a great voice and perfect pitch. But, he makes Bob Dylan look like Mick Jagger. I don't think he moved the entire night. I wouldn't change a thing about Bongo. However, you were keeping an eye on him like he was a three-year-old looking for trouble. You always managed to look over at me just before your solos, but otherwise you had Bongo on the brain. Have I adequately pissed you off yet?"

"Not at all. You made some very good points. Eli always was and always will be a statue. He's just a natural introvert who was blessed with a golden set of pipes. Bongo even tried giving him a hotfoot at practice one night. Once the fire was out Eli went back into cadaver mode. I didn't pick up on Eddie. That's probably because I was so focused on you and Bongo. He didn't always play like that. I'll see what I can do about loosening him up. Meanwhile, if you catch me unconsciously staring at Bongo again, give a nod toward him the next time I look at you and I'll cut it out."

My *Watching the Detectives* ringtone sounded. "What's going on, Flannery?"

"I'm bringing Rose Amanesco to the stationhouse for questioning at 3:30. Are you interested in watching from the observation room?"

"I'm interested, but I thought we were having a snow day."

"Suck it up, Duffy. If you want to work on your tan go back to California."

"What prompted the formal interrogation?" I asked.

"Her alibi for the night Louie was killed didn't check out. She said she was at her girlfriend's house visiting, and the girlfriend confirmed it. But I since learned that the girlfriend volunteers at her mother's nursing home, and found out she worked the dining room the night Louie was killed. According to the Volunteer Coordinator she didn't leave the facility until 7:30."

"How about if I meet you at your desk at 3:15?"

"I'll be bringing her in. Check in at the front desk. The sergeant will have somebody walk you to the observation room. We can talk afterwards," he said, and hung up.

"Do we have a backup plan for plowing the driveway if Bongo doesn't make it?" I asked.

I filled him in on Flannery's development. Patrick made a phone call and a neighbor with a pickup truck plow had it cleared by 1:30. My uncle dropped me off at police headquarters and went next door to the Steamtown Mall.

A uniformed officer showed me to the observation room at 3:15 and departed. Flannery and Rose arrived at 3:47. When they were both seated he calmly laid out his findings regarding Rose's alibi. Then he turned up the heat.

"Why did you lie about being with Denise Delveccio the night Louie was murdered?"

"I *was* with Denise. Ask her."

"I spoke with the Volunteer Coordinator at her mother's nursing home. She told me Denise worked dinner that night and didn't leave until 7:30. The coroner says Louie died between 6:00 and 7:00."

"I was never much of a clock watcher, detective. Denise and I definitely got together in the early evening that night. With the sun going down so early at this time of year it's hard for me to keep track."

"When was the last time your Glock was fired, Ms. Amanesco?"

"I try to practice a couple of times a week."

"Why do you need so much practice?"

"I'm a female who lives alone in an upscale neighborhood. I like the idea that my neighbors and their help know I have a gun and know how to use it. Do you have an issue with the Second Amendment, Detective Flannery?"

"My only issue is with using human targets."

Rose turned her head toward the mirror and appeared to look right at me. She twirled a finger around one of her ringlets and smiled for just an instant.

"Was Louie behind in his support payments?"

"Yes."

"Did you ever threaten him?"

"Louie was the love of my life. We had spats the whole time we were married and that didn't change with the divorce decree. But I never threatened to kill him."

"Ms. Delveccio is in a lot of trouble for lying to the police in a murder investigation. Are you telling me that after an hour or two of questioning she's not going to remember you making any threatening comments about your ex-husband? She's no Tony Montana. If you're counting on Omerta from her you're in for a big letdown."

"You don't understand, detective. You're a big strong man who gets to carry a gun on his belt all day long. I'm the kind of woman that criminals dream about. If I let people see my vulnerable side I might as well paint a target on my back. So I talk tough and I sometimes act tough. If people think I'm a hard case they're less likely to try and take advantage of me."

"That doesn't change the fact that you lied about your alibi and probably talked Ms. Delveccio into corroborating it."

Before Rose could respond, a briefcase-toting man in a $2000 suit walked into the interview room. "Unless you're charging my client, this interview is over."

Flannery handed Rose a card. "If you feel like unburdening yourself give me a call."

Rose glanced again at the mirror and winked. A minute later Flannery led me into the same interview room.

Flannery asked, "Do you understand now why we're working the snow day?"

"Because sharks steer clear of cold waters, especially sharks with $2000 skins."

"He was probably curled up next to a fire in his smoking jacket reading Proust when he got the call."

"What did you think of her scared little girl routine?" I asked.

"I think she was giving me a preview of her witness stand prowess. What do you think?"

"I've seen drunk and salacious Rose. Now I've seen cornered and caught in a lie Rose. Both times she's gone to the vulnerable card. It's not quite what I expected. Patrick painted her as a fighter. I was sure she was going to ask for her lawyer the minute you blew her alibi out of the water."

"Maybe her life of luxury has her in a state of arrested development. Like a teenager, she thinks she's invincible. Daddy will get her out of any problems that come her way," he said.

"I believed her when she said that Louie was the love of her life. That doesn't mean she didn't kill him. But I do think it means she can't ignore the situation by hiding behind her lawyer. She put herself at risk by talking to you, and she's probably catching hell for it right now."

"I wonder where she practices with her Glock."

"When I visited her last week I saw a big piece of plywood that was pretty beat up at the back of the property. It definitely contrasted with the décor."

"Any sign of it being used recently?" Flannery asked.

"I saw a stand about thirty feet in front of it, and I remember seeing contrasting spots on a nearby snow mound. They were probably shell casings. I wonder if she uses traditional targets or posters of her least favorite people."

"Maybe Diane Delveccio can enlighten us when she's brought in. A black & white was dispatched to her house as soon as we got here."

Flannery spent the next five minutes making three calls. He did not appear happy.

"One of Delveccio's neighbors said she asked him to collect her newspapers and mail for the next two weeks. She told him she needed some January sunshine. I'm guessing the volunteer coordinator didn't keep her yap shut like I asked."

Flannery looked like he wanted to punch a wall. His face was flushed, making his freckles more pronounced.

I stood up and said, "I'll give you a call if anything happens on my end."

I called Patrick as I walked out of the stationhouse. "It's a little late to start cooking. How about if we find a restaurant here in town?"

"Meet me at the car." Patrick sounded stressed.

"What's going on?" I asked, buckling my seatbelt.

"Dakota Rainwater called me a half hour ago. Bongo's had a standing date with her every Friday night for the last ten years. She said today was the first time he didn't call in the early afternoon to talk about their plans for the evening."

"He probably got behind in his plowing because of a late start. You said yourself that he was likely to tie one on after talking about Buzzy."

"She's been calling all afternoon and getting voice mail. I tried, too."

"Bongo strikes me as the kind of guy who occasionally forgets to recharge his cell phone," I said.

"I'm sure you're right about that, but I also know that Bongo is a creature of habit. If his phone was dead he'd hit a bar in between plowing jobs and call Dakota. I promised her we'd look for him."

"Where to?"

"He easily could have gone off the road in that storm last night. But it's too dark to drive around looking for fresh skid marks, especially with snow and slush all over the roads. I talked to the bartender at the Ranger Room and she said he left about ten minutes after us, but didn't say where he was going. I'm sure it was another bar. Since we're in town we can start at Thar Saile's Lounge."

Friday night happy hour was definitely suffering from the snowstorm. There were only about 20 patrons. Most of them looked like they spent their snow day pounding the pints. Patrick spoke with the owner and exited without placing an order.

"Let's head back up the mountain and start with the bars between the Ranger Room and Bongo's trailer."

My stomach was grumbling, so we hit a fast food drive through in Daleville. All Patrick ordered was a large coffee. The sixth pub that we hit was called Paulie's Bar Chord in Moscow. The outdoor sign featured a large plastic guitar with a hand forming an A minor bar chord. Patrick approached a plump bald man of about his own age sitting at the far end of the bar.

"Paulie, was Bongo in here last night?"

"Bongo's in here almost every night."

"What time did he get here last night?"

"Somewhere around midnight, I suppose."

"Did he meet anybody?"

"Is he in jail again, Patrick?"

"No, he's missing. I promised Dakota I'd find him." Patrick pinched his white soul patch. "I'm afraid he might have gone off the road in the storm last night."

"No shit."

"So, did he meet with anyone?"

"Just the usual crew. He came in alone and left alone."

"Did he get any calls?" I asked.

Paulie gave a quizzical look, and Patrick made the introductions. "As a matter of fact I think he got a call just before he left."

"What kind of shape was he in?" Patrick asked.

"For Bongo, I'd say a little better than usual. He calls my place *third base*." Patrick furrowed his brow. He must have been thinking about the musical instrument instead of baseball. "You know - the last stop before heading for home."

"How long was he here?" I asked.

"Fifteen minutes at the most."

"Could you hear his end of the call?" I asked

"I was right here. He was hanging in the middle of the bar. When the call came in he walked over by the dart board. The jukebox was going all night. I don't think anybody heard anything."

"Did he talk to anyone after the call?" I asked

"Nope. He just chugged what was left of his beer and walked out the door."

"Did anybody walk in shortly after he left?" Patrick asked.

Paulie shook his head. "The snow was coming down pretty good by then. Bongo was the last one to stop by."

Since we were less than two miles from Bongo's trailer we headed up Van Brunt Street and soon left the village behind. Patrick put the Prius into a lower gear to climb a steep hill after passing an old WPA stone bridge. When we crested the hill Patrick drove no faster than 15 miles per hour. He instructed me to look for any sign of a vehicle leaving the road on my side, and handed me a flashlight from his glove compartment.

Before we reached Bongo's place, Patrick received a call from Dakota. It was clear that she still hadn't heard from him.

The trailer was set in from the road about fifty feet. There was no pickup truck in front and the driveway wasn't plowed. The snow in the driveway held no tracks.

"He never made it home last night," Patrick said.

"What do we do now?"

"Let's head home and I'll call every bar he could have hit. With all of this snow I ought to be able to get the bartenders to answer a couple of questions."

Over the remainder of the night Patrick called every bar he could think of, and then every other one listed in the phone book. The answer was always the same.

Chapter 13

My uncle woke me up at 6:30 on Saturday morning. I felt like I had been up all night. It's rare that I remember my dreams, but occasionally I'll wake up with the feeling that I had been working on a problem all night long. Unfortunately, no big revelation was coming to mind as I dragged myself out of bed.

Patrick uncovered a plate of bacon, eggs, and home fries when I reached the dining room. "After last night I thought you might need something substantial."

I cut a piece of bacon and asked, "What's the plan for today?"

"We can't file a missing person's report until tomorrow. But, I have friends on most of the local police forces. We'll visit the ones on the mountain before heading into Scranton."

"Did you talk with any of the other band members?"

"I called all of them, starting at five o'clock this morning. Eddie has a few friends in the State Police. He'll get them looking for signs of a car leaving the road on the area highways. Eli will check hospitals and use the computer in every way possible to get the word out. Russell's going to focus on finding Bongo's truck. He'll contact the supervisors of the plow crews all over the area, and also work the cab companies."

About three quarters of the way through breakfast a thought shot across my brain, and I responded as if I'd suddenly gotten a chill. I knew right away that it was the result of my all-night pillow pondering, and didn't know how to tell Patrick.

"What was that? Are you getting the flu? Your mother's going to kill me."

"It's nothing. I'm fine."

"You're not fine. Get back into bed right now. I'll go out by myself today."

"I'm not sick, Patrick. I just had a thought about Bongo that caught me by surprise. It's probably nothing."

"Tell me."

I stared at Patrick without speaking for at least 15 seconds.

Patrick broke the silence. "Saying it out loud won't make it happen. We need to consider all possibilities. Tell me, damn it!"

"There was a lot of talk on Thursday night about the rock you used to hang out on at Nay Aug Park; the one where Buzzy died. What if Bongo went back there?"

"In a Nor'easter when he was just two miles from home?" he asked.

"You're right. It wouldn't make sense." I replied.

"Get your coat and see if you can fit into my high boots. I'm going down to the basement for my hip waders."

Forty-five minutes later we reached the entrance to Nay Aug Park in Scranton. Two lanes had been plowed in front of the park. On my right were a number of Christmas displays adorned in lights. A large sign read *The Twelve Days of Christmas.*

We made a left onto a road that obviously received no more than one pass by a snow plow. The rear end of the Prius slid a bit as we rounded the corner.

"Take it easy, Patrick."

He answered with a stern look. A few more light displays appeared on our left. A minute later I spotted a huge tree house on my right that could have held the whole Swiss Family Robinson. I surmised that it overlooked Roaring Brook. I saw a set of cages up ahead and had to ask.

"What's that?"

"It was our zoo. It's been closed for a few years now."

I looked at the tiny cages and thought about the expansive environments of the San Diego Zoo and the Wild Animal Park. It was like comparing Bongo's trailer to Rose's mansion. Patrick stopped.

"Why don't you put on the hip waders, Jason? My boots aren't going to keep your legs dry."

I could tell by his tone of voice that Patrick was steeling himself against a grim possibility. I held off on the macho man argument about the hip waders, handed him his boots, and put them on. We then trudged down a fairly steep road covered with 21 inches of snow. The closer we got to the bottom of the hill, the louder the brook became, and the faster my heart beat. The road swung to the right as we neared the bottom, and we were suddenly in front of a very modern covered bridge.

Patrick pointed to the left. "The rock is over there, on the other side of the bridge. A couple of pine trees block the view from this angle."

The covered bridge was open on both sides, affording a spectacular view of Roaring Brook. I expected Patrick to take a moment and knock the snow off of his pants above his boot line, but he continued his purposeful stride. About 20 feet past the bridge he stopped.

"The rock is about 50 feet in. It's pretty steep when we first leave the path, so take it easy and concentrate on your balance."

Patrick leaned back a bit as he stepped forward. After noting his form I strained to find an opening in the foliage 50 feet ahead, but no large rocks came into view. I took one step forward, leaned back, and my legs went out from under me. After my coccyx took a mean one-two punch I plowed into the back of Patrick's legs, sending him face-first into heavy powder. A football referee would have thrown a penalty flag for clipping.

"Are you alright?" Patrick asked.

Dusting myself off I replied, "My ass hasn't felt like this since the day Dad caught me smoking a cigarette behind the garage."

My comment failed to lighten the mood. "Can you walk?"

"I'll be fine."

We passed through a stand of pine trees on a path shaped like a fish hook. At the point of the hook was the rock, blanketed in snow. It was about fifteen by fifteen and slanted toward the brook, which was visible to the right but totally obscured by pines to the left.

Patrick immediately began sweeping the front of the rock furiously with his gloved hands. I moved to the left side and started digging at a more controlled pace. Soon we had removed all of the snow that could be reached from ground level, and climbed onto it.

"Take it easy up here, Jason."

Over the next ten minutes we managed to push about two thirds of the snow off of the rock without falling.

"Oh my god!"

Patrick jumped off of the right side of the rock and disappeared from my view.

"Bongo!"

I spent the better part of the next three hours suffering the indignity of getting my tailbone x-rayed at a hospital conveniently located at the entrance to the park. After looking into the frozen face of a man I had just accepted as a band mate I wasn't up for the moon jokes and butt puns that came from well-meaning staff members. Patrick drove me over, but I insisted that he return to the crime scene to oversee the collection of forensic evidence.

"I'm sure the Crime Scene Unit can handle it without me," he said.

"I know nothing about what can and can't be done to find footprints made during a snowstorm. But, if the local police relegated their least tenured detective to work Louie's case, I wouldn't leave anything to chance on what they'll do for Bongo."

Patrick tried to give me his best poker face, but I could feel the reality of the situation hitting him hard. He turned his head as he got out of the waiting room chair.

"Call me when they're done with you."

About an hour later the phone rang. I was expecting an update from Patrick. Instead, it was Walter Shamansky, a San Diego homicide detective and my contact within the department. We worked closely on my top three cases, the most recent just a month ago. It might be good to talk with a friend right now.

"What the hell are you doing in Scranton? I scheduled you for a deposition on Monday morning, and your father tells me you're off helping his no good, pain in the ass brother on the other side of the country."

"Could you not use the phrase *pain in the ass* anymore?" I told him about finding Bongo and my current medical status.

Shamansky said, "It doesn't do any good to bust the bad guys if you don't do what it takes afterwards to put them away for their crimes. I expect you to get your sorry ass on a plane tomorrow and meet me in the lobby of the DA's office at 10:00 AM on Monday." Cell phone silence signaled the end of the discussion.

There was no way I could burn Shamansky and continue to be an effective PI in San Diego. He wouldn't be asking me to drop what I was doing if the deposition wasn't vital to the prosecution's case. So, I used my phone to make flight arrangements for tomorrow.

The doctor told me that my coccyx wasn't fractured, but that it would be plenty sore for the next few days. He also told me to avoid sitting as much as possible. I wondered if it would be possible to flirt with a flight attendant in the galley from a standing position for nearly six hours.

"I have to fly across the country tomorrow. There's no way I can postpone it."

"Stop at any pharmacy and tell them you need a donut."

I no longer had to worry about getting my flirt on. The best I could hope for from the flight attendants was that they held their laughter until I was out of earshot.

Patrick picked me up and drove me to a neighborhood pharmacy for my donut; a big, red, shiny one. It was the same color and texture as a whoopee cushion. I wondered if they were made by the same manufacturer, and if they ever made a few gag donuts on casual Friday.

"Flannery wants me to drive you over to the scene. He'll come up to the car to talk with you."

"I take it that putting Flannery on the case means they think it's related to Louie's murder," I said.

"Probably."

When Patrick didn't elaborate I said, "Or, you think that with Bongo's long sheet of minor offenses they don't want to pull anybody off of the Society Page Slasher case."

"I'm glad Flannery has both cases. Related or not, it'll make our lives easier."

When we turned onto the road leading to the zoo I noticed that it had been widened considerably by a snow plow. A large section had been cleared across from the zoo, and several official vehicles were parked in a less than uniform fashion. I spotted Flannery making his way up the road from the covered bridge, which was also now plowed.

He stuck his head in my window, looked down at the red donut, and to his credit, refrained from cracking wise. "Patrick, can you give us a few minutes?"

My uncle walked over to a coroner's office staff car that was parked 30 feet in front of us and knocked on the window. He then climbed into the back seat.

"Patrick wasn't very clear when he explained how you two came to look down there for Bongo."

I spent the next five minutes explaining, in the least incriminating way possible, about how Bongo recounted the night Buzzy died shortly before disappearing. "Was Forensics able to find evidence of another set of prints?"

"The Nor'easter took care of that, if there was anyone else down there."

"What do you mean *if*?"

"We won't know until the tox report comes back, but the coroner is calling it an OD for right now."

"Two guys from the same band are found dead in consecutive

weeks and you don't suspect foul play?"

"Louie took care of Bongo like a brother. He was undoubtedly depressed. It's a well known fact that he had a big drug problem. And, when I asked Patrick if anything else unusual was happening in Bongo's life, he told me about his big win at Mohegan Sun."

"Shouldn't the money make him less depressed?" I asked.

"What do you think druggie's do when they come into a lot of money?"

"Did you find drugs on him?"

"Enough to kill him five times."

"How did he get down there?"

"Patrick told us the band used to park up on the hill, where Luna Park used to be. I walked up and found his pickup truck. Forensics is going through it now to see if there's any sign that he had a passenger, but I wouldn't count on it."

"Bongo wasn't depressed. I agreed to fill in for Louie at the upcoming reunion gig, and Bongo was the most enthusiastic guy in the band. I was sitting across from him at the Ranger Room when he talked about Buzzy. I'd say he was nostalgic, but definitely not the least bit maudlin."

"Jason, sometimes there's a fine line between excessive celebration and excessive depression for long-term druggies. He might have taken the first couple of snorts to celebrate; a couple more for Buzzy; a couple more for Louie; pretty soon he's passed out in the middle of a big snowstorm."

What Flannery was saying made sense, but my gut wasn't buying it. "What about the phone call he got at Paulie's in Moscow? Who was it from?"

"We didn't find a phone."

"I heard Bongo always carried a phone. Don't you think that's suspicious?"

"Patrick said it was a cheap burner. Maybe the battery died and he tossed it. With the casino winnings to spend it's certainly a solid possibility."

"It also conveniently prevents us from being able to learn

who called him at Paulie's."

"I'll try to keep an open mind, but I plan to spend most of my time working Louie's case," he said.

"I'm going back to San Diego for a couple of days to give a deposition on the Concert Killer case. I'll call you as soon as I get back here."

Chapter 14

I felt terrible leaving Patrick right after Bongo died. From Shamansky's tone I got the distinct impression that a delay in my deposition would be a win for the Concert Killer's defense team. I knew that Shamansky juggled working active cases with providing testimony on a regular basis. Justice is never served by sloppy follow through after the arrest. If I wanted to continue building my reputation at SDPD I needed to fulfill all expected obligations.

Kelly picked me up at Lindberg Field late Sunday afternoon. She was anxious to talk about the family therapy sessions that I set up before my departure.

"Andy Stelzner is seeing them twice a week. He asked me to attend the first one, and it went pretty well."

"Are you going to be included on a regular basis?" I asked.

"I don't think so. Since I don't live in the home and I'm not part of their drinking circle, I'll only be making the occasional guest appearance if my presence becomes necessary."

"Do you like Andy?"

"I do. He told us he practices Reality Therapy, which is what Danny should expect if he gets sentenced to prison. Andy also told us that a good progress report might possibly keep my brother out of jail. He made a strong case for securing their cooperation. Whether or not they can stay sober long enough to complete the program remains to be seen."

Upon entering my house, our seven-month-old German Shepherd, Colonel Hogan, nearly knocked me on my battered and bruised behind. This prompted a discussion on why I was walking funny. I glossed over the part about how broken up Patrick was regarding the loss of another friend.

"I guess I won't have to worry about you pulling any more slick moves to get laid," she said.

"I'm sure sex would be very painful in any position right now. And, do you know what? It would serve me right for the way I treated you just before leaving."

"You're impossible," she said, and left the room.

I used the moment to hobble into the bathroom for a much needed pit stop. I've never been a big fan of jet johns. Turbulence and peeing just don't give me that *friendly skies* feeling. I feel sorry for the women who have to sit on those seats, knowing that most of the men were about as accurate as a drunk trying to write his name in the snow. I took a few extra minutes to wash up after my flight.

When I emerged from the bathroom Kelly called to me from the bedroom. She was dressed in a sexy nursing costume she wore for Halloween the year before last.

"Your doctor wants me to start the examination without him. I'll need you to drop 'em and lie down on the examining table."

Whoever said *payback's a bitch* didn't know Kelly.

Later in the evening I gave Kelly a fairly complete rundown on what was happening in Scranton. She was very interested in exploring my similarities with Uncle Patrick and the origins of his feud with Dad. She was also enthralled with Aunt Megan, her hippie upbringing, and how those values impacted her life with my uncle.

By 9:00 PM I was getting tired. The combination of east coast time change and pain pills for my battered butt caused me to fade fast. Kelly insisted that I lay my head in her Nurse Nancy-clad lap, and tickled my face with her long chestnut hair a couple of times before allowing me to turn in for the night.

I arrived at the DA's office lobby at 9:50, and scanned the room for Shamansky. After a couple of minutes I was approached by a woman in her late thirties wearing a conservative green business suit, and with black hair pulled back so tight it drew her eyebrows up into a constant look of surprise.

"Are you Jason Duffy?"

"Yes. I'm waiting for Detective Shamansky."

"He called a few minutes ago and isn't going to be able to make it. My name is Regina Holmeyer. I'll be conducting the deposition."

Over the next three hours I recounted my role in the Concert Killer case and answered numerous questions. Regina was thorough, professional, and about as stiff as a Snickers Bar after a week in the freezer.

When it became clear that our meeting was drawing to a close I asked, "Is it going to be a problem that Detective Shamansky wasn't here today?"

"Not at all. We won't be going to trial for at least another five months. As long as he gets the dep done in the next month we're fine."

"Then what was the emergency in getting me back here today?"

"I didn't insist on today. Detective Shamansky asked if I'd be available to meet with you today, and I moved a couple of things in my calendar to make it happen. No need to thank me, it's all part of the job."

I managed to maintain a cordial face as I bid farewell. Below the surface I was picturing myself sharing my pain with Shamansky by burying my Timberline in his gluteus maximus. When I got to the lobby I called him immediately, but reached voicemail and didn't leave a message. He'd need his Kevlar vest if I did a proper job of venting my anger.

A voicemail from Mom said that Dad was at Casey's Bar, and she'd love to have a late lunch after my deposition. I waited until I got back to my car to place the call. She was anxious to hear about Patrick, and I agreed to come right over.

I considered taking a pain pill on the short drive from

downtown to Little Italy. But Mom is very perceptive and would pick up on it in no time. At least I was off of the hard plastic chair at the DA's office.

The instant I walked in the door I was glad my senses were fully functional. The smell of Mom's homemade chicken soup brought me back to a simpler time, and a feeling that everything was going to be alright.

After a hug and kiss Mom said, "Jason, you look terrible. Why are you walking like that?"

I explained what happened and she directed me to the most comfortable chair in the living room – my father's recliner.

"I'll get you set up on a TV tray and we'll eat in here."

I answered questions over lunch about Patrick's state of mind, and she told me about his relationship with Aunt Megan. It was apparent that Mom loved them both, and felt badly that she wasn't able to engineer a truce between the two brothers.

"Did I tell you that I spoke with Megan the afternoon before she died?" Mom said.

"No, you didn't. Did she sound anxious or concerned about any of the patients she was seeing?"

"She did sound anxious, but not about her patients. She was scheduled to meet with a reporter the next day about the reunion concert, and she was worried about saying the right things to get the band's old fans motivated enough to come out to the show."

"Nothing at all about anyone acting in a threatening way?"

"Megan loved working in a helping profession. She never talked specifically about anyone in particular. But we had a close enough relationship where she felt comfortable expressing concerns and disappointments when her clients were regressing. I'd say she was pretty pleased with the progress of her evening group members."

Dad walked in the front door, and the healing qualities of Mom's chicken soup leaked out.

"If it isn't my son, Benedict Arnold. What the hell are you doing in my chair?"

"He has a badly bruised bottom," Mom said.

"I hope it's from somebody trying to kick some sense into you."

"Jim, that's a terrible thing to say to your son," Mom said.

"Did you put Shamansky up to ordering me back here for a deposition that isn't due for another month?"

"Maybe he was just pissed that you'd turn your back on your old man to help some pinko commie sympathizer."

"How did he happen to learn about your lifelong vendetta? Did you invite him over to play the home game of Family Feud?" I asked.

The next ten minutes are too embarrassing to recount. Suffice it to say that he compared me to Judas Iscariot, and I told him he was a hypocrite and a bad Catholic for receiving communion every Sunday with brotherly hate in his heart.

By the time I left their house my head was pounding, my heart was racing, and my tailbone felt like it had been inflated by an air compressor. I took a double dose of the pain pills and headed for my office. I arrived 20 minutes later, and still wasn't feeling the effects of the medicine. The office door was locked.

Jeannine left a note on my desk that said she got called in to work at the golf course cocktail lounge, and would be out for the remainder of the day. Since I was still fully in the mood, I placed another call to Shamansky, but again got voicemail and hung up.

The golf course wasn't far away. When I exited my car I felt a bit lightheaded. I pictured some of the compressed air in my tailbone travelling up my spine and into my brain, like a 60s television commercial from an episode of Mad Men. Cory's van was nowhere in sight.

Entering the club, I was met by a linebacker of yesteryear wearing the country club's employee shirt.

"Sorry, no guests in the lounge today."

"What's going on?"

"Private party."

"I need to speak with one of your cocktail waitresses, Jeannine Joshlin." I said. My tailbone pain was now a non-issue.

"She's working the party, and you need to leave now."

"I'm her brother, Jason, and I need to see her on a very important family matter."

"Your sister is a very nice girl. We love having her on the staff. You wouldn't want to jeopardize her job by making a scene, would you?"

"I just flew all the way across the country to deal with this emergency, and I have to fly back in a few hours. The instant I walk out of here I'm going to call Jeannine, tell her that her employers don't give a damn about her or her family emergency, and insist that she quit her job immediately. I guarantee today will be her last day."

Linebacker dude looked genuinely perplexed. "Stay right here," he said, and walked into the lounge. A minute later he returned with Jeannine.

"I'm afraid I have some bad news about Aunt Louise," I said. "Let's take a little walk."

The bouncer gave her a nod.

"Where's Cory?" I asked.

"He's tailing Vinnie and one of his golfing buddies. We think the two of them and one of the golf cart boys are planning a jewelry store heist."

"What led you to that conclusion?"

"The golfing buddy, Hubert, works at a high end jeweler here in La Jolla. Cory saw them both enter the store after hours twice in the last three days. Once it was just the two of them, and once with Benjamin, the cart boy."

"Anything else?"

"Cory took a picture of Vinnie and Hubert walking out of Vinnie's house yesterday. Hubert was holding a tennis bracelet up to let the sun reflect off of the stones. We're assuming it belongs to Mrs. Vincigura."

"I'm sure there could be an innocent explanation. Maybe

Vinnie was getting a loose stone reset."

Jeannine asked, "How does the cart boy fit into the innocent explanation?"

"I'll have to check Cory's timelines and photos before I hazard a guess at that one. Why is there muscle on the door today?"

"They've got a *money on the table* Hold 'Em poker game going on. I'm told it only happens once a month. I knew Vinnie would be getting in, so I agreed to work it."

"I thought you said Cory was tailing him."

"Vinnie and Hubert both lost in the first round. I should probably get back in there. By the way, are you OK? You look a little strange."

"I took a fall, I'll be alright. I'm on a pain med that has me a bit lightheaded."

"Stay here. I'll be right back."

Jeannine jogged to the lounge in her racy outfit. The sight left no doubt in my mind why the bouncer agreed to her unscheduled break. Two minutes later she returned.

"Give me your car keys," she said.

"I'm fine," I said.

"You're not fine and you're not driving. I took the rest of the day off. Hand 'em over."

"But you don't drive, Jeannine."

"I know how, I just choose not to."

"Do you have a license?"

"No, and you're not going to have one either once you start sideswiping cars on Pearl Street. Hand 'em over. I know what I'm doing."

Ten minutes later we pulled up behind Cory's van on Prospect. It was getting dark, and the coastal breeze had just a hint of a January nip. I thought of Patrick's hip waders. Jeannine got covered in canine kisses the instant she opened the back of the van. I, too, received a royal welcome from Hoover.

"What's going on?" I asked.

Cory told us that the store clerk departed when Hubert arrived.

98

Vinnie stayed in his car until the clerk was out of sight. Then he went into the store's glassed-in interior office and closed the blinds. Hubert locked up a few minutes before we arrived and joined Vinnie in the office. Hoover did his bark-over thing every time Cory spewed a four letter word. For the first time, the bark-over didn't disrupt my ability to focus on Cory's content.

"Let's hang out for a bit and see where they go," I said.

While we waited Cory quizzed Jeannine on her driving history. Apparently she never made it past her high school driver's education course. In fact, she never made it out of the school parking lot. She became so fixated on the little pebbles on the driver's side floor mat that she hit a light pole in the middle of the lot. Good thing I picked up a two-for-the-price-of-one deal on car detailing last month.

At 6:10 PM a fairly new Mustang parked in front of the store. A young man with a surfer haircut, tan, and a Belvedere Heritage Country Club shirt walked to the front door and knocked.

"Do you have your directional listening device?" I asked.

Cory said it wouldn't work through the store's bulletproof glass. He asked if I thought they were trying to crack a safe.

"Hubert looks like a trusted employee, or maybe even a partner. He probably has the combination." I said.

After a few minutes Jeannine asked, "When are you flying back to Pennsylvania?"

"Tomorrow morning. I'm hoping to get back in time for a wake."

"You should spend the night with Kelly. Let Cory drive you home in your car. He can take a cab back. I'll keep an eye on the diabolical duffers while Hoover keeps me company."

"What if they leave while we're gone?" I asked.

We all looked down at the mats on Cory's floor. He told us he'd plant a tracking device on Vinnie's Cadillac, and Jeannine assured us she'd stay put. Five minutes later we were on our way.

I decided not to bring my problems home with me, so I called

Mrs. Vincigura while Cory drove. She was as unpleasant as ever. At first it sounded as if she wanted to shut down our surveillance since we had yet to uncover any evidence of infidelity. But, when I made it clear that Vinnie could be involved in a criminal endeavor that could jeopardize her financial well being with huge legal fees, she opted to continue the operation.

Kelly and I both went out of our way to try to make it as enjoyable an evening as possible. I had no idea how long I'd be gone.

When I worked as a counselor for two years after college I did my best to get clients in touch with their feelings. But in Kelly's case, instead of discussing her dysfunctional family, I opted to tell her all about Uncle Patrick, Aunt Megan, Louie, Bongo, and the others in hopes of getting her to care about their plight. I wanted her to understand why I needed to see the case through to the end. I think I won her over when I launched into Mom's long-term relationship with Megan, and her genuine concern for Patrick.

Several times during the evening I considered calling Shamansky and leaving a message that fully expressed my own feelings about his bogus emergency. But I mashed those feelings down like grapes in a vat because I knew it would kill the mood with Kelly. Besides, burning my number one bridge into the San Diego Police Department would be foolhardy. Perhaps I'd downgrade his free lunches to eateries that offered plastic toys and cardboard crowns.

Chapter 15

Charger fever was everywhere, as our local football team made a definite statement in the playoffs two days ago. I spotted a street vendor selling small Chargers blankets as we neared the airport. Kelly pulled over while I bought a cover for my butt donut. At least I wouldn't be heckled by the bullies of the friendly skies, or showered with unwanted attention by motherly flight attendants.

Patrick picked me up just in time for a quick trip back to his house to change into appropriate clothes for Bongo's wake. I suspected that there was a very real possibility that his killer would be in attendance, so I opted to forego any more pain pills.

The funeral home was located in South Side, about ten blocks from Thar Saile's Lounge. I hoped there were enough unshoveled sidewalks between the two establishments to prevent Irish wake histrionics and other acts of unruly drunken comportment. The funeral home itself was large enough to accommodate a doubleheader. But Bongo didn't have to share the limelight. There were about 40 people in attendance when we arrived, about 45 minutes into a three hour viewing.

"At least half of these people are musicians," Patrick said, as we made our way to the casket.

The funeral home did a nice job on Bongo. I wasn't sure if we'd be seeing an open casket. I said a short prayer and followed Patrick to the back of the room where the remaining Luna Parkers had gathered.

Russell gave Patrick a hug. "This is too much. I don't think my heart can take any more."

Eli shook my hand, and embraced Patrick once his brother let him go.

Eddie was standing in a small circle next to us with his wife, daughter, and another couple. Patrick tapped him on the shoulder.

"Patrick, I'm so sorry you had to find him that way. It was hard enough hearing the news without actually being there."

"I don't think anyone expected him to live to a ripe old age. But finding him in the same place as Buzzy is making sleep damn near impossible," Patrick said.

Turning to me, Eddie said, "One of my friends on the force told me you were the one who thought to look there. Whatever gave you that idea?"

"He was locked in on talking about Buzzy at the Ranger Room, and mentioned your rock by Roaring Brook. I thought it was worth checking out."

Eddie's daughter, Kristen, gave me a finger wave and a sad smile. I thought her black dress looked more fitting for a cocktail party than a funeral home. Patrick gave me a shoulder tap.

"Jason, I'd like you to meet Dylan Conway. He's our promoter for the reunion show."

Before we could shake hands, Bongo's girlfriend, Dakota Rainwater, threw her arms around Patrick and began to sob.

Dylan said, "Let's give them a little space."

I followed him to a quiet spot in front of the restrooms. He appeared to be in his early 50s, with black and silver hair combed neatly to the side.

"Eddie told me you agreed to fill in for Louie."

"I'm sure that's a moot point right now," I said.

"We all found out yesterday that Dakota charged the wake and funeral on her credit card. She barely makes minimum wage as a retail clerk. I've talked with Eddie and Eli so far, and they're both willing to do the show as a benefit concert for Dakota if everybody goes along. It was originally going to be a benefit when Megan was alive."

"What do we do for a drummer?"

"Eli said Russell has been playing drums since the Luna Parkers were the hottest band around here. He's not as good as Bongo, but he knows all of the songs and Eli says he keeps a good beat."

"I made a commitment to play. If the band is still willing to do the gig, I'm in."

Dylan patted my shoulder. "Glad to hear it."

"I understand you worked closely with Megan on marketing the event five years ago."

"Your aunt was a saint."

"She died the night before she was to meet with a reporter from the Times. Did you two go over talking points for the interview?" I asked.

Dylan put his hand on a lighted display cabinet against the wall adjacent to the restrooms. For a moment he stared into the cabinet, deep in thought. The display cabinet held a small shrine to Penn State football.

"The only thing that stands out is that she wanted to talk about misconstrued lyrics in their big hit, *Parkers Luna Sea*."

"I saw that in her notes. What's it all about?"

"I don't remember exactly. But it had to do with the line: *That's why it took the ten of us to bloom*. Back in the day, there was all kinds of speculation on who was being counted among the ten since there were only five band members."

"What was misconstrued?"

"Ask Patrick. I'm sure Megan explained it to me five years ago, but her death knocked me for such a loop that I honestly don't recall any more details."

The remainder of the evening was spent fielding questions from numerous musicians. Someone mentioned that I played a couple of gigs with Doberman's Stub, and that ended my ability to have any more quiet conversations. I tried keeping an eye out for suspicious looking characters around the casket.

But with so many musicians dressing in a manner that Bongo would appreciate, and so many drug & alcohol buddies arriving in various states of cosmic awareness, Ziggy Stardust on acid wouldn't stand out in that crowd.

I asked Patrick if he learned anything significant on the ride home from the wake.

"I talked with Bongo's sister. She had him over for dinner just before band practice. She said he was in great spirits because of you coming along to help make the reunion concert happen."

"So she thinks suicide is off of the table. What about an OD?"

"I can answer that one, Jason. Bongo used whatever he could get his hands on since the early years of the band. He knew more about dosages, side effects and contraindications than most pharmacists."

"Yes, but it's probably been a long time since he was flush enough with the bucks to afford whatever his heart desired. You heard what they found on him."

"I couldn't tell this to Flannery for obvious reasons, but the scene was a set up. There's no way Bongo would have brought that big of a stash out with him on a warm summer night, let alone in the middle of a snowstorm."

"Maybe he was reveling in the big spender role. I hear it happens all of the time after huge gambling wins."

"Bongo was a realist. I had enough heart-to-heart chats with the man over the years to know that. He didn't win the Mega Millions Lottery, he won ten grand and had more creditors chasing him than a Florida real estate developer in 2009. Bongo wasn't a dealer, and would never carry more of his stash than he planned to use in one night."

"What do you think happened, Patrick?"

"Whoever called him at Paulie's Bar Chord talked him into making one more stop before going home. If the set up was a one man job, Bongo was convinced to drive 12 miles in a Nor'easter to Nay Aug Park. If it was more than a one man job he could have been OD'd anywhere, and the accomplice drove his pickup to the park."

"How did Bongo feel about driving in snowstorms?" I asked.

"He wasn't afraid, but he also wasn't stupid. I'm sure it would have taken a pretty compelling reason to get him out there on a night like that."

"Could it be to score some primo drugs at the right price?" I asked.

"I don't think so."

Chapter 16

Most people consider seven to be a lucky number. When I saw it on Patrick's porch thermometer as we left for Bongo's funeral on Wednesday morning it lost most of its magic for me. My face felt numb by the time we got in the car. The leather seats reminded me that my butt was still on the disabled list.

We were directed to a little chapel in the Moscow graveyard. I sat in a metal folding chair for about three seconds before opting to stand in the back. Just as the caretaker was about to close the chapel door, Rose Amanesco slipped in wearing a large black hat and sunglasses. She realized her cover was blown the instant I nudged her and nodded.

It was apparent that the preacher knew Bongo by reputation only. He made a few minor references to the benefits of a wholesome lifestyle, but quickly ended the sermon when Russell began coughing. Dakota gave a passionate eulogy that any musician would have loved. It was too bad that there were only about twenty people in attendance.

The bereavement luncheon was at a small restaurant about a mile from the cemetery. I wasn't surprised to see that Rose passed on the opportunity to chat with Louie's friends. I listened to one story after another about Bongo's most memorable moments. The only thing worth reporting was that the band scheduled a practice for the following evening, again at Eddie's house. I received a call from Flannery as the luncheon wound down.

"I'm in the restaurant parking lot. Are you and Patrick up for a look inside Bongo's trailer?"

"We'll be right out."

We followed Flannery into town and up Van Brunt Street until we reached the trailer. The driveway had been plowed and a path had been hastily shoveled to accommodate the forensic unit's gear. Flannery stood next to his vehicle with one hand in the air. We pulled in behind him.

"What's up?" Patrick called from alongside his car.

"Somebody's been here since we processed the scene."

I walked around the vehicle to bring Flannery into view. "How do you know?"

"I left the shovel by the front door. I see drag marks in the path. Whoever was here used the shovel to obscure footprints, and probably tossed the shovel when he got back to the plowed driveway."

"Good eye, Flannery," said Patrick. "Can we go in now?"

Over the next forty-five minutes we picked through Bongo's treasures. Patrick gave a running commentary on mementos Bongo had saved from his glory days with the Luna Parkers, as well as pictures from other groups that Bongo had played with over the years.

"What's missing, Patrick?" Flannery asked.

"A well stocked bar," he replied. "I need a drink. Why don't we go down to Paulie's and kick it around."

Flannery didn't look too pleased with his answer, but agreed and we led the way to the bar.

Alone in the car with Patrick I said, "I can see the wheels turning, Patrick. Let's hear it."

He responded by shooting me an uncertain look.

"The day we stop being partners on this thing is the day I go home."

"I'm trying to figure out whether or not to tell Flannery."

"What?" I asked.

"Rose gave Louie a new briefcase for his birthday the year before they split up. Louie gave his old one to Bongo. It was one of his prize possessions."

"But it wasn't in the house."

"It wasn't in his pickup either," he said.

"What was in it?"

"Sheet music, pictures, handbills from big shows, a few sets of drumsticks, and few tools for his drum kit."

"What's the harm in telling Flannery?"

"It'll probably put each of the band members under the microscope," he said.

"If you don't tell him and somebody else like Dakota mentions it, you look like you're covering something up."

We pulled into Paulie's parking lot. "I'll figure it out by the end of my first drink."

The three of us sat at a table near the front window, away from Paulie and the five people occupying the bar. Patrick asked for our orders and walked up to the bartender.

"Did the forensic unit find anything helpful at Nay Aug Park?" I asked.

"The snowstorm wiped out any usable trace."

"Is it possible to uncover footprints after a storm, like an archeologist at a dig site?"

"Not when we're dealing with a Nor'easter. The wind is too much of a factor. Even if snow print archeology was a real science, and our department approved the huge expense, chances are it would be excluded in a pretrial motion."

"So what did you find?"

"Enough drugs for the DA to call it an accidental overdose."

I wanted to pass along Patrick's comment that Bongo would never go anywhere with a big stash. But considering the bad habits of my uncle and his friends, I thought it best to let him share anything of that nature in his own way.

He returned from the bar with a beer for me, a soda for Flannery, and a double Wild Turkey for himself. "Did I miss anything?"

"You tell me, Patrick. What was missing from Bongo's trailer?"

Patrick immediately told him all about the briefcase.

"What could have been in there that cost Bongo his life?" asked Flannery.

"Only two possibilities are coming to me. It could be that Louie's killer didn't find what he was looking for in the wall safe, and thought he gave it to Bongo to hold for him. Or, they both had a copy of the same document, and the killer wanted the documents and absolute assurance of their silence."

We sipped our drinks and processed those possibilities. Flannery had Patrick describe the briefcase in detail. Patrick told him it was highly unlikely that the briefcase contained a secret compartment where Louie could have hidden something without Bongo's knowledge. He also pointed out that Louie was not likely to expect Bongo incapable of losing the briefcase during one of his inebriated escapades.

"What's happening with Rose?" Patrick asked.

"I stood next to her at the cemetery chapel this morning," I said.

"I saw you," Patrick said with a hint of disgust in his voice. "I was asking Flannery."

"I paid her a visit yesterday to hear what she had to say about Bongo. At first she wasn't particularly broken up about him. But when I asked if she thought there was a connection between the two murders she cried and fixed herself a drink that would have knocked Bongo on his ass."

"Did she come on to you?" I asked.

"I left when she started getting flirty."

"Was there any surveillance on her during the snowstorm?" Patrick asked.

"I'm still flying solo, Patrick. She said she was home alone, and would rather wear a dress from Wal-Mart than drive during a Nor'easter."

"That tops a *swear to God and hope to die* in Rose's world."

"I figured as much." Flannery stood. "Is there anything you're not telling me, Patrick?"

"Just that I'm wondering if I'll be next."

When we returned to Patrick's house I spent about an hour on the phone with Jeannine. She is truly an exceptional Internet researcher. I asked her to get everything she could on Louie, Bongo, Megan, and Buzzy. Patrick accepted Megan's death as an accident, but the timing was too coincidental for me.

My uncle kept drinking until after dinner, then mixed in some pot. To avoid debating him on the merits of pot as an antidepressant, I told him I was turning in early and brought my laptop into the bedroom. Jeannine called a half hour before she needed to leave for the country club.

"I'm sorry to say I don't see any real common denominator."

"Was there much info on Buzzy?" I asked.

"Just an obit that had been scanned into the local paper's archives. It read like his mother wrote it, and made just a casual reference to his status as a musician."

"How about the others?"

"The other three all died within weeks of the scheduled reunion show. Megan's death cancelled the first one. But when Louie's murder didn't cancel the next try, Bongo got added to the victim list. It seems like somebody really doesn't want the show to go on."

"Patrick said my aunt's connection to the show was serving as publicity coordinator. Were there any articles written about the show in the Scranton paper or any surrounding community publications?"

"The only thing I saw was a little teaser ad in the Scranton Times. It asked, 'Are you a real Luna Parkers fan? Take the Luna Parkers quiz in the Entertainment Section of Sunday's paper and win two free tickets to their upcoming reunion show.' That was the whole ad, and the only direct reference that I could find."

"Did you check the Sunday paper?" I asked.

"Of course. But by that point Megan had died and the show was cancelled, so no quiz."

"Anything else I should know about?"

"I slapped a dirty old man at the country club last night."

I had to ask. "What did he do?"

"He grabbed a frill on my uniform bottoms and snapped it. The manager took me into his office and threatened to fire me."

"What did you tell him?"

"I told him exactly what happened and he was very unsympathetic. He actually said my tips should more than cover any minor embarrassment. Then he said I could turn in my uniform today and collect my final paycheck on Friday."

"So, how did you keep your job?"

"I told him that the average cost of winning a wrongful termination suit is over $150,000, and that I was sure my cousin would be willing to file all of the necessary paperwork at no cost to me."

"And that did the trick?"

"He stared at me for about a minute before calling the bouncer and telling him to bring the dirty old man to his office. When they arrived he told the drunken degenerate that he could either apologize to me or immediately lose all club privileges. The drunk said he was sorry and that was that."

Jeannine got agitated as she conveyed the tale. I spent a few minutes reprising my therapist role before ending our conversation.

Chapter 17

I woke up on Thursday morning and immediately touched the tip of my nose to my palm. Did I dream that I was the lead dog in the Iditarod? A horrifying vision appeared in front of me - my breath. After pulling on more clothes than a homeless person, I trudged to the living room and found Patrick passed out on the sofa. The fireplace was colder than my sniffer.

Patrick woke up as I crunched kindling on top of a few crumpled newspaper sections. "Do you know what you're doing?"

"My band played the snowboarding resorts of Big Bear quite a few times," I said.

"I was afraid you got your training at the Burning Man Festival."

Patrick looked like he was ready to face the day after fifteen minutes in the bathroom. I dished out the pancakes and sausage I had prepared, and we settled into our usual spots in the dining room.

"What's on the agenda for today?" I asked.

"I tried figuring that out last night and didn't do a very good job. You must be wondering how I ever made a living as an insurance investigator. I haven't contributed much since you got here. I need to start pulling my weight, but it's like my brain shuts off as soon as an emotion floats through."

Since Patrick was already partially incapacitated I thought it might be the best time to bring up a question that needed to be asked.

"I spent a few minutes with Dylan Conway at the funeral

home."

"What did he have to say?"

"I asked him what Megan was working on for the reunion show just before she died. He said she was about to do an interview with the Times, and planned to tell them about misconstrued lyrics in *Parkers Luna Sea*. What was he talking about?"

Patrick rubbed his temples. "Do we really have to do this now?"

"I know that talking about Aunt Megan is painful for you. But this topic keeps coming up. Stop and think like an investigator for a moment. All of these deaths took place shortly before the reunion. There has to be a connection. Megan died the night before she was going to talk with a reporter about the misconstrued lyrics. Louie died next to an open wall safe where he kept his sheet music. Bongo died, and the only thing missing was his briefcase where he kept his music."

Patrick stood up and poured himself another cup of coffee. He added a dollop of rum and returned to the table.

"I never took a close look at the lyrics angle because it inferred that someone connected to the band was in on it."

"What are the lyrics, Patrick?"

"You know from our practice sessions that the song is about the band, and how in spite of the fact that we sometimes drive each other crazy we always make great music. The lyric that Megan was going to tell the reporter about was: *That's why it took the ten of us to bloom.*"

"I was going to ask you about that after band practice. There were only five band members; six if you count Buzzy. Who were the other four?" I asked.

"That question got the song a ton of local buzz on the radio. In fact, the buzz is probably what generated the national attention."

"So, what's the answer? Who were the other four?"

"You're not getting it, Jason. There was no other four; no ten of us. Our fans misinterpreted what Eli was singing, and the new version took on a life of its own."

"What were the original lyrics?"

"Who knows? That was around 40 years ago."

"How could you not know? It sounds like that error was the biggest catalyst your band ever experience."

"I always thought of it as an edit. We change things all of the time when we're composing. If one thing doesn't work we try something else. I do my best to forget the older versions so that I don't inadvertently play the wrong one during a show."

"Still, it was a huge turning point. Did you ever really try to remember?"

"Jason, you're a vocalist; I'm not. The words need to have contextual meaning in order for you to express them with the proper emotion. I'm a lead guitarist, but we both know that the title is a misnomer. Lead guitarists actually follow and react to the other instruments. When you sing lyrics, I'm not thinking about the message, I'm reacting to your tonal qualities, your emotion, the notes you hit, and the amount of volume you project. To me, your voice is just another instrument that I need to respond to."

It took a moment for Patrick's words to sink in. I couldn't help but wonder if Michael Marinangeli, lead guitarist for Tsunami Rush (and now, Doberman's Stub) felt the same way.

"Who would know the original lyrics?" I asked.

"Louie and Eli collaborated on the song. Ask Eli at practice tonight."

We spent the day getting ready for band practice. I would normally be out and about searching for clues. But with all of the murders pointing back at the Luna Parkers, I felt it best to get the songs down with Patrick so that I could stir up a little trouble at practice and focus my attention on any subtle responses.

Kristen Pohanick met us at the door wearing a slinky cocktail dress that was so short Vicky's secret was sure to become common knowledge in no time.

"It looks like you'll be starting your weekend a night early,"

I said.

"Just a little clubbing with the girls later on. You're welcome to join us after band practice."

"Aren't you going to freeze in that outfit?"

"Tonight I'm dressing like the Cake song: *Short Skirt/Long Jacket.*"

The Shapiros had already arrived. Russell was seated behind a purple, top-of-the-line Tama Starclassic drum kit. Eddie was using an electronic tuner on his bass, and Eli adjusted the PA while holding a wireless mic. After some informal acknowledgments Patrick and I tuned up. Over the first hour we worked on five of the band's original songs. Russell didn't have Bongo's professional style, but did a very credible job of keeping the beat. We adjourned to Eddie's bar for beers and a confab.

Eddie asked Patrick, "How's Jason coming on the set list cover tunes that we haven't practiced?"

"We spent the whole day practicing. He's a quick study."

Eddie turned to the Shapiros. "Russell, ya done good."

"Thank you, Eddie. Drumming has been my hobby for many years."

I couldn't help but wonder if Russell had been biding his time waiting for Bongo's inevitable demise. The conversation stayed on the set list throughout the break.

"Does anybody have any questions?" Eddie asked while looking at me.

"Just one," I said. "Can anybody tell me the original lyrics that got misconstrued in *Parkers Luna Sea*?"

"Why do you want to know that?" asked Eddie.

"It's come up in a couple of conversations, and now it's turned into one of those things that will bother me until I find out."

"Don't you remember, Patrick?" Russell asked.

"I told him lyrics aren't in my job description."

"Discarded lyrics are like discarded band aids. Once you throw them away you should never put them back on. Let's get back to work," Eddie said.

Eli still had two slugs of beer left in his bottle. I lingered behind with him while the others filtered into the next room.

"C'mon, Eli. I need to focus in there."

Without any expression he said, *"That's why it took the tender's prune to bloom,"* and walked out of the bar.

Even after the full day of practice I messed up at least four times in the second hour. I couldn't keep myself from speculating on the meaning of the lyrics. The band was talking about getting me high again when Kristen walked into the room.

"Daddy, your office is on the house phone. Your secretary said it's an emergency."

"What now?" he asked, and quickly followed her upstairs. "Young lady, you're not leaving this house in that dress."

Over the next ten minutes I worked with Eli on backup vocals for two songs. When Eddie returned he was wearing his coat.

"The police just arrested Myron Banner's son, Dane, for the Society Page Slasher murders. Myron asked for me."

"We have just over a week to get ready for the show, Eddie," said Russell. "If you take this case we might as well just forget about playing the gig."

"I'll be delegating most of it to my staff, but I need a little face time with Myron and his son tonight. Bear with me, guys. We just put two hours in. Let's pick it up back here tomorrow night."

"I'm bringing my drums home tonight so that I can practice. Let's reconvene at my place tomorrow at 7:00."

"You've got a deal, Russell. Keep practicing without me if you like, and help yourselves to the bar." Eddie turned and departed.

Patrick said, "Let's bring beers back in here and work on the start of the second set."

We spent another 45 minutes practicing before packing it in.

"I'm thinking about hitting the Bar Chord on the way home," Russell said.

"We're in," Patrick replied.

There were about 40 people in the Moscow hotspot when we arrived. A few of them yelled a greeting to Patrick. It was obvious that Russell and Eli were known but weren't regulars. We found a table along the wall, across the room from the bar. I had hoped that Russell asked us to the bar to reveal something that would help our investigation. Instead, it appeared to be about his insecurities as a drummer, and his need for Patrick's approval. Considering the ordeal that the band had been through since the first of the year, I couldn't complain.

When Russell seemed appropriately assured I asked, "Do you two have any guess as to what was taken out of Louie's safe?"

They looked at each other. Eli shrugged, and Russell said, "I assume it was something related to his business."

"Then why kill Bongo, too?" I asked

"The police told me it was an accidental overdose."

"We don't think so," Patrick said.

"Bongo worked for Louie, and they've been lifelong friends. If the killer didn't find whatever he was looking for in the safe, maybe he thought Louie gave it to Bongo. It still could have been business related," Russell said.

Russell's phone rang and he took the call at the table. It was apparent his wife wanted him to come home. He departed a few minutes later.

"Don't you have to go, too?" I asked Eli.

"Russell came straight from work. We took separate vehicles tonight."

Over the next twenty minutes Eli quizzed me on how comfortable I felt about every tune on our playlist. I had to rate each song on a scale of one to ten while he took notes. The minute we finished he put on his coat and departed. Before we could drain our beers a waitress came by with another round.

"Compliments of Paulie," she said.

Patrick waved him over to our table. He extended condolences and told a couple of stories about Bongo doing some good deeds.

117

I expected the tales to improve Patrick's sullen mood, but they didn't.

"Let's take a walk up the street," he said.

"It's freezing outside," I replied.

"I need a smoke, and the temperature is up into the mid-twenties. There's heavy cloud cover tonight and it's acting like a big insulating blanket in the sky. This is as warm as it's been since you got here."

I agreed, and we made our way up Van Brunt Street. Patrick held off on lighting his joint until after we passed the lights of the Borough Building which also serves as police headquarters.

"I don't know why we keep pushing to have this reunion show. It's been nothing but one disaster after another from the beginning," he said.

"What about the money that Dakota's going to get from the gate?"

"God knows she needs it. But I'm sure Russell donates three times what could come from the show in charitable contributions every year. It's not like we have to do this."

When we reached Grove Street I heard a vehicle a couple of hundred yards behind us, and angled my path to the left side of the street. A football-sized chunk of snow had rolled onto the road and Patrick gave it a kick. It managed to clear the four-foot snow bank that the plow created on each side of the street.

I was about to compliment Patrick in hopes of lightening the mood when I glanced over my shoulder in time to see a large black pickup truck heading straight at us. Patrick saw my startled expression.

When I yelled, "Jump!" we both dove over the snow mound, rolled fifty feet down a steep embankment, and stopped next to a stream. I heard the truck door slam, and directed Patrick to the far side of a snow-covered boulder next to the stream. We stood in a foot of freezing cold water.

"Fuck this," Patrick said.

Before he could take a step forward, a hail of silenced

automatic gunfire sprayed the plot of ground where we landed. I thanked God for providing the insulating blanket of clouds that was obscuring the moon and keeping the gunman from seeing us.

My feet were numb. I peeked around the corner of the boulder, and up at the snow bank above.

"Shit," I whispered.

"What?" Patrick asked.

"He's wearing night vision goggles."

I peeked again and saw him starting to climb down the hill toward the spot where we landed. On the other side of the stream was another embankment. I saw a rock outcropping about 40 yards upstream and 20 yards up the embankment. Our assailant was about half way down the hill. As much as I hated to do it, I took off a glove and plunged my hand into the bed of the stream.

"He's almost all the way down," Patrick whispered. "Ouch!"

"What?"

"I stepped on something," he whispered.

"Which foot?"

Patrick pointed to his right. I reached down and pulled out a fairly round stone, about the size of a golf ball. I didn't need to peek around the boulder to see the gunman any more. His last few steps were a little too quick, and his left foot stepped into the stream. Before he turned around, I hurled the stone with all of my might at the outcropping.

The gunman was in the process of turning our way when the stone made a distinct noise at the top of the hill. He charged up the other side of the embankment, and we quietly made our way back to Van Brunt Street. I wanted to get the license plate from the pickup truck. But since it was parked directly across from where the gunman was climbing, we opted to jog back to Paulie's, where we called the cops. The Moscow Police were brave enough to drive us back to the scene, but the pickup was gone.

Flannery made it to Moscow by 2:00 AM. He used yellow crime scene tape to section off where the casings from the automatic rifle probably entered the snow, relative to the footprints on the top of the snow bank. One of the Moscow cops stood guard all night, and Scranton PD sent a Crime Scene Unit van up at daybreak. By 7:30 AM they found two casings.

Just so you don't think we were completely crazy, I should report that Patrick and I spent most of that time soaking our feet in buckets of warm water courtesy of our host, Paulie. We also managed to soak our livers in glass buckets of Jack Daniels after Flannery took our statements. Patrick and I were too concerned with frostbite to speculate on the identity of the gunman as we waited for dawn. Or, maybe it was the constant presence of Paulie the town gossip that kept us from mentioning any of the Luna Parkers.

Chapter 18

After getting to bed at 8:30 AM on Friday morning, I was none too pleased to hear my phone jar me from a sound sleep. My move to retrieve it from the nightstand gave my tailbone a déjà vu experience. The adrenaline from last night must have suppressed the pain caused by bodysurfing a Moscow hillside.

"Hello."

"What the hell is going on out there? I just read that my damn fool brother almost got you killed last night!"

"I thought Mom switched you over to decaf."

"Don't give me any smart answers, son. I want you on the next flight to San Diego. Do you hear me?"

"I wouldn't do that to a client, let alone a family member. Don't worry about me. I'll be alright."

"If you're not coming back then I'm coming out."

"Good, we could use your help. I'll take the couch and you can have the guest room."

"I'm not sleeping under the same roof with that pinko."

"It's pretty cold for a camp-out, Dad."

"Book me a room at the hotel that used to be the old D&L train station."

"I have no idea what you're talking about."

"Then do a little detecting," he said, and hung up.

The clock radio told me it was 11:07. I pulled on some warm clothes, including a wool scarf, and spotted half a pot of coffee on the kitchen counter before seeing Patrick reading the paper in the living room.

He eyed my unstable gait as I entered the living room. "I was going to make bacon and eggs, but it looks like you'd be better off with a red donut and a Vicoden."

"I just got a call from Dad. He's about to join the east coast branch of Duffy Investigations."

Patrick closed his paper, walked over to me, and held up the end of my wool scarf a few inches from my face. "If you think it's cold now, wait until hell freezes over."

"He said he wants to stay at the old D&L station, whatever that is."

"It's an historic building that was converted into a Radisson. You're going to like it. They have acoustic acts in the lounge during happy hour, and rock bands at night."

"Dad will be thrilled. I better make sure his room isn't above the lounge when I book the reservation."

"I'll be glad to take care of that for you," Patrick said with a smile.

"I had better handle this one myself. Did you eat breakfast yet?"

"Flannery called an hour ago. We're having lunch with him at The Glider Diner at 12:30."

"We didn't get much of a chance to talk last night, with Paulie doing the frostbite bucket brigade. Do you think it's possible that one of your band mates could be behind this?"

"I don't know what to think at this point," he said.

"I wouldn't be surprised if Flannery asks that question over lunch, so I suggest you give it some thought."

"I've given it plenty of thought. I just haven't come up with any answers."

"Then let's review. Eddie got called in to work, but said he was planning on delegating a lot of the preliminary work on the case until after the reunion show. We got attacked around midnight. Somebody needs to find out where Eddie was at that time."

"I forgot to put my slide in my guitar case last night. I could pop by Eddie's house later on and see if I can get his wife to tell me when he got home, and if she thinks he really can delegate the Society Page Slasher case to his staff over the next week. That might prompt her to tell me what he did and didn't do last night. We can try to fill any gaps tonight at practice."

"How about the Shapiros?"

"Either of them could have been waiting for us to leave the bar," Patrick said.

"What about the pickup truck? Do any of them own a pickup?"

"No. Bongo was the only one in the band with a pickup. You looked up at the guy when he was on the snow pile. Did he look like anyone in the band?"

"The only streetlight was about 100 feet away, and cast a shadow over the front of him. It was hard to get a body type reading, and he was wearing a hoodie and the night vision goggles."

"How about when he got to the bottom of the hill?"

"It was dark, and I was focused on hitting the rock pile when I threw that stone. Did you see anything familiar?"

"You were standing in front of me. I tried to lean out of the way of your arm without moving my feet when you reached back to make the throw. I didn't see shit."

"What are you going to say when Flannery asks why we were walking on Van Brunt Street at midnight?"

"I was about to show you the WPA bridge at the end of the next block," Patrick said. "I really was."

The Glider Diner is almost directly across the street from Scranton's Memorial Stadium. I spotted Flannery at a window booth as we pulled into the parking lot.

"Order the hot roast beef platter with French fries," Patrick said, walking toward the front door.

"I usually go with a lighter lunch."

"You'll be picking your father up at the airport at the end of the afternoon, and we have practice at Russell's house at 7:30.

This is your dinner."

Flannery was reading a pocket notepad when we arrived at his table. The waitress appeared within seconds, and we all ordered the same thing without the benefit of menus.

"Did you learn anything new since last night?" I asked.

"How about if we start with what you two were doing on Van Brunt Street at midnight?"

"Patrick was about to show me an old WPA bridge one block up from where we got attacked," I said.

"If you're not going to be honest with me I don't see the need for a deputy."

"He's covering for me," Patrick said. "I'm the reason we were out there on Van Brunt Street."

We both looked at Patrick with rapt attention. "Go on," said Flannery.

"Paulie told a story about something Bongo did for a guy who was down and out, and it really got to me. I was about to lose it in the bar so I just grabbed my jacket and headed for the door. Jason followed me. When we got outside it took me a while to get it back together. When Jason asked where we were going I told him about the bridge. But it was really about me not wanting to look like a wuss in the Bar Chord," Patrick said.

Our lunches arrived covered in gravy. Flannery appeared to accept Patrick's story.

"Will you be getting any help on the case now that the Society Page Slasher is in custody?" Patrick asked.

"Two more detectives are assigned as of Monday."

"Why wait until Monday?" I asked.

"The guys just finished back-to-back 70 hour weeks. They're getting some well-deserved time with their families."

"Any new developments?" I asked.

"That's why I asked you to lunch. Patrick, do you know Nello Lapaglia?"

"Never heard of him."

"He's Rose's handyman. According to her neighbors he does

more than electrical and carpentry, if you catch my drift."

"Sounds like he does plumbing, too," I said.

Flannery shot me a glare. "Nello is the proud owner of a new black Ford F-150 pickup truck. Could that be the make and model of the vehicle your perp was driving last night?"

"It could have been," Patrick said.

"When you said F-150 I flashed on seeing the front grill. It was definitely a black F-150," I said.

"What have you learned about Nello Lapaglia?" Patrick asked.

"He's 35 years old, had a DUI ten years ago, but nothing else on his sheet."

"Do you want me to drop in on Rose again and see what I can find out?" I asked.

"Actually, I could use some help with a stakeout."

"Where does he live?" Patrick asked.

"Lake Winola, about 15 minutes from Rose's house. How about if you two watch him until 1:00 AM, then I'll do the night shift?"

"No can do," said Patrick. "We're doing a benefit concert to pay Bongo's funeral expenses in a week, and we're practicing at Russell's house tonight."

"What's more important, Patrick?" he asked.

"My father's flight gets in later this afternoon. He's a retired San Diego police detective, and I'm sure he has no interest in watching band practice. How about if he takes the first shift?"

"Call me after you ask him," Flannery said, and stood up. He tapped his wallet and I shook my head.

Once he was out the door I asked, "Did you pick up your slide from Eddie's house?"

"I did. Eddie's wife took an Ambien while we were practicing and was out cold all night."

"I don't suppose Kristen was home in time to give him an alibi."

Patrick shook his head. "She slept over at a friend's house.

I'm relieved we have a suspect that won't be at band practice tonight. Are you sure your father is going to want to freeze his ass off on a stakeout. His blood is probably pretty thin from all of those years in the sun."

"If he tells me his blood needs thickening I'll bring him here and pump some gravy into his veins."

Chapter 19

Upon our return to the Duffy abode, Patrick wanted to practice a bit more before picking Dad up at the airport. Instead, I spent the next two hours doing research on the Internet in tandem with Jeannine. Between the two of us we got a reasonable handle on Nello Lapaglia. We learned that he's a member of an exclusive gun club that is believed to be connected to a paramilitary group. But unlike most militia's, this group is not about race. It's all about money. An Internet blogger said they use a subtle form of intimidation to influence lobbyists, politicians, and shareholders on behalf of presumably wealthy corporate clients. I say "presumably" because we weren't able to identify anyone specific as yet.

Jeannine discovered that Nello earned an MBA under another name, and that the entire degree was funded by a dummy corporation. The fact that an MBA graduate with a 3.8 grade point average was working as a handyman for rich clients put us on high alert. I wanted to keep digging with Jeannine, but the welcome wagon needed to be at the airport for Dad, and I certainly wasn't about to send Patrick. He agreed to lend me his car around 4:00 PM, just before heading to bed for a nap. I made a snap decision shortly after he turned in, and called the Radisson to modify my reservation.

At 5:15, I spotted Dad's white hair above a group of women heading toward the baggage carousels. I'm sure my greeting must have looked strange to the casual onlooker. I smiled, hugged, and welcomed. He stood stiff as an icicle, rolled his eyes, and remained silent. As we approached the escalator heading down to baggage, I stepped in front of him and directed him to a mezzanine with rocking chairs, overlooking the baggage area.

"We need to talk privately for a couple of minutes," I said.

"Can't we do it while I'm getting my bags?"

"It needs to be now. There's been a break in the case, and the lead detective, Colin Flannery, is hoping you can help with a stakeout tonight. I reserved a rental car in your name. If you don't want to do it I can go over to the rental counter while you're getting your bags and cancel the reservation."

"And what? Rely on my pinko brother to be my chauffer while I'm in town? No thanks."

"What about the stakeout?"

Dad pointed to a baggage carousel, stood up, and said, "I'm getting my bags. Are you coming?"

It was seventeen degrees when I left Patrick's house. Standing next to the parade of luggage inside the terminal it felt substantially colder. Benedict Arnold Duffy was not about to catch a break on today's episode of Family Feud.

With bags in hand, we walked to the parking lot and I loaded them into the back seat. All attempts at initiating casual conversation ended with Dad making a sarcastic comment. On the drive to the rental lot I thought of lyrics from *Hey Jude*: "It's a fool who plays it cool by making the world a little colder." I opted not to share this tidbit of Macca's wisdom with the last man in America to continue to call the Beatles a fad.

I led the way out of the rental lot and onto the entrance to Interstate 81N. It took Dad all of about six seconds to pass me once we were on the highway. I spent the 10 minutes it took to get from the airport to the hotel trying to remember the Catholic Church's position on forgiveness, and how to deal with the "Honor thy father" argument that was sure to follow.

Dad was hauling both bags when I caught up with him on the front steps to the hotel. I snatched one out of his hand before he could argue. Smalltalk about the amazing building we had just entered seemed futile, so I simply trailed him most of the way to the front desk before heading him off.

"The reservation is in my name and on my card. I'll need to deal with the clerk," I said.

Instead of replying, Dad gave an *after you* hand gesture, set his bag down, and wandered around a bit, checking out the old train terminal renovation while I transacted our business.

"Where did you park? I need to get your license plate number," I said.

"Back of the lot, where you can look down and see Spruce Street."

I exited the building, got his license number, and made a stop back at Patrick's car.

"What the hell is this?" Dad asked as I walked in the door with two more suitcases.

"I'm staying with you. We've got a suite," I said.

"I suppose this was your uncle's idea."

"He doesn't know I've moved out yet."

Dad showed a brief hint of a smile.

"I appreciate that you've come out here to help. You'll need to be brought up to speed on what's happening with the investigation, and I can do a lot better job of that if we're roomies. Besides, you're my dad and I've missed you."

"What time are we meeting Flannery?" he asked. This was as close as Dad would get to any kind of reconciliation.

"He's meeting us in the bar at 6:30."

"Is Patrick going to be with him?"

"No. Patrick and I will be working a different angle of the case tonight. I'll give you all of the details as soon as we have some time to go over it. You'll be working a new suspect that just came to light earlier this afternoon. He's a dangerous guy who likes to play with guns. I don't want you doing this if you're tired or if you're going to let your mind wander to your feud with Patrick."

"Don't tell me how to run a stakeout, Jason. It's three hours earlier in San Diego, I slept on the plane, and I've been around bad guys my whole life."

"Fair enough."

The suite was a little smaller than I anticipated, but it was immaculate, had well appointed furnishings, and a spectacular view. Dad took the room closest to the bathroom.

Trax Lounge was packed for Friday happy hour. A solo guitarist was set up in the far corner. I led the way, scanning for Flannery, and found him fending off a chair seeker at a table for four.

"Dad, this is Detective Colin Flannery, Scranton PD. Flannery, this is my father, Jim Duffy, San Diego PD, retired." They shook hands and we sat down.

Flannery said, "Before you get comfortable, the happy hour spread here is excellent, and if you're planning on helping me out on the stakeout, this will be your last chance to eat. Why don't you two hit the buffet right now?"

The heavy lunch was still with me, but I made myself a small plate. Dad loaded up on chicken wings and pizza on two little plates, then handed me another one and piled it high with pasta. Airline peanuts and pretzels must not have done the job for him.

Flannery gave Dad a rundown on what he had said about Lapaglia over lunch. I then filled them in on what Jeannine and I had learned this afternoon. Flannery looked at me with a bit more respect.

"I see you've been busy," he said. "I'd like to tap your database."

"I'm afraid his database is already spoken for, Flannery," Dad said.

I quickly added, "Most of my research comes from my assistant, Jeannine. She's dating one of my best friends."

I glanced at my phone for the time. I left Patrick a note to pick me up here in the lounge at 7:15. It just dawned on me that he could pop by before the happy hour ends at 7:00. I thought it best that the brothers Duffy not air their dirty linen in front of Flannery and the staff of our new home away from home. I excused myself and headed toward the restroom. Once out of sight I called Patrick and explained why I needed him to be punctual.

When I returned to the table Dad and Flannery were in Irish cop mode, smiling and swapping stories.

"What time do you expect Lapaglia to get started on his Friday night?" I asked.

Flannery looked at his watch and said, "We had better get rolling, Jim."

"Are you going to swear him in as a deputy?" I asked.

"I'll ask my captain first thing on Monday."

"What if he needs to assert some authority tonight?" I asked.

"Give him your badge, Jason. He'll need it more than you on the stakeout."

I reluctantly handed it over, and they departed. Ten minutes later Patrick walked in the door.

Chapter 20

"I guess I missed him," Patrick said, taking the chair his brother had occupied.

"Just barely. He's on his way to Lake Winola with Flannery."

"I read your note and was sorry to hear you won't be staying with me any longer."

"Dad needs to be brought up to speed on the case. Plus, it's obvious he thinks I've sided with my cool uncle over my dad. First of all, that isn't true. Nobody's choosing sides like this is a pickup football game. Second, Dad could be a real asset on this investigation if he can focus on the facts and not be distracted by a fight that should have been worked out decades ago."

"You're right, Jason. I'm glad to hear you say it. When I first read the note I was afraid you were moving out because of my pot smoking."

"I try not to be judgmental, Patrick, but I think the pot and the booze are keeping you from recognizing some significant aspects of what's happening around you."

A cocktail waitress asked Patrick if he'd like a drink. He hesitated and waved her off.

"It wasn't always like this. Ever since Megan died I've been hitting it harder. I know that. But I also know I've been an investigator since before you were born and can still pull my weight in the field."

I stared at my uncle without responding.

"You obviously don't agree. I realize pot isn't your thing, and I'm sorry that I insisted that you smoke to show the guys you're cool with our habit," he said.

"It's not about smoking pot, it's about getting wasted. Just like there are social drinkers who have one or two cocktails after a hard day, I know there are social smokers who have one or two tokes to wind down. Don't forget, I live in California where medical marijuana clinics could soon outnumber Starbucks coffeehouses. It's all a matter of degree. Getting blitzed every night on both pot and booze has a cumulative effect. You saw what chronic abuse did to Bongo. Why do it to yourself?"

Patrick looked at his watch. "Let's talk in the car."

Just before he reached the hotel front entrance I grabbed his shoulder. "We can see the parking lot pretty well from here. Look for a black F-150."

Two minutes later Patrick was behind the wheel. "You said my substance abuse was keeping me from recognizing some important things. Like what?"

"Like how Aunt Megan could have been murdered by the same person who killed Louie, Bongo, and tried to kill us."

"Megan was killed by a hit and run driver. It wasn't anything like—"

"Like how the black pickup tried taking us out last night?" I asked.

We rode in silence the rest of the way to Russell's house in the Green Ridge section of Scranton. Actually, it was a mansion that was probably four times the size of Eddie's opulent abode. We were greeted at the front door by Russell's wife, Becky. Her youthful glow, pageboy haircut, and sincere smile could have made her an excellent choice for AARP Magazine covergirl.

"Becky, you met my nephew Jason at Bongo's luncheon," Patrick said.

"I did. We were on opposite sides of a round table, so we didn't get much of a chance to talk."

"You have a beautiful home," I said.

"Thank you. Its upkeep is my full-time job."

"Is everybody here?" Patrick asked.

"They are. Why don't you take the elevator down to the ballroom? Nice seeing you again, Jason," Becky said, and walked away.

"Wait until you see this," Patrick said.

We carried our guitars to a section of the foyer wall slightly off of the main walkway. In front of us was what appeared to be a small red theatre curtain. When we got to within four feet, the curtain retracted to reveal an open mirror and brass elevator.

"Down," Patrick said, and off we went.

The ballroom held table seating for about 200, a huge dance floor, and a stage that was bigger than most of the clubs I've worked over the years.

"How did our amps get here?" I asked.

"One of Russell's peeps picked them up this afternoon. C'mon, we're late."

The rest of the band was in no hurry to get started. Each of them had questions about our brush with death last night and expressed concern for our safety.

"Did you see any security men on the way in?" Russell asked.

"Not a soul," said Patrick. "I'm getting a flash of the hospital scene from The Godfather."

"They're supposed to be invisible. I gave them a picture of all of us so they wouldn't hassle anyone on the way in," Russell said.

"Why don't we get started," said Eli.

Over the next two hours we worked without a break. Russell had hooked up top-of-the-line recording equipment to give us instant feedback on the quality of our performance. Eli moved into the role of taskmaster and was unrelenting in pointing out every minor flaw. He was especially critical of Russell, who was clearly trying his best, but not as professional as Bongo. I fully expected a fight to break out, but Russell suffered through each berating with little more than the occasional glare to express his feelings.

"I need a break," Eddie said a few minutes before 10:00.

We moved into the adjoining bar where Russell played bartender while Eddie blasted Eli on his rancorous attitude.

Eli replied, "We're a week away from the show and nobody looks like he's ready. You're about to go into Perry Mason mode, filing a series of motions for Banner's kid, we've got fill-ins on rhythm and drums, and Patrick is playing with the passion of a zombie. We're going to look like a bunch of old guys who should have stayed in our rocking chairs."

"What are you saying, Eli? Do you want to call it off?" asked Eddie.

"Hell no! I want a little focus from Patrick. I want a little commitment from you, Eddie. I want my brother to stop thinking and start feeling. Jason, it's clear that you're the only one here who could pass for a full-time musician, but we're throwing a lot of new material at you, and it'll take a lot of work outside of these sessions to play them like Louie, back in the day," Eli said.

"We're not back in the day, Eli," I said. "No amount of practice will ever turn back the clock. When you set that kind of standard, you're setting the band up to fail. We sound good; very good at times. I think the audience is going to be amazed at the sound we'll be producing next Friday night. The only thing that could derail that happening is if we let the pressure get to us and implode before the show."

"Jason's got a lot more perspective on this than we do," said Eddie. "Clubbing each other over the head in practice is going to make us worse instead of better."

We put in another hour and a half before calling it a night. When the five of us got in the elevator, Russell gave a voice command to go to the second floor. Without a word, he crooked his finger at us and we followed him to a room at the end of the hall. It was a small room filled with a wide range of firearms. I noticed a retinal scanner in front of a lead door with no handle that was slightly ajar. It was undoubtedly the entrance to the

Shapiro safe room.

"I think we all need to be ready in case of another attack," Russell said. "Pick out whatever weapon floats your boat."

I spotted a pair of Glock 17s that reminded me of the weapon I borrowed from Dad recently.

"My father just arrived today. Can I take one for him, too?" I asked.

"Whatever you need, Jason."

Eddie and Eli stated that they both had weapons of their own, and were more comfortable with something familiar.

"Megan would turn over in her grave if I ever armed myself," Patrick said.

"Be practical, Patrick. You could run into another ambush on your way home tonight," said Russell.

"I'll take my chances."

"At least your nephew will be armed," Russell said.

Patrick opted not to argue. "Let's get going."

Walking back to the elevator Patrick said, "I got a call from Dylan Conway today. He has video from some old gigs, and wants to do a tribute to Louie and Bongo at some point during the show. I told him I'd discuss it with everybody tonight."

"I don't have any problem with it," Eli said.

"Fine with me," said Eddie.

Patrick said, "I'm concerned that I might lose it onstage if I look up and see Louie over my shoulder."

We rode the elevator to the first floor in silence.

At the front door Eddie said, "Why don't we let Dylan make his tribute after we finish the show. We can go backstage and drink a beer. When he's done we go back out, play *Parkers Luna Sea* as our encore, and leave the audience with tears in their eyes and a song in their hearts."

"Brilliant," said Russell, and we all agreed.

Chapter 21

I woke up at 8:00 AM on Saturday morning. Dad was in a sound sleep, so I walked a block to the Northern Lights Espresso Bar for a caffeine infusion, banana nut muffin, and a reading of the Scranton Times newspaper. Eddie's picture was on the third page, along with a brief bio highlighting other major cases he had worked over the years. It also discussed Eddie's long-term relationship with the accused killer's father, Myron Banner. It said that the Banners were prominent members of Scranton's high society, and that was how Dane was able to get close to his victims. With a bail hearing coming up on Monday, and other motions pending, I had to wonder how Eddie was going to keep his word about being at nightly practice sessions for the next week.

When I returned to the hotel Dad was dressed and hungry. "So, you went to breakfast without me."

"Just caffeine and the newspaper. I'm ready to eat."

We got a window table at the hotel coffee shop. I had a view of railroad tracks and a snow covered college soccer field.

"How did the stakeout go?" I asked.

"Lapaglia left his house just after 8:00 and drove to a gun shop outside of Clarks Summit. I put my winter hat on and followed him in."

"Not the Elmer Fudd hat," I said.

"It's called a sheepskin winter hat."

"I'll twy to wemembew that."

Dad laid an eyebrow lift on me. "He bought 6 boxes of Buffalo Bore HP 77 grain ammo. I heard him tell the clerk it was for a Ruger SR-556c Carbine Semiautomatic. Flannery told me they found .223 Remington shells on the scene, but they're interchangeable in that Ruger."

"Maybe he changed it up, knowing what he left behind." I said.

"Lapaglia went straight from the gun shop to Rose Amanesco's house, and was still there when Flannery relieved me at one o'clock."

"Were you able to see anything through the windows?"

"The curtains were closed, and there were no other vehicles in the driveway. I took a picture of the F-150 tire tracks."

"You should send the picture to Flannery."

"I told him about it and he took one of his own. He expects you to work a shift later today," he said, handing back my deputy shield.

"Who's on him now?"

"One of the new detectives coming onboard on Monday agreed to work 7:00 AM to 1:00 PM. You've got 1:00 to 7:00."

Stakeouts are my least favorite aspect of detective work. It's the main reason I hired Cory. My initial reaction was to call and tell him to get on a plane immediately. But the thought of leaving Jeannine alone while working the gig as a field operative was out of the question.

"I don't think my tailbone's healed enough to take a shift yet," I said.

"That's what your donut is for, son. Don't be an embarrassment to the family."

"Speaking of which, we need to get you and Patrick together before I do anything."

"Don't get me started. Our breakfast just hit the table."

"The only way this is going to work is if we function as a team. I'm sure you worked with plenty of guys in the department over the years that you didn't care for. It's your turn to suck it up for the sake of the case," I said.

"I don't have to suck it up for anything."

"I'm convinced that Aunt Megan was murdered by the same guy who killed Louie and Bongo."

Dad popped half of a sausage into his mouth to give himself time to think. "I'm sure I can make a significant contribution to the team doing the sort of things I did last night."

"You're here because the murderer tried to shoot me. I'm going to be standing next to Patrick most of my waking hours until after the reunion show. You're not going to be keeping me safe sitting in a car in the next county."

"Maybe it's time the two of you stop trying to be rock stars and start spending your time actually working on the case."

I spent the next ten minutes explaining how the three murders and the Thursday night attack all linked to the Luna Parkers. I finished by telling him about the misconstrued lyrics, and how the attacks on Megan, Patrick, and myself all happened almost immediately after bringing the topic to light.

Dad said, "Assuming Megan was one of the ten, have you figured out who the other four are, besides the three surviving band members?"

"That would be a good conversation to have with Patrick. I'm going to invite us to his house for lunch."

"Forget it."

"Then why did you come out here if you aren't planning on being anywhere near me? Patrick's working with Flannery, too. Do we really want to explain all of this to him?"

Dad remained silent.

I said, "Last night you were in Wyoming County. That's where the Yankee-Pennamite War took place. Did they teach you about it in high school history class?"

"The name rings a bell. What does that have to do with anything?"

"In the mid-1700s, both the Pennsylvanians (or Pennamites) and the Yankees from Connecticut had charters that granted them Wyoming County. They battled over it for years until the Revolutionary War happened. Then they joined forces, defeated the British, and went back to fighting each other immediately afterwards. I don't see why you and Patrick can't do the same thing to keep me from getting what's left of my ass shot off."

"Where's the restroom?" he asked.

Five minutes later he returned. "Make sure you tell your little story to Patrick before you set up the lunch. I don't want any hippie love-in crap coming my way."

"I'll call him now," I said, and walked into the hotel's empty dining room.

Thirty minutes later we were in Patrick's living room. I served as moderator in getting each of them to discuss the case. I only had to play referee three times in the first hour, and that was to break up verbal sparring before it could escalate. At 12:10 I called Flannery and learned that Lapaglia was at an indoor shooting range in Scranton. We agreed that I would be relieved at 6:00 PM so that I could stop for a bite to eat before band practice at Russell's house.

After finishing my call I asked, "Which one of you wants to lend me his car?"

Patrick said, "Why don't you take Megan's vehicle? I've kept it in good shape. It's in the garage, and the keys are on the hook next to the kitchen light switch."

The key was attached to a large brass peace symbol. That should have been my first clue. In the garage, I pulled a quilt cover off of a Volkswagen Microbus with murals of white doves flying through blue skies with white puffy clouds above green fields of deer and bunnies.

I returned to the living room. "Patrick, do you really think I could manage a discreet surveillance in a Peter Max-mobile?"

"You're going to be out in the country. You'll probably blend right into the background."

"I'm going to be parked in front of a Scranton indoor target practice range. Lapaglia will be the least of my worries if I have to sit right behind Bambi all day."

"OK, take the Prius. I'll take the V-dub to Russell's."

I took Dad's silence on the matter as a good sign, and left without making them swear to maintain the peace.

Detective Frank Navorocki appeared to be rapidly approaching mandatory retirement age. His eyelids were at half mast when I tapped on his passenger window. The door lock flipped up, I hopped in, and immediately winced from the pain.

"What's wrong with you?" he asked.

"Just a pain in the butt."

"More good detectives are taken out by roids than by bullets," he said.

"Tell me about Lapaglia's day."

"I tailed him from Amanesco's to his house at Lake Winola around 9:00 AM. Then he headed down here at 11:30."

"Did you see what he brought into the range?"

"It was in a case. So far everybody who walked in there was carrying at least one case."

"By the way, I'm Jason Duffy."

"Navorocki." We shook hands.

"Thanks for working the shift. I heard you logged a lot of hours on the Society Page Slasher case."

"I haven't been able to wind down since the arrest on Thursday. It's like overtime jet lag."

"Why don't you head home and try to sleep. We can talk on Monday." I opened the door.

"Take my parking spot and get a picture if Lapaglia walks out the door with anybody."

"Will do."

Twenty minutes later he exited alone and rushed to his immaculate black pickup truck. I tailed him to center city where he parked on Adams Avenue, directly across from the courthouse. I found a spot on the opposite side of the street and watched him enter an Irish bar/restaurant called Carley's. We were close to my hotel. I knew that the University of Scranton was less than two blocks away, so I grabbed one of the hardbound books

I had noticed on Patrick's back seat and walked into the bar. It was less than a quarter filled at that hour. I had no problem spotting Lapaglia seated at a cocktail table behind a trio of empty barstools. I took the one in the middle, opened my book, and ordered a bottle of Becks beer.

I stood up for a moment, took off my coat, and discreetly slid my stool a foot to the left so that I could see the table in the mirror behind the bar. Lapaglia sat with two men who were 10 to 15 years older. One was wiry with thick gray hair combed straight back. The other was overweight with a comb-over that couldn't cover a two dollar bet. They were both dressed in winter country club casual. All three displayed the bombastic voices of the self-important.

Wiry guy said he needed Lapaglia to get 10 of his best men to attend their stockholders meeting on Friday morning. Comb-over said the union would be making a show of force, and he needed a counterbalance. A glance in the mirror told me that Lapaglia wanted more clarification. Comb-over said they were to shout down the dissidents. Wiry guy added that the board members might need a security escort back to their cars after the meeting.

Instead of responding, Lapaglia made eye contact with me in the mirror. I looked down at Patrick's book. Seconds later he was standing next to my barstool.

"Are you enjoying our conversation?" he asked.

"Do I know you?"

"After listening to us for the last fifteen minutes I imagine you know us pretty well."

"If I need a moment to think when I'm studying I look up from my book. I saw you staring the last time I looked up. Frankly, it was kinda creepy," I said.

"Don't give me that crap. I know you've been spying on us. Who are you?" he asked in a louder voice.

"There's a mental health unit at the hospital up by Nay Aug Park, it's just a few blocks from here. Paranoid delusions should be on the seventh floor. If you leave now you might still be able to get your dinner order in."

Lapaglia's voice switched from bombastic to threatening. "I don't like you!"

The bartender looked like he was in between workouts at Gold's Gym. "Is there a problem here?"

"This guy keeps trying to ask me out, and won't take the hint that I don't play for his team," I said.

Lapaglia pointed to his left. "That's not true. I'm with the men at that table," he said, as if the bartender would recognize them as men of status and back down.

"Look buddy, I can understand why you want to trade up, but *no* means *no* in my bar. Unless you want me to walk you to the door, I suggest that you dance with the guys that brung ya, and go back to your table."

"Thank you," I said. "I'm going to be leaving now. If this guy follows me out will you call the police?"

The bartender placed both hands on the bar, displaying arms that were bigger than wiry-guy's legs. He leaned across the bar so that his nose was less than two inches from Lapaglia's. "I can do a lot better than that."

I took an indirect route back to the car and called Flannery. After filling him in on all of the details we decided that Lapaglia's radar would be on high alert, and that I was off of the stakeout squad. I was crushed. Flannery showed up twenty minutes later and relieved me. I described wiry-guy and comb-over, and Flannery said he'd get license plate numbers before heading to Lake Winola.

Dad's absence from the hotel suite wasn't surprising. I thought he took a walking tour of his home city. But a phone call to his cell left me shocked. He was still at Patrick's house. I joined them a half hour later. When I walked in the door they were both seated on the same side of the dining room table, which was covered in newspapers.

"We've been going over all of the stories relating to Megan's death," Patrick said.

"What have you come up with?"

"Jim, you have the fresh perspective. Tell your son what you see."

Dad stood up and crossed his arms. "Megan ran a therapy group on Wednesday nights for Vietnam War Vets who had a lot of problems. One or two of the vets would always hang around afterwards with personal questions, and Megan accommodated them. Once everyone left she'd lock up, walk across the street to the parking lot, and go home. The night she died, she was hit by a car as she crossed the street.

"At first it looked like a random hit and run. But three days after it happened, one of the nuttiest in the group, Carlton Burke, drove his car off of a cliff. One of the group members told a detective that he thought the guy was in love with Megan, and upset that she didn't return his affection. Another one of the group members said he went straight from the meeting to a Dunkin Donuts down the street from the mental health center, and saw Burke's car go flying by as he was finishing his coffee. After getting time estimates from the two men who stayed after the meeting, Scranton PD estimated that Burke's car went past the Dunkin Donuts just seconds after Megan was hit."

"Did the other group member actually see Burke in the car?" I asked.

"No," Patrick said, "just the car. Go ahead, Jim."

"It sounded like a very plausible explanation. Patrick tells me Burke's doctor confirmed that he had anger management issues, and his rap sheet shows that he was popped a half a dozen times for assault."

"Once I heard all of the facts I accepted that Burke did it, and couldn't live with himself afterwards. It wasn't until you pointed out the similarity to Thursday night on Van Brunt Street that I questioned it," Patrick said.

"Did you learn anything new from these newspapers?" I asked.

"Burke had a sister who lived in Pittston. She told a Luzerne

County paper that her brother hadn't had any fights since he went on a drug called Ativan. She also said he was in love, but not with Megan. He never gave up on the high school sweetheart that he left behind when he went to Vietnam. The old girlfriend had a restraining order on Burke, and the sister said that was one of the issues that he was working on with Megan," Dad said.

"It still could have been a case of transference," I said. "Patients fall in love with their therapists all of the time."

"The article went on to say that Burke refilled his prescription for Ativan the morning he died," Dad said.

"I got to know the lead detective pretty well. He told me that the tox screen showed a normal amount of his prescribed medications," said Patrick.

"Did they find any injuries that were inconsistent with the car crash?" I asked.

"The car flipped about six times on its way down a 300 foot ravine, and Burke wasn't wearing a seat belt. The crash erased any chance of getting trace evidence from Megan, and pulverized Burke in the process," Dad said.

"Very convenient if Burke wasn't the perp," I said.

Dad asked Patrick, "Do you know anything about the patient at Dunkin Donuts who reported seeing Burke's car?"

"He looks solid; long-term job, long-term marriage, no rap sheet. One of Megan's coworkers told me he's in the group because of war dreams and insomnia. No history of problems with Burke, Megan, or anyone else in the group," said Patrick.

"Any luck with Rose's boyfriend?" Dad asked.

After Patrick winced I told them about my afternoon. Dad agreed to start his shift at 6:00 PM. I was tempted to ask if they resolved any of their differences, but opted to keep my hands off of Pandora's box.

Band practice was fairly uneventful. Becky Shapiro was thrilled to be getting her first *girls night out* since the Society Page Slasher hit town. Russell played much better. I was convinced that Eli scored some tranquilizers, especially after Eddie revealed that he might have to miss part or all of two practices because of Dane Banner's immediate needs. The most notable difference was in Patrick. His leads had a soulful quality that I never heard from him before.

On the ride back to the hotel I asked him about how things went with Dad after I left for my shift. He told me that they focused on the case, and that it was heartening to be in the same room with him for so long without fighting.

Chapter 22

I couldn't believe Dad woke me up at 5:45 to attend Sunday Mass with him. Four and a half hours of sleep just doesn't cut it for me.

"Don't they have services at normal hours like everybody else?" I asked.

"Quit your bellyaching and do something for your father for a change. I flew all the way across the country to help you out. It's the least you can do."

Dad insisted that we walk six long blocks in a wind that chilled me all the way down to my soul. Two blocks from St. Peter's Cathedral, Dad told me that Flannery arranged for us to visit the stationhouse at 9:30 AM to go over the hardcopy reports on Aunt Megan's death.

"Why didn't you tell me this at 5:45?" I asked.

"I needed to get your blood boiling before taking you out in this cold wind."

I held off on my reply as we reached the steps of the cathedral. During the five minutes that we waited for mass to start, I thought about what to look for in the police files. That calm, reflective state was short-lived. Once services started I was reminded of why I rarely attended church with my parents. Dad has the annoying habit of needing to be a half-second ahead of everyone else for all of the responsorial prayers. Mom says he's a natural leader. I'd tell you what I think, but I'm sitting directly below an ancient light fixture that will undoubtedly crash down on my head if I entertain such thoughts in church.

I reverted to an old trick from my high school years, and

recited the responsorial prayers a half-second after the rest of the congregation. It always reminded me of the *Row, Row, Row Your Boat* song, and would ensure that I wouldn't be getting any more predawn Sunday morning wakeups.

Dad drove us over to Smith's Restaurant in South Side after mass. I tried checking my messages on the way over and discovered that I left my phone at the hotel.

"What was Lapaglia up to last night?" I asked.

"He played the role of Rose's security guard in the parking lot of Patzel's Restaurant in Clarks Summit while she had a leisurely dinner with the hoity-toity crowd."

"Russell's wife, Becky, did the same thing. She was thrilled to be getting out now that the Society Page Slasher is behind bars."

"Did Eddie mention how his client is going to plead?" Dad asked.

"He told us before practice that he'd be missing a couple of sessions, starting this afternoon. Considering the band's reaction, I'm not surprised he didn't mention the case again."

Dad recounted a story about eating breakfast with his family at Smith's back in the late 50s. I enjoyed hearing about my grandparents, who died before I was born. Although he didn't mention Patrick, I knew he was present and part of those fond memories. I resisted the urge to point this out to him, knowing that we'd be pent up in a small records room for the next few hours.

When we arrived at police headquarters it was impossible to find a parking spot. "I thought this place was supposed to be on skeleton staff at this hour," I said.

"That's what Flannery told me." Dad made a left out of the entrance and pulled into the Steamtown Mall parking lot next door.

Flannery walked us to an interrogation room as soon as we arrived. Every cop on the force had to be in that building.

"What's going on?" I asked as soon as the door closed.

"The Society Page Slasher struck again last night. The body was found at 8:00 AM. Didn't you get my message?"

I shook my head. "What about Dane Banner?"

"Either he isn't the guy, or we have a copycat. But it's almost certain that Banner isn't the perp."

"Why?" asked Dad.

"We withheld something from the press that half of the guys on the task force didn't know about. I can't even tell you."

"Where did it happen?" I asked.

"The Philharmonic had a concert at the Cultural Center last night. The vic had an early dinner at Posh with three friends. They all got up to walk to the concert when the vic spotted an old friend on her way out. The others went on to the concert without her. When she didn't show up they figured the old friend may have been an old lover, and didn't get alarmed. A churchgoer spotted a hand sticking out of a hedge about a block from the restaurant this morning."

"I guess this means we won't be getting our reinforcements tomorrow," I said.

"It also means we won't be doing any work here this morning. But don't worry. I have an alternate plan in place. Follow me."

Flannery led us to the captain's office, where he swore Dad in as a deputy, and allowed Flannery and I to carry two boxes with Megan's name on them to Dad's rental.

"Patrick is expecting you. I have to attend a mandatory briefing in fifteen minutes. I'll stop by as soon as it's over."

Patrick had a full pot of coffee made, and the dining room table was cleared and ready for action. He also placed a 4'x6' bulletin board on a wooden easel at the far end of the table. A stack of index cards and marker pens sat next to it.

Over the next two and a half hours we read through the files and posted significant items to the bulletin board. Flannery stopped by about halfway through to check up on us before leaving for Lake Winola.

"Who's watching Lapaglia now?" Dad asked.

"I get to keep Navorocki for the time being because Rose is a potential target as a prominent member of the society set."

"What happened after I left last night?" Dad asked.

"Lapaglia had a sleepover at Rose's and headed home around 9:00 AM. What's the most significant thing you've found in the files, so far?" Flannery asked.

Team Duffy looked at each other, and Patrick said, "On the neighborhood canvas after Megan's death, a neighbor reported hearing Burke shouting at someone in front of his house."

"Let's check him out," Flannery said.

"I'll take a ride over while the rock stars go to practice," Dad said.

We worked in silence for about an hour. As Patrick and I were putting our coats on, Dad said, "Sit down a minute, Patrick. You need to hear this.

"It's a report from Detective Walling. He was at the door of the Amanesco's house on the Elmhurst Boulevard just before Louie and Rose were about to leave for Megan's wake. I'll skip down to the significant part.

"I spoke with Louie Amanesco for about five minutes in the entryway to the house. Mrs. Amanesco was nowhere to be seen. I didn't know she was there, and I'm sure she didn't know of my presence. I was about to leave the premises when I heard Mrs. Amanesco loudly state, 'I don't know why I have to go to this damn wake. I never liked the bitch and I'm sure she felt the same way about me.' End of quote."

Patrick looked hurt. I said, "We'll work on that one this afternoon. Here's my key to this house. If you want to work on the files some more after interviewing the witness, you'll be able to let yourself back in."

The ride to Russell's house was a quiet one. I tried speculating on the identity of the person the witness heard arguing with Carlton Burke, but Patrick was stuck on Rose's comment.

Turning onto Green Ridge Street I said, "Rose was never in

Megan's league as a human being. It shouldn't be surprising that she resented her. Focusing on an insensitive comment made by a total ass will only serve to render you useless to the band and our investigative team. Show your brother that you can pull your weight by getting over the slap and concentrating on the tasks at hand." We pulled into Russell's driveway. "We need to play well and keep our ears open for anything that might help us to figure out what's going on."

Patrick lightly tapped his cheeks and shook his head. "You're right. Thanks for the kick in the butt. Let's rock & roll."

Becky answered the door with red eyes and smeared mascara. She dabbed at her eyes as she led us into the mansion.

"Did you know the victim?" Patrick asked.

"We were on a couple of charity boards together over the past year. The woman was a saint. I can't imagine who would do such a thing to someone who's done so much for the community."

Patrick gave her a hug. "Jason was at police headquarters at 9:30 this morning and tells me that every cop in the city is working the case right now. That monster will be brought to justice, Becky. Why don't you get some rest?"

"Thank you. I'll try, Patrick."

The Shapiro brothers were on stage without Eddie.

"I isolated Eddie's bass line from the songs we completed, using Russell's Pro Tools. We should be able to get by without him for at least one set," Eli said.

"Did you hear from him?" Patrick asked.

"He's supposed to get here in about an hour and a half. He and his staff are drafting the motion to dismiss. Let's get started," Russell said.

Working without Eddie was a pain in the ass. With Russell on drums instead of behind the controls, stopping a song to smooth out a rough spot meant a lot of running back and forth to the recording equipment for Eli and Russell. It also meant letting some mistakes and glitches slide. Without Eddie we were not in the mood to make beautiful music. Russell suggested a bong break, and I gave Patrick a long stare.

He said, "Jason plays like shit when he's stoned. Why don't we let him go upstairs and make himself a sandwich while we do our thing?"

Russell called his wife and she met me at the elevator. We walked into a kitchen that easily could have fed a fine dining establishment.

"What would you like, Jason?"

"I can make it. Why don't you lie down?"

"Being alone with my thoughts isn't helping. Let me make you something."

"Whatever you've got in the fridge will be fine."

Becky didn't belabor the issue by citing menu possibilities. "Russell tells me you were the detective that caught the Concert Killer last month."

"I worked with police departments from all over the state on that case. Were you friends with Megan?"

Becky stopped what she was doing for a moment when I changed the subject. "Most of the time."

"What does that mean?" I asked.

"Initially we were very close. We sat next to each other at all of the band shows, and were in each other's weddings. But as Russell earned more and more money, Megan was constantly reminding me of all of the good we could be doing if we donated most of it to charity. Russell was reinvesting the majority of it into his business, and I got tired of the guilt trips. So we drifted apart."

"Were you surprised when she was killed?"

"Today is a picnic compared to that day. I felt like if I had been a better friend she never would have died. Tell me, how self-important does that sound?"

"The police think there may be a connection between her death and everything that's happened to the band members since Christmas."

"Why would there be such a long lag time between their

152

deaths?" she asked.

"All four incidents, including what happened to Patrick and I last Thursday night, happened shortly before a scheduled reunion show. It seems like someone doesn't want that show to happen. Can you think of any reason why?"

Becky placed her right fist under her chin and supported her elbow with her left hand. She maintained that pose while leaning against a huge kitchen island.

"I can't imagine anything that could lead to murder," she said.

"Something came to mind, though. What was it?"

"Band members have disagreements all of the time. I'm not telling you anything you don't already know."

"What was the disagreement about?" I asked.

"Eli was hoping that the band would schedule regular gigs after the reunion. Nothing stressful, maybe just one show per month. But Louie insisted that the reunion was a one-time deal."

"Was Eli angry?"

"He was disappointed. Eli never married and has no children. Being lead singer for the Luna Parkers was the high point in his life. I think he was hoping to recapture some of the magic from his youth."

The doorbell chimed and I followed Becky to the main foyer where she welcomed Eddie with a hug. We took the elevator to the ballroom where the band was reassembling on the stage. The practice session broke up at 6:30.

On the drive back to Patrick's I asked, "Did you know that Eli & Louie had a disagreement about scheduling more shows after the reunion?"

"Of course. Louie was my best friend."

"How did the rest of the band feel about it?"

"Bongo loved the idea. I wasn't too enthused before Megan died, but afterwards I said I'd go along to give me something to do. Eddie said he'd play the gigs, but wouldn't commit to a regular practice schedule."

"Why didn't Louie want in; especially after he split up with Rose?"

"Actually, he was fine with the idea before the split."

"I don't get it. I'd think he'd have a lot more time on his hands afterwards."

Patrick said, "I don't like badmouthing band mates, but Eddie didn't get Louie a very good settlement with Rose in the divorce."

"What does that have to do with playing gigs?"

"Rose was afraid Louie would slack on his job after the divorce. She wanted to make sure he kept his eye on the ball, and didn't get sidetracked by the band. She insisted on a clause that entitled her to 50% of Louie's music-related earnings above and beyond her monthly alimony."

"Louie didn't want to give Rose any more than he was already giving," I said.

"And, it was a way of distancing himself from Eddie for screwing him over."

"What does Eddie say about it?"

"He claims that he made Louie very aware that he's a criminal attorney, and told him to get a proper family practice attorney for the divorce. But Louie always liked doing business with people he knew and trusted. That time it cost him dearly."

Dad's rental was in the driveway and smoke was billowing from Patrick's chimney. I checked the thermometer on the way in the house and hastened my step after reading 16 degrees.

"Any new developments, Dad?"

"I read through the canvass reports from Burke's neighbors. They all thought he was an asshole, but one guy in particular sounded like he had a particular ax to grind. I took a ride over to his house and he invited me in for a beer."

"Mighty nice of him," Patrick said.

"He was watching an NFL playoff game and didn't want to miss any of the action."

"That explains it," he said.

"I waited until his team gave up a touchdown before asking him about what Burke did to piss him off. By that point he was ready to cut loose."

"What did he say?" I asked.

"Burke had a broken-down old RV parked in front of his house. He parked his white '89 Impala in front of the neighbor's house all of the time. The day before Burke supposedly committed suicide he used spray paint on his right front fender to cover the Bondo he applied a week earlier. The Bondo took up approximately three square feet and was beige in color. The neighbor was mad that he got white paint on his curbstone and grass."

"That means Aunt Megan's patient in Dunkin Donuts should have noticed the Bondo," I said.

"Did you call the patient?" Patrick asked.

"Since confidentiality issues were involved I let Flannery handle that. The patient told him he was sure there was no Bondo on the car that he saw."

"So, whoever killed Megan set Burke up," Patrick said.

"It sure looks that way," Dad replied.

Chapter 23

Dad and I met Patrick for breakfast at the Radisson coffee shop on Monday morning. Flannery would be joining us at any moment. Large snowflakes streamed past our window booth.

Before Patrick could order a coffee, Dad said, "I expect you to tell Flannery about your band buddies when he gets here."

"It's all speculation, Jim. It's not going to do any good."

"I don't like the idea of covering up a very plausible theory because it involves your musician friends."

"Dad, we're in the process of working the case from the inside. If we tell Flannery, and someone in the department says something that gets back to Eddie or Russell, that would be the end of our inside advantage."

"Jason's right, Jim. Both of those guys have a lot of friends at City Hall," Patrick said.

"I still don't like it."

"Our inside advantage is good through the reunion show. Come Saturday morning, if we aren't any closer to solving the case we can tell Flannery everything," Patrick said.

"It's your case. I'm here for support. Just don't put me in any compromising positions," Dad said.

Flannery's skull cap was covered in snow when he arrived. "I got a confirmation from another neighbor about the Bondo. She saw him putting it on about a week before he died."

"Thank God for nosy neighbors," Dad said. "I don't know what the next generation is going to do when all the potential witnesses are on their couches playing video games with ear buds blocking out any possible connection to reality."

"That means Megan's patient was definitely set up as the fall guy," said Patrick.

"And killed before he could defend himself," Dad added.

"How can we find out who did it and why?" I asked.

Flannery looked me in the eye. "Your father told me you and your secretary are pretty slick at finding info on the Internet. I was hoping you could coordinate with her while I tap into all of the law enforcement databases."

"It would help if I had the name of Lapaglia's gun club."

"The Conservators of Justice Gun Club. Their charter is listed in Newton-Ransom," Flannery said.

"Where is that?" I asked.

"Just a few minutes west of Clarks Summit," Patrick said.

"I'll call Jeannine as soon as I get to Patrick's house."

"What do you want me to do?" asked Dad.

"Jason, I heard about an electronics store here in Scranton that sells those tracking devices that people put on their spouse's cars to find out if they're cheating. Do you happen to know if they really work?" Flannery asked.

"As a matter of fact, I had occasion to use one a few times."

"I hear you can track vehicles on a laptop. I'll bet it's a great way to follow someone without getting too close, especially on a snowy day," Flannery said.

"By the way, Flannery, I'm not sure Patrick's computer is modern enough to do the research you need done. I sure wish I had a tablet," I said.

Flannery reached into his overcoat pocket and produced the latest in miniaturized technology. "Why don't you take this with you?"

"Do The Conservators of Justice have an actual building?" I asked.

"It's more like an executive suite where a receptionist answers the phones for two floors of sole proprietorships. Their office is probably little more than 100 square feet."

"I could pose as a prospective tenant and check them out,"

Patrick said.

"Why don't you go along with him, Jim? Who knows, maybe one of you could look around while the other takes the tour," Flannery said.

I wanted to tell Flannery about the lock picking skills I learned from my college tutor, but decided the less said the better. He finished his coffee and departed before breakfast was served. I pulled out the computer while we were eating and found a post-it stuck to the tablet screen. It simply listed the name and address of an electronics company on Penn Avenue, about eight blocks away. We purchased a tracking device before heading to Patrick's house.

I called Jeannine as soon as we got in the door. The phone rang five times before she answered.

"Did I wake you up?" I asked my administrative assistant, who a friend insists is a dead ringer for a 25-year-old Reese Witherspoon.

"I was in the shower. In fact, I'm dripping all over my bedroom floor."

"Get dried off, I'll wait." It was 7:10 AM in San Diego.

Two minutes later she asked, "Are you alright?"

"I'm fine, but I need your research skills ASAP. Can you go into the office now?"

"I'll call you as soon as I get there," she said, and hung up.

"I just got off the phone with Navorocki. Lapaglia is at the Viewmont Mall Home Depot. He's probably getting supplies for a maintenance job. We're going to wait here until he gets busy then go to Newton-Ransom," Dad said.

"I'm going with you."

"Flannery wants you to coordinate with him on the research."

"Did you get a look at that computer he gave me? I could do the research from anywhere. You'll need me to get into the gun club office," I said.

Dad gave me his *less than proud papa* look. "Patrick and I

will case the place today. I'll ask a lot of security questions so we'll know what we're up against if it becomes necessary to send you in."

I thought I could manage without the recon, but decided not to argue. The more time those two spent together, the more likely they could get past their differences.

The minute they left I began making a list of all of the info searches that Jeannine and I would divvy up. She called while I was proofreading the list.

"Before we get into the assignments, what's happening with Vincigura?" I asked.

"I don't have any solid evidence, but it sure looks like he and his golfing buddy are about to pull the caper."

"What makes you say that?"

"It started with a few late night meetings, and has since escalated. Cory got a shot of them bringing suitcases to a hotel in the South Bay on Saturday afternoon. They changed into disguises and had a rendezvous with a couple of other guys who were doing the same thing. They met up in a bar, then visited Hubert's jewelry store and an art gallery that has been handling some high ticket pieces."

"Have Cory email the photos to me. In the meantime, I have a full day planned for you."

I proceeded to get her working on The Conservators of Justice and Nello Lapaglia. I would be focusing on Rose and her possible connection to the group. Patrick had mentioned that he was executor of Louie's estate. I hoped to use his access to see if Rose made any contributions to the group from a joint account, and if so, to pinpoint when they started.

I began my research by calling Patrick and getting permission to review the estate files in his desk. His tone of voice revealed that the Duffy brother's peace treaty was being tested. I kept our conversation on the Amanescos, and learned that Rose had her own checking and savings accounts throughout the marriage.

At 12:40 PM I brought up a credit report on Rose. Before I

could find anything significant I got a call from Kelly. She should have been in the middle of an arithmetic class with her second graders.

"What's going on?" I asked.

"My father was just led out of the mental health center in handcuffs. He punched Andy Stelzner during a therapy session," she sobbed.

"Where are you now?" I asked.

"I'm in the school parking lot trying to get it together enough to drive down to the jail."

"I'll call Shamansky and ask if he can meet you. Then I'll call Andy and find out what I can."

"I wish you were here, Jason. I miss you, and I really need you."

"I miss you too, Kelly, and I love you. Stay in the parking lot for a few minutes. I'll ask Shamansky to call you back right after I talk with him."

Shamansky answered on the second ring. "What?"

"Kelly's father just got popped for punching his therapist and is about to be processed at county lockup."

"I take it you're still in the middle of the sibling dispute," he said.

"Dad's here now. In fact, the brothers Duffy are checking out a lead together as we speak. Who knows, the feud could be over by the end of the day."

"Or, you could be calling your Scranton PD connection at any minute and dealing with assaults on both coasts."

"Thanks for the support. Kelly is on her way downtown. Could you meet her and help her get through this?"

"I thought she was used to bailing her family out."

"Bar fights don't carry the same weight as an assault on a mental health professional who does a lot of work with the courts. The therapist is a friend and my former boss. I'm going to call him after I get off the phone with you. I was hoping we could do some damage control before statements and formal complaints went into the system."

"Give me Kelly's number."

After a few failed attempts, I caught up with Andy in the lunch room of the mental health center where I worked for two years before starting my PI internship.

"Jason, I've been expecting your call." His voice had a very nasal quality.

"I understand my future father-in-law had a breakthrough this morning."

"You are correct. He broke through my septum with a sucker punch. By the way, congratulations. No one mentioned that you gave Kelly a ring for Christmas."

"It's not official yet. I'm waiting for Valentine's Day, so don't let the cat out of the bag."

"I'll do my best to keep it strictly business at his trial," he said.

"What happened?"

"The old coot has been on a bender since New Year's Eve. He showed up with alcohol on his breath for the third time in three sessions. I confronted him and he cold-cocked me."

"Is there any way of keeping him out of the system, Andy?"

"The system is what he needs right now. His wife has been enabling him for years. I'd be willing to recommend probation, contingent on a monitored Antabuse program, but I'm not sweeping it under the rug."

I called Kelly and gave her the news.

"The Antabuse program might save his life," she said.

"Or the life of one of your other family members," I added.

We talked for another three minutes before she put Shamansky on the line. I told him about my conversation with Andy.

"I managed to get him parked in a holding cell for the time being. I'll see if I can keep him out of the drunk tank after processing. Kelly seems to know what she has to do at the bail bonds office."

"Thanks for the help."

"You owe me one," he said.

"I thought we just got back to even after you made me fly across the country for a meeting that the DA told me could have taken place any time in the next two months." Shamansky hung up before I could complete my point.

I didn't feel like jumping back into the plodding research on Rose's finances. My adrenaline was pumping, and sitting at a keyboard did not seem feasible. I changed into the jeans that got battered when I fell at Nay Aug Park and put on the heavy flannel shirt that Patrick wore the last time he chopped firewood. Large flakes were falling, although it was obviously not an accumulating snow. I used to chop wood at the cabin my band rented at Big Bear during college winter break. Patrick's pile of split logs, stacked six feet from the garage, had dwindled considerably since my arrival. He clearly had enough seasoned whole logs to get through winter. It felt good to get a rhythm going with the ax.

My arms got heavy after 45 minutes of hard work. I planted the ax in the splitting stump and went into the kitchen for a bottle of water. I checked my messages as I chugged. Nothing from Kelly, but Jeannine left three.

"What's going on, Jeannine?"

"Were you being chased by a bear? You sound out of breath."

"Just a little wood chopping, what's up?"

"I watched a show about bears on the Discovery Channel last week. There are a whole lot of bears in Pennsylvania. Did you know that, Jason?"

"I do now. What did you find out about the gun club?"

Jeannine hesitated. I knew she was still thinking about bears, and was probably picturing me being chased around the forest like a male version of Goldilocks. Obsessive Compulsive Disorder hijacked her emotions at least once each month.

She said, "The Conservators of Justice Gun Club began in 2003. It's officially a non-profit organization. Nello Lapaglia is their Vice President."

"Very good. What else?"

"The gun club, in and of itself, appears to be on the up-and-up. They host competitions, provide shooting and safety lessons, and coordinate hunting expeditions."

"But, you didn't call three times to tell me it's a dead end," I said.

"I found an article in a small weekly paper. It was about one of their members whose house burned down last winter. He said that if it wasn't for The Conservators of Justice Gun Club and the work they got him with Select Sentinel he never would have survived."

"Select Sentinel?"

"This is where it got interesting. Select Sentinel is a security company that specializes in corporate bodyguards. Their discreet ad campaign always mentions that they work exclusively with clients whose values are in keeping with the mission statement of the organization."

"What does that mean?" I asked.

"That's the interesting part. There is no mission statement on their site. There's also no pricing for services, endorsements from satisfied clients, or description of services. There is only a Contact page that asks several questions of the prospective client and gives nothing in return."

I gave her Rose's contact info and asked her to find out if she had any connection to either of those organizations. Call waiting told me that Kelly was on the other line.

"How are you holding up?" I asked.

She sighed heavily. "Shamansky was a big help. But Danny and Sean are playing the blame game and at each other's throats. I'm going straight home to decompress."

We talked for another five minutes. She didn't push for me to return to San Diego. The fact that Dad was here in spite of his ongoing feud told her more about the seriousness of the situation than what I had let on. She didn't feel the need to try to drag the details out of me, and I wasn't about to load her plate up with any additional anxiety.

When we disconnected I called Mom and told her what was happening. She said she'd give Kelly time to get home, and give her a call.

"I can't believe your father and Patrick have been out and about all day. Have you checked to make sure they're both still alive?"

"I'll do that as soon as we get off of the phone."

Chapter 24

I heard a vehicle coming up Patrick's quarter mile long driveway before I saw it. Flannery's drab green SUV navigated without a slip over the two inches of snow that accumulated since morning. When he pulled to the parking area at the rear of the house I admired my stack of firewood next to the garage forty feet from the back door. I glanced at Patrick's wrought iron log holder next to the fireplace and saw that just three logs remained.

"Your uncle must love his privacy," Flannery said as I held the door for him.

"My mother told me that Aunt Megan never cared for tan lines."

Flannery smiled. "That explains it."

I poured him a cup of coffee while he removed his boots. "What brings you out to God's country?"

"It only took 15 minutes to get here from the stationhouse, so no big deal."

I gave him the full rundown on the relationship between The Conservators of Justice and Select Sentinel. He agreed to use the various law enforcement databases to learn what he could about the private security firm.

"Did you have any problems with that computer I lent to you this morning?"

"As a matter of fact I did. But I stopped by an electronics store on Penn Avenue, picked up a piece of software that helped me gauge its responsiveness, and it's been working fine ever since. At least it was the last time I talked with Dad and Patrick."

"Why don't you give them a call?"

I tried Dad first and it went to voicemail. Patrick answered on the first ring.

"Your father is as bullheaded today as he was 45 years ago."

"Where are you?"

"At a sporting goods store in Scranton. Your father is buying a kit to clean the guns you got from Russell."

"Uh-oh."

In unison, Patrick and Flannery asked, "What do you mean, uh-oh?"

"Dad likes to clean his guns when he's really pissed off. I take it the Vietnam War came up in conversation."

"Only for about two hours."

"Ask him what's happening with Lapaglia," Flannery said.

"I heard him. Put it on speakerphone," Patrick said. "Hello, Colin. The software that Jason installed is working great. Lapaglia brought materials for a carpentry job to a house on East Mountain, and stayed there until about an hour ago. We followed him to a neighborhood bar in North Scranton."

"I thought you said you were at a sporting goods store," I said.

"It's the same place that we bought your wool socks. It's only a few blocks from the bar."

"I'd rather you keep an eye on the door and see if any familiar faces go in or out," Flannery said.

"That's what I told Jim, but he insisted on getting the damned gun cleaning kit. What time is our relief coming, Colin?"

"I'll have Navorocki call you in a few minutes. What did you find out at the executive suite?"

"Not much. The gun club HQ was on the first floor, and the place only had open offices on the second floor. Jim took the tour while I excused myself for a restroom break. All of the doors have glass panel inserts, so I took pictures of everything I could shoot from the doorway. Nothing appeared to be particularly suspicious."

"Call me if there are any new developments," Flannery said, and I hung up.

"Your turn," I said. "What did you come up with?"

"I hate to tell you this, but I got stuck calling people who used a credit card to purchase tickets to the concert at the Cultural Center Saturday night. All of the local politicos are catching heat from their top contributors, and the shit is rolling downhill like nobody's business."

My Irish temper made a brief appearance. "So, in spite of the fact that we just found a link between a solid citizen who was killed five years ago, and two people who were killed in the last month, the department opted to take everyone off of the case."

"It was just for the day, Jason. Memories of small details fade fast. There were over a thousand people at the concert, and 657 of them paid by credit card. That's a hell of a lot of conversations, especially since it's a work day, and many calls were redirected to business numbers, where phone tag usually preceded making the contact."

I glared at him.

"I'm authorized for overtime to work with you guys tonight. I'll run Select Sentinel through everything before I call it a night," he said.

"I've got work to do," I said, and Flannery left.

Over the next hour I coordinated with Jeannine in eliminating a couple of dead end leads. Five minutes after putting a pan of stuffed pork chops in the oven, Dad and Patrick entered the house in the midst of a heated debate. Apparently the war in Southeast Asia was still raging.

"Where are those Glocks?" Dad asked the minute his boots were off.

I stopped the battle by telling them about Kelly's crisis. When I finished, Dad opened his cleaning kit on a living room TV tray, and Patrick loaded two of the three remaining logs into the fireplace.

"I split some logs today, Patrick. I'll bring in an armful if you two can remain civil for the next five minutes."

Neither of them replied. I put on my Nordic wear and walked out the back door. Patrick had a large deck on the back of the house, with a set of stone stairs leading to the driveway that ran along the east side of the house. I grabbed the toboggan that Patrick used for hauling wood, and pulled it 40 feet to the woodpile. After placing a log on the toboggan, I heard wood splinter directly behind me. I jumped over the four-foot stack, landing on my back. A lightning bolt shot from my tailbone to the base of my skull.

My first thought was to call for Dad. But I quickly realized that it could easily get him killed. I put my hat on a stick and peeked around the side of the woodpile. I saw a flash come from a rock ledge above the driveway, about 10 feet past the rear deck on the house. A second flash sent my hat flying. I could see that the gunman was closing in on me. To my right was the splitting stump with the ax sticking out. Just beyond was the garage.

A grapefruit-sized ball of snow rolled down the hill ten feet closer to me than the last flash. I scooted to the opposite side of the woodpile, grabbed the ax, and opened the side door to the garage. Two bullets hit a few feet from my head, and a third broke a window in the garage. I looked around for a place to get the jump on the gunman, but there was nothing but open space between the door and Aunt Megan's microbus. I slid the side door open, climbed in, and held the ax over my head.

When my eyes adjusted to the light I spotted the garage door opener sitting on the console. I placed the ax on the floor, crawled to the console, grabbed the opener, and resumed my position, hitting the opener in the process. Before putting both hands on the ax handle, I used a finger to slide the microbus curtain enough to see the side door. A large figure holding a rifle was standing behind the woodpile. He stepped almost to the threshold, stuck the gun out in front of himself and sprayed the area to the left of the door. He then reversed the direction of the gun, sprayed to the right, and replaced the magazine in his rifle. Eyeing the microbus, he took two steps toward me and started shooting. Immediately after ducking below the windows, I heard gunfire coming from the house. Footsteps went past the van toward the front of the garage.

I peeked out the back window and saw the gunman removing his silencer. This would improve his accuracy in dealing with Dad. When he cut loose with the first spurt I picked up the ax and positioned myself next to the open van door. I was hoping to go Lizzie Borden on him before he heard me coming. But the next spurt came from outside the garage. Looking through the side door, I saw the back of the gunman behind a tree, about halfway between the woodpile and the house. Dad was on the far side of the stone steps leading to the deck.

The gunman took two tentative steps toward Dad's car when my father took four shots in rapid succession. I saw a chunk of bark fly off of the tree behind the gunman. He ran back to the tree when the bullets started flying, but reversed his course as soon as he realized Dad's magazine was empty. I prayed that Dad had another one. I sprinted to the gunman's tree while he ran toward Dad's rental car.

"Out of bullets, old man?" he asked, and sprayed the stairs with six rounds.

When Dad didn't reply the gunman walked out from behind the car and approached the stairs slowly. I knew at that moment that Dad would have taken the shot if he had any more ammo. The gunman was now a mere six feet from where Dad was crouching.

Desperation can cause us to take wild chances. Without thinking, I gripped the ax handle in a throwing position and took a crow hop out from behind the tree. The plan, if you can call it that, was to hurl the ax as if I was making a throw from shortstop to first base, with the gunman being the first baseman. He heard me as soon as I started my crow hop. As he was bringing the gun to bear on me I heard a shot ring out. The gunman dropped his rifle and grabbed his right arm. He started to bend down for the gun when another shot spit snow up next to the rifle. The gunman broke into a sprint down the driveway.

"Gimme the gun, Patrick," Dad called.

By the time Patrick reached the stairs I heard an engine turn over beyond the bend in the driveway. We all went into the house, and I called Flannery. Twenty minutes later six police vehicles bathed Patrick's snow covered lawn in red and blue flashing lights.

"Do you think this might merit a full day of police work?" I asked Flannery.

Chapter 25

I expected Patrick to be stressed about missing band practice last night with the reunion show just four days away. I was wrong. His entire world was focused on what Megan thought about him using a gun, looking down from heaven. He got the notion into his head that she would be standing him up at the Pearly Gates, and he would spend eternity searching for her.

I expected Dad to tell Patrick to man-up and take a little pride in the fact that he saved his brother's life. I was wrong again. My father has a lot of good qualities. Empathy is not one of them. Yet he stayed by his brother's side and offered words of support throughout the evening. The whole thing reminded me of a mad scientist cartoon where brains are swapped in vastly different characters. The only thing that kept the transformation from being complete involved Patrick glancing over at his stash box every two minutes.

Flannery was staring at Patrick's bulletin board when Dad and I walked in on Tuesday morning. Patrick clutched a framed picture of Megan.

"There's something important that I'm missing on this board. I just can't figure out what it is," said Flannery.

Dad and I flanked him on either side, bent down and read the file cards. Nothing new had been posted.

"I'm getting coffee," Dad said.

No insights came to me, so I checked on Patrick. "Did you get any sleep last night?"

"I never should have dragged you into this. With all of my

pain over what Megan would think about me using a gun I never even thought about the fact that you and your father came damned close to being killed."

"How about doing your part in keeping us alive by focusing on the case for a while? Flannery thinks there's something important that we're missing about your bulletin board. Will you join us in the dining room?"

"Good morning, Patrick," said Dad.

Patrick nodded. "Jim."

My uncle immediately started yanking push pins and reconfiguring the alignment of the cards.

"What are you doing?" asked Flannery.

"I do this all the time when I'm working insurance cases. Sometimes it's just a matter of looking at things a little differently."

All of us reread the cards in their new configuration. Dad shook his head. Flannery shrugged. I gave it another reading but nothing came to mind.

"Do you see anything, Patrick?" I asked.

"Give me a minute."

He unpinned the card listing all of the items Eddie mentioned that might have been in Louie's safe.

"It's not what I'm seeing, it's what I'm not seeing that bothers me."

"Like what?" asked Dad.

"Jason, do you remember the day we met Eddie at his office? I asked him for a copy of Louie's Master Settlement Agreement and he refused because he said Rose is so litigious."

"We never did get a copy of the agreement. Rose mentioned it when she was drunk and told me about the insurance policy."

"Wouldn't that be exactly the kind of document Louie would keep in that wall safe?" Patrick asked.

"We moved Louie's file cabinet to an evidence locker," said Flannery. He called Navorocki and told him to look for the MSA.

"Why don't you get the ball rolling on requesting a copy from Family Court? It could save us some time if it doesn't turn up in the file cabinet," said Dad.

"Navorocki is at HQ. He should be calling back within the half hour."

I introduced the idea that we start speculating on the possibility that one of the Luna Parkers was the killer. Patrick made Flannery aware of the fact that Eddie and Russell had a lot of friends in high places, including his bosses. We spent the next twenty minutes talking about Eddie. Before we could move on to other members Navorocki called back. After listening for a minute, Flannery told him to start processing a request with Family Court, and to do everything possible to expedite it.

Jeannine called as he was hanging up. "I have an emergency situation, and I have some research you asked for. What do you want to hear first?"

"Let's go with the emergency."

"Last night I overheard a conversation at the country club that makes me think Vinnie and Hubert are planning something big for tomorrow night."

"What did you hear?" I asked.

"Two of the golfers that I actually consider to be gentlemen were speaking very quietly about Vinnie and Hubert hosting a hush-hush stag costume ball fundraiser tomorrow night. I think they'll probably be playing poker too because one of the men said to bring lots of cash; no credit cards. Cory thinks Vinnie, Hubert, and Benjamin will wear disguises that will completely hide their identities, and bring real guns to the party."

"You two have been doing all of the work on this case, so I'm going to trust your instincts. Have Cory pick up a costume that will allow him to hide a camera and an audio feed. I'll call Shamansky and try to get an undercover van outside of the party."

"What about me?" she asked.

"I'll ask Shamansky if he can get you in the van. If he says yes, you're to stay put when the action goes down."

"Don't worry about me. I have no interest in being in on the action. But a front row seat would be wonderful," she said.

"You deserve it, Jeannine. What's the other thing you mentioned?"

"I found out that Rose's father was the defendant in a criminal negligence case six years ago, and Edward Pohanick was his attorney."

"Good work, Jeannine. I'll get back to you after I talk with Shamansky."

When I returned to the dining room table the conversation was on Eli. I told them about Jeannine's research find and we went back to speculating about Eddie.

"You've known this guy your whole life, Patrick. What do you think?" Dad asked.

After 30 seconds Flannery said, "The longer you hesitate, the worse you make your buddy look."

"It's just that I don't want my brother and I to go back to having a feud. We're finally getting along after all these years."

"Say what you have to say, Patrick. It won't change the fact that you saved my life."

"Eddie could have become an epic rock bass player. When we were teenagers he used to pour his heart and soul into his music. The studio engineer that recorded us told Russell that he was the best bassist he had ever seen. Eddie's father was a high powered attorney back in the 60s and 70s. He pushed hard to have Eddie follow in his footsteps. But all Eddie wanted to do was wail on his bass.

"We got signed to a big label right after high school and spent the summer recording our first album. The label insisted on demoting Russell to a support role and got us hooked up with a big-time manager who had experience taking bands to the top of the charts. We thought we were set. The only thing standing in our way was the Vietnam War and the possibility of getting drafted. All of us had been accepted to attend area colleges, and the plan was for us to attend while playing a modified tour around our class schedules.

"The first day of orientation the dean announced the end of college deferments and we were told that we'd all be subjected to the results of the upcoming draft lottery. I remember lottery day like it just happened. The five band members plus Russell sat in Eddie's GTO in front of Gallucci's Music Studio in a driving rain storm, listening to the radio. The only one with a draft number under 150 was Eddie. He drew number 5. We all acted like he was diagnosed with cancer.

"Eddie's father said he could pull strings to get him a deferment, but would only do it if Eddie agreed to switch majors to Prelaw and follow through with a career in law. Eddie refused. It wasn't long afterwards that he got his notice to report for his physical. A week before he was to report, our album was released to strong reviews. Four days later our well-connected new manager got busted with a pound of pot crossing from Canada into the US. The next day our tour got cancelled, and Eddie told his father he'd get into the family business.

"Eddie was never the same after that. He kept playing with the Luna Parkers, but never with the soul that he had before he was forced to swim with the sharks. The rest of us dealt with the disappointment in our own ways, but Eddie was the only one who seemed like he went on to become a different person."

"Why didn't your label just assign somebody else to take over for the new manager?" I asked.

"You two can talk about that later," Flannery said. "Right now we need to figure out what we're going to do with this information."

"I'll let you guys get started without me. I've got a situation on a case in San Diego that requires my immediate attention."

I walked into the guest room I had used. Much to my surprise, Shamansky answered on the second ring.

"You're welcome," he said.

"Thanks for helping Kelly. To show my appreciation I'm

giving you a hot tip on a possible armed robbery planned for tomorrow night."

I spent the next ten minutes telling him about the Vincigura case. His only response was to laugh when I told him that Cory, my Tourette's impaired employee, was going undercover in a costume rigged with audio/video equipment.

"I work Homicide, not Robbery. Call me if somebody gets killed."

"The only backup we have right now is Jeannine sitting in Cory's van. I was hoping you could get your own van of officers together to make the bust, and keep an eye on Jeannine in the process."

"Why don't you just come back here and run the show yourself?"

"The case I'm working is coming to a head. Dad and I took a lot of gunfire last night. There's no way we leave my uncle here by himself."

"I almost forgot; he's the pacifist."

"The pacifist winged the bad guy last night and saved all of our lives."

"I'll see if I can round up a buddy to help out, but we won't be getting a van," he said.

"You can use Cory's van. It has all kinds of tech toys you can play with, and Jeannine can keep you company."

After a five minute walk down memory lane, where Shamansky reminded me about a trip the three of us took to a prison near the Mexican border, he reluctantly agreed to her presence. I assured him that all he would have to do is watch a group of elderly golfers get their party on while Jeannine regaled them with stories about which ones pinched her butt. Being a lifelong admirer of the female form, Shamansky was fully onboard with the plan.

I spent the remainder of the afternoon coordinating plans with Cory, and working out a strategy with Patrick on how to approach Eddie after practice. Dad offered a third party perspective without getting judgmental about Eddie's reaction to being drafted. At times I felt like I was taking a helicopter tour of an active volcano and getting far too close for comfort. But Dad kept his cool.

An exciting and disturbing development came just after dinner when Kelly called. "I have wonderful news."

"What's going on?"

"Andy Stelzner offered to drop the charges against my father."

"How did that happen?" I asked.

"My mother dropped in on him today carrying a book called *Codependent No More*, and he said he'd drop his complaint if she'd read the book aloud to her husband and sons and they all agreed to live by the principles outlined in the book."

"That's a tall order," I said. "Where did she get the idea to approach him like that?"

"From *your* mother. She gave my mother a call last night and they met at a coffee shop in Santee. Your mother brought the book along and convinced her that she could change everything by not being an enabler anymore. My mother stayed up all night reading the book and ambushed Andy as he was leaving the clinic for lunch."

"I'm glad Mom was able to help. But don't get your hopes up too high. There are no guarantees."

"Andy said he'll write up a contract that includes all four of them going on Antabuse. If Sean refuses to sign it because he's not in trouble right now he'll have to move out of the house."

Over the next ten minutes I told her about the latest chapter in the Duffy brothers' feud. She was ecstatic over what was going on with both of our families. The minute I got off of the phone it dawned on me that Andy might have said something about me planning to give her an engagement ring for Valentine's Day. Oh, what a tangled web . . .

I hoped to pick up on a vibe from one of my band mates at

practice that would help me to figure out who was involved and why. This is not the kind of detective work I could discuss with Dad, Flannery, or Shamansky without getting a lecture, unless I used the word *hunch* or *gut* which would have made it OK. There were no subtle traces of nervousness among the surviving Luna Parkers. Everyone was barely hanging on to his composure after two deaths and two more murder attempts in the past month. We sounded as bad as we felt, but no one was assuming the role of task master. At 10:00 Eddie announced that he had to call it an early night because he was presenting a motion in court first thing in the morning. I gave Patrick a head gesture, and he told the Shapiro brothers that we were leaving as well.

I caught up to Eddie in the mansion's guest parking lot and told him we needed ten minutes. He led us to a small bar on Green Ridge Street.

"This place has an excellent solo acoustic act on Tuesday nights," he said as we entered.

"I'm not here for the music, Eddie."

We found a table near the stage area. Patrick took our drink orders and headed to the bar.

"My assistant told me this afternoon that you represented Rose's father in a criminal negligence case six years ago."

"I represent lots of criminal cases."

"Wasn't it a conflict of interest when you represented Louie in his divorce?"

"You wouldn't believe how hard I tried talking Louie out of using me as his divorce lawyer. I told him it could be construed as an ethics violation. He said he didn't care, and he'd sign anything that got me off the hook with the Bar Association's Ethics Committee. I took him up on that offer."

Patrick returned with beers. "Did I miss anything?"

"Eddie was just explaining about representing Rose's father before taking Louie on as a client."

"No wonder he got screwed so badly in that settlement!" Patrick was pissed.

"I was up against the top divorce attorney in Pennsylvania. I warned Louie that it would be a lions versus Christians fight if he didn't get a lawyer who specialized in divorce settlements, but he wouldn't take no for an answer. You know how he was when he set his mind on something, Patrick."

"I was surprised you didn't include Louie's MSA as one of the documents that was probably in his safe," I said.

"I didn't list any documents in his safe. We spoke hypothetically."

"God knows you didn't want any of us getting curious about that document," Patrick said.

"You're right. It wasn't my best work. I felt badly about getting smoked by the competition, especially when representing a lifelong friend." Eddie did his best to look contrite.

"So tell me, Eddie," I said, "have you received any more checks from Rose or her father since you started representing Louie?" I asked.

"We're clearly in the area of privileged information here. I can't answer that."

"Can't or won't?" asked Patrick.

Eddie stood up. "I'm not going to be bullied into betraying confidences. Goodbye."

"Are you ready to head out?" Patrick asked me.

"Eddie was right about one thing," I said. "This musician is an excellent solo act. Let's finish our beers, and you can tell me why the Luna Parkers didn't just get a new manager after your hotshot new manager got busted at the border."

Over the next half hour Patrick explained how the phrase *15 minutes of fame* had an almost literal translation back in the day. "Last year I heard Russell explain it as being like a stock market day trader dealing with a hot stock. Once the opportunity to catch momentum had passed, everyone jumped off of the bandwagon and moved on to the next big thing on the horizon."

"Why not just delay the release until you could find someone else to drive airtime?"

"The bust happened immediately after the release date. Radio Programming Managers were sure to interpret the absence of support as a lack of enthusiasm for the album by the record company. The timing left us DOA in the record stores and everyone knew it. End of story."

Chapter 26

Dad was dressed and ready to start his day at 7:00 AM Wednesday morning. "Are you coming to breakfast, Jason?"

"Go ahead without me. Amanesco Construction headquarters is less than two blocks from here. I'm going to pop in and try to talk with Louie's uncle."

"Do you want me to go with you?"

"I'm a near stranger. If I brought you along I think he'd get cautious. But he might just tell me something he wouldn't say in front of Patrick in a casual one-on-one."

"I understand. I'll meet you back here in the room."

The cold air hurt my lungs the instant I exited the hotel. My eyes stung as I walked into a headwind. It was hard to imagine that my grandparents endured these conditions every year of their lives. An appreciation for my father's willingness to start a new life in San Diego grew a bit in that very moment.

Connie's secretary recognized me the moment I walked in the door. She told me that Connie was in a meeting with a subcontractor, but she would do her best to get me in right afterwards. She practically jogged back to her desk as soon as she got me seated, so I didn't bother her with random questions. Twenty minutes later I sat across from Connie.

"Thanks for seeing me without an appointment."

"Any idea who done it?" he asked.

"We're getting closer, Connie."

"I seen in da paper ya come pretty close to meetin' my nephew a couple two, tree times."

"Bongo died since I was here last. I was hoping, as his employer of many years, that you might be able to tell me something."

"Ya got my full attention. Fire away."

"As you know, Louie was found under an empty wall safe. Bongo's house was searched shortly after he was murdered. Whoever killed them was obviously looking for something. Do you have any idea what it might have been, Connie?"

Connie reached under his desk and came up with a good sized set of barbells. The septuagenarian started doing curls as he stared out onto Lackawanna Avenue. I felt it best not to interrupt his unorthodox cognitive process. After about a minute he set one barbell on the floor and tapped his thin gray hair five times. He resumed his arm exercises for another minute then suddenly stopped.

"Louie and Bongo got into a fist fight at da Steamtown remodel da week after Tanksgiving."

"What was it about?"

"Louie wouldn't say shit. So I called Bongo in for a little heart-to-heart."

"And?"

"He said somethin' about a movie producer wantin' to buy the rights to their big song."

"Did the movie producer contact Louie directly?"

"Fuckifiknow."

"Did Bongo mention their lawyer/band mate, Eddie Pohanick?"

"Now dat ya mention it, yeah he did."

"Did he say anything else?"

"Fuckifiknow." Connie tapped the top of his head five more times. "It ain't da steel trap it used ta be. I tink I'm gettin' the oldtimers."

"If you think of anything else will you let me know?" I asked, handing him a business card.

"Anyting fer Louie."

Dad was watching CNN when I returned to our hotel room.

182

"Flannery called earlier. I'm going to relieve Navorocki at noon. Did you learn anything we didn't already know?"

I told him about the movie producer, and called Patrick. After a few minutes we decided to drop in on Dakota Rainwater at work. I arranged to meet up with Dad for dinner before going to band practice.

Dakota worked behind the counter of a gas station/sub shop/convenience store. We arrived just after 11:00, avoiding the lunchtime crush. Her blondish white hair was pulled back into a ponytail, making her appear even thinner than when I met her at Bongo's bereavement luncheon.

"Hello, beautiful. How are you holding up?" Patrick asked.

"One day at a time, Patrick. Hello, Jason."

"We were hoping to ask a few questions before the lunch crowd rolls in," Patrick said.

"Just act like you're looking at the candy under the counter if I get customers. I'll ignore you till they're gone."

"This morning I found out about the fight Bongo had with Louie over the movie rights to *Parkers Luna Sea*. What can you tell us about it, Dakota?" Patrick asked.

"You should ask Eddie. He knows a lot more about it than I do."

"Eddie never said a word about it, and I expect he'll tell me the absolute minimum unless I know which questions to ask. Whatever you tell me can only help to get to the bottom of what's going on."

Dakota looked relieved to see a customer approach the counter. Her relief was short lived as he was merely paying cash for gas.

"Eddie met Bongo for drinks early last month. He said that all of the band members who played on the song would get a nice chunk of change if it got put into the movie, but that Louie refused to option the rights. He said that since Louie and Eli were listed as the composers he couldn't do the deal without both of their signatures, and Louie was refusing."

"So Bongo agreed to try to persuade Louie?" I asked.

"Eddie gave him $50 just for agreeing to try, and promised another $100 the day Louie signed."

"What did Bongo say about the fight?" Patrick asked.

"He said that Louie didn't want to give Rose any more than she was already sucking out of his veins. Bongo was mad that Louie was thinking about himself, and that as soon as the store remodel was finished Bongo would be going on unemployment for the rest of the winter."

"Did Bongo say anything else that might help us?" I asked.

"A few hours after he met up with you two at that horrible Irish bar in South Side he told me he thought the rumor about Buzzy and Becky had something to do with it."

"What did he mean by that, Dakota?" Patrick asked.

"I haven't the foggiest idea. He was pretty drunk and said it just before he passed out."

Four construction workers lined up behind us. Dakota gave us a wave and we departed.

After buckling my seat belt I asked, "Why didn't anybody tell you about this deal?"

"We're going to know the answer to that question before I turn my amp on at practice tonight."

"Speaking of which, I need to leave at 9:30. A robbery is supposed to be going down involving my case in San Diego, and I need to be in constant contact with my peeps."

Patrick replied, "My fist might be in contact with my peeps, so don't worry about it. We'll use Russell's recording of your tracks if we need them."

"Tell me about the Becky and Buzzy rumor."

"I didn't think you went in for idle gossip."

"When a guy makes that kind of comment and ends up dead a few days later I don't consider it idle gossip," I said.

"Back in high school, Russell suspected that Becky was having an affair with Buzzy. Louie and I broke the news to him that she was actually having an affair with cocaine, and was just sneaking off with Buzzy to score."

"Did he believe you?"

"I don't know. But I was sure he believed Bongo when he pointed out that Becky always ground her teeth when she was on coke. Russell started telling her how unattractive he found the teeth grinding, and Becky stopped sneaking off with Buzzy. That was about six months before he died and I thought that was the end of it."

Five minutes after we arrived at Patrick's house I got a call from Dad. "What did those two characters look like who were with Lapaglia at Carley's?"

I gave him a brief description. "Why?"

"The three of them are having lunch with Rose Amanesco at Cooper's Restaurant."

"Are you close enough to hear their conversation?"

"They were seated in the main dining room. I got the table closest to them but it's not close enough," he said.

I filled him in on the conversation with Dakota. Dad insisted that we have dinner at Cooper's after getting a whiff of their lobster bisque.

Most of my afternoon consisted of conversations with Cory, Jeannine, and Shamansky. Jeannine learned that most of the men would be dressing in their wives' evening gowns for the party. I instantly thought of the Hogettes, a group of 12 male Washington Redskins football fans who wear women's dresses, garden party hats, and pig snouts to all of the home games.

Since Cory would be going undercover he would need a similar disguise. He is 5'6" and tops out at 140 lbs. I called my sister, Lisa.

"One of my employees will be going undercover tonight and I'm hoping to borrow one of your evening gowns."

"What do you mean *one of my evening gowns*? The last time I wore an evening gown my no good ex-girlfriend, Noreen, was getting married for the third time. That was two years ago."

"It sounds like the dress might be bad luck. Can I borrow

it?"

"I thought you were at Uncle Patrick's with Dad."

"I am. Like I said, it's for one of my employees."

"Jeannine's a bit bustier that I am. I don't think it will fit her."

"It's not for Jeannine."

"Don't tell me you hired another girl."

"OK, I won't."

"What aren't you telling me, Jason. I always know when you're trying to pull something. If you were here right now I'd have it out of you in five seconds," she said.

"Have you ever watched a Washington Redskins football game?"

Fifteen minutes later Lisa agreed to lend me the dress, but only if she didn't have to deal directly with Cory. I don't think she cared about the foul language that comes with his Tourette's as much as the notion that they were the same dress size.

Jeannine informed me that Cory already secured a mask/ headdress with more feathers than a Las Vegas showgirl. I was certain that it had more to do with camera mounting infrastructure and probably nothing to do with getting in touch with his inner Sally Rand.

Cory walked me through the equipment set up so that I would get a live feed of everything coming through the headdress cam. Shamansky, his partner, and Jeannine would get the same feed in the back of the van parked outside the hall. On my instructions, Cory also rigged an office laptop computer to receive the video feed.

I called Mrs. Vincigura and told her that I expected a highly significant development to occur tonight, and thought it best that she witness it in real time. She agreed to stop by the office before closing to pick up the laptop. She was far less combative than usual. I took this to mean that Vinnie's behavior tipped her that something was about to happen, and she was relieved that her overpaid sleuths were cutting her in on the action.

Shamansky informed me that his buddy wasn't thrilled about giving up his night off to do the stakeout. He felt that the least Duffy Investigations could do was to show a little appreciation by asking Jeannine to wear something sexy. I told him I'd have a word with her about her wardrobe before the end of the day. At first I thought it might be a great way to pay him back for my 6000 mile round trip on top of an inflatable donut. I considered lending Jeannine what Kelly refers to as her Miss Frumpington outfit, but decided that cruel and unusual was not the way to go, especially after he had since intervened on Kelly's behalf. I ended up telling Jeannine that she might have to sneak into the party if Cory's equipment goes down, so she should bring the Zorro hat and mask in my credenza, and wear a sexy outfit that would keep the golfer's eyes away from her familiar face. I justified this by thinking of Shamansky as an art lover who was doing me a favor.

Patrick, Dad, and I were seated in an interesting room next to Cooper's main dining area. About every ten minutes a model train would traverse the room on tracks built close to the ceiling. Old pictures of Scranton during its glory years adorned the walls. Dad refused to entertain work related questions until he finished a bowl of lobster bisque. At his insistence, I ordered one for myself and gave him a heartfelt thank you when I finished.

"Why would Lapaglia bring Rose along to the meeting?" I asked.

"That's the $64,000 question, son."

"Do you think there's any chance I could poke around Select Sentinel to get some answers?" I asked.

"I wondered the same thing. Flannery and I took a ride over there after my shift was over, and their security is tighter than the skin on a grape. But The Conservators of Justice office might give us what we're looking for," Dad replied.

"Any ideas on how to get past the receptionist?" I asked.

Patrick said, "The office next door to them is called Giles

Import/Export. I peeked through their mini-blinds. There wasn't anybody in, and the room was half full of boxes. If we send you in with a hand truck, clipboard, and a set of keys you could tell the receptionist that Mr. Giles sent you over to locate a few packages and make a delivery."

"I need to find out more about their product line, and a few facts about Mr. Giles, but it could work. In fact, I'm sure it will work if a certain lessee prospect comes back for a second look while I'm doing my thing," I said.

"I'll charm the pants off of her," Patrick said.

"Geez Patrick, I'm eating," Dad said.

Chapter 27

Patrick was quiet during our five minute ride from Cooper's to Russell's house in Green Ridge. I assumed he was plotting how he would confront his band mates. His driving reflected the rise in his adrenaline. By the time we reached Russell's abode, Patrick bounded into the driveway like a racecar driver making a pit stop. Within seconds two men aimed automatic weapons at us from opposite sides of our vehicle. A third man walked out of the shadows and instructed Patrick to cut his lights.

"Sorry about that, Mr. Duffy. Until the murderer is caught please refrain from driving onto the property as if you're about to mount an assault," he said.

"Go away," Patrick said. He turned to me and added, "Although that's exactly what I'm about to do."

We grabbed our guitars and approached the front door. "Why don't you go down to practice and have your talk with the guys. I'll tell Becky you have some band issues to discuss before practice and see if I can get her tell me about Buzzy."

"Good idea," he said.

Becky answered the door in black slacks and a pink sweater. "You're the last ones here."

"Patrick has some Luna Parkers business to discuss before practice. Do you mind if I wait up here with you for a few minutes, Becky?"

"Not at all, Jason. Would you like a drink?"

"A hot chocolate might help to get me defrosted."

I followed her into the kitchen and took a seat at an arched tile counter that faced the stove and several cooking appliances.

189

The set up looked like it was designed for a televised cooking show.

"This is an interesting view," I noted.

"Russell and I are both gourmet chefs. We used to be members of a small epicurean club where the guests observed the chefs during all phases of meal preparation."

"Becky, I need to ask you about something that's a bit delicate in nature. It came up today as part of our investigation into Louie and Bongo's deaths."

"Go ahead." She stopped tinkering with a machine that looked far too complicated for the making of hot chocolate.

"A few days before Bongo died he said that he thought Louie's death had something to do with the rumor about you and Buzzy."

A minute of silence was broken by the sound of steam escaping from the hot chocolate time machine.

"I can't imagine how the two could be related," she said.

"Most teenagers sow a few wild oats before settling down. It's natural, "I said.

"I never had an affair with Buzzy. Our relationship was strictly business."

"What do you think may have prompted Bongo to make that statement?"

"I'm told that alcohol poisoning and confabulations go hand-in-hand for long term abusers," she said.

"Patrick told me that it was Bongo who debunked the rumor in the first place. I had a long talk with Bongo just a few hours before he died and the topic of conversation was Buzzy. That's what prompted me to look for him at Nay Aug Park. And, sure enough, he was found in the exact spot where Buzzy died. I think you can see why I'm having a hard time accepting this tie-in to Buzzy as coincidence."

Becky handed me the best cup of hot chocolate I ever tasted in my life. Normally I'd drop a compliment. But it was her turn to respond and I didn't want her to change the subject. She leaned across the counter as if she were about to confide in me, when the phone rang.

"I'll send him right down," she said, and hung up. "You've given me a lot to think about, Jason. I'll let you know if I come up with anything relevant."

I was anxious to find out how the movie rights conversation was resolved, and fully expected to find out soon. I've been involved in enough band practice arguments to know the usual process. It's like the opposite of a boxing match, where the contestants fight for three minutes then take a one minute break. In band practice fights, the break happens while a song is being played. In the case of a well practiced band rehearsing material they've been playing for years, they have the time to think of counterarguments during the song, and use the time in between songs to introduce their new perspectives.

But that didn't happen. We had our best practice session since Bongo died, and not a word was spoken relating to the movie rights issue. At 9:30 they all knew that I would be leaving, and no one tried to guilt me into staying.

I called Jeannine as soon as I arrived at Patrick's house. She was in the van with Cory, Shamansky, and his SDPD colleague. Cory got on the phone and walked me through the set up of my live feed. The test of his headdress cam told me that Jeannine was wearing a slinky black mini-dress. Shamansky would be pleased. We then tested the audio feed to make sure I could communicate with him inside the party, and talk with everyone inside the van. Everything worked fine. The final test involved the camera mounted on top of the van, which gave me an unobstructed view of the front door of the private banquet facility.

"Cory, it's highly likely that your video could provide important evidence in a court case some day. But once you see guns drawn, your main objective is to get out of harm's way. Don't try to be a hero," I said.

On my computer monitor I saw two male septuagenarians in

evening gowns and wigs enter the party. Cory assured me that he'd use good judgment when the shit hit the fan. I got a look at him in the outfit Lisa wore to our parents' 30th anniversary party as he departed the van. His headdress looked like two pheasants were locked in the throes of passion on top of his head.

"Who's on the headset?" I asked.

"It's me," said Jeannine. "Shamansky and his partner moved to the front of the van when Cory started talking to you. I think the partner was offended by the potty talk."

"How are you doing?"

"Better, now that Cory left. I wish I hadn't worn this outfit. One of Cory's feathers poked through my cleavage and got stuck in my bra. Shamansky's partner blessed himself and turned away."

"What about Shamansky?"

"He offered to help, and told me he delivered a couple of babies in the line of duty."

"Did he . . . help you?"

"Don't be silly. I wouldn't let him do that. Let's just say that Cory's flock of seagulls got a little trim from my cuticle scissors, and leave it at that," she said.

Following Cory's instructions, I toggled over to the headdress cam and instructed Jeannine to do the same. "Tell Shamansky it's showtime."

We watched for a few minutes as Cory walked around the banquet hall to give us a feel for the layout. The room was relatively square, with a poker table in each of the four corners. Although only 15 minutes past the start time, two of the poker tables had games in progress, and the other two held players awaiting the start of a game. There were about a dozen people milling about the middle of the room, and half that number at the bar. Vinnie and Hubert sat at a table away from the door where they exchanged money for poker chips.

"That's Benjamin talking to Vinnie at the table," Jeannine said.

Benjamin was dressed in harem pants, a turban, and a silk vest. Looking around the room I saw three other men of about Benjamin's age wearing similar costumes.

"Who's Benjamin?" asked Shamansky.

"He's a cart boy at the country club," she replied.

"Benjamin has been at a couple of meetings with Vinnie and Hubert. We think he may be in on the heist," I said.

Cory made a series of unusual sounds.

"What's that?" asked Shamansky.

"Cory's wearing his mouthpiece to keep his Tourette's from becoming the center of attention," I said.

"Like that sound isn't going to draw attention," said Shamansky.

"He's miked in case he needs help. He sounds a lot louder to us than he does to anyone near him," I said.

"Lucky us," said Shamansky's partner.

"The turban and harem pants make me wonder if this is some kind of Shriners initiation ceremony," Shamansky said.

"I'm pretty sure Shriners don't drink at official ceremonies, and I don't think they'd have open gambling at one of their parties," I said.

"What do you know about Shriners, Duffy? You're a Catholic. The closest you'll ever come to the Shriners experience will involve driving a compact car." At least Shamansky was having fun.

A man in his mid-fifties, wearing a designer gown, blond wig, and a tiara approached Cory and held one of his headdress feathers between his thumb and index finger.

"Well aren't you the hottest thing since Lady Gaga," he said. "What's your name?"

Cory reached under his mask and removed the mouthpiece just long enough to blurt out his name.

"I'm going to have a glass of champagne. Would you like one, Cory?" asked Tiaraman.

Cory nodded, and Tiaraman headed for the bar.

"How is he going to drink with the mask, microphone, and mouthpiece all in there?" asked Jeannine.

"He was just getting rid of the guy. The place has really filled up in the last 15 minutes," I said.

"Vinnie's been doing big business. The guy in the aqua chiffon just plunked down a brick of hundreds," said Shamansky.

"Is Mrs. Vincigura able to hear us?" asked Jeannine.

"She has a video only feed. I'll call her after the deal goes down," I said.

Over the next 45 minutes we watched as the room continued to fill. Cory managed to avoid Tiaraman while giving us a good look at the crowd. Then something very curious happened. Two large men with shaved heads wearing harem pants approached one of the poker tables. All of the Hogettes stood behind their chairs as they watched the table be covered by a large clear plastic sheet that was gathered at the base and secured by bungee cords. One by one, the eunuchs secured all four tables. It appeared they were making sure no one helped himself to anyone else's chips during an upcoming break. Upon finishing they exited the front door and stood guard at the entrance.

Cory gave us an unobstructed view of Vinnie from about 15 feet away. He pulled a table microphone out and said, "Will everyone please move to the perimeter."

Four of the harem pants boys got behind what appeared to be a large gymnastics mat that was rolled up against the wall opposite Vinnie's table. Once unrolled, the mat was indeed the size of those used in gymnastics floor exercise routines.

"Ladies, you've been very naughty tonight," Vinnie said. "All of this drinking and gambling and cavorting around in lacy under-things means you need to be punished. So, if you'll prepare yourselves, the harem boys are about to give you what you deserve."

"This is it," said Shamansky's partner. "Let's go!"

"Let them make their move first," said Shamansky. "I'd rather bust them coming out the door with the money."

We watched in horror as all of the men disrobed and moved onto the mat. Six harem boys were seated on armless chairs, and began giving out spankings.

"Where have you been? I've been looking all over for you, Cory," said Tiaraman.

On our monitors we saw a hand draped over Cory's shoulder. Then we saw Tiaraman's masked face. Finally, the camera slowly panned down his torso before Cory's rapid movements turned our video feed into a blur. By the time the camera stabilized he had removed his mouthpiece.

Being one of the few who speaks fluent Cory, I could tell he was trying to say: *Get the hell away from me, you perv*. But the heavy interlacing of four letter words rendered his intent meaningless to Tiaraman.

"Talk dirty to me, Cory. I love it. Let's get you out of that fetching frock."

Cory spun toward the door and tried breaking into a sprint, but ran directly into a man in his late 70s making his way to the mat.

When the camera settled on the elderly man, Jeannine was shocked. "Mr. Sandoval! What are you doing in there?"

"Jeannine, stay here!" I heard Shamansky shout. But it was too late.

Toggling to the outside camera I saw her wearing my Zorro hat, tying on the mask. I couldn't hear what she said to the eunuch guards, but they allowed her to pass into the hall.

Headdress cam picked her up almost immediately after she entered, since Cory was headed for the same door at the time.

"Cory, give me a hand," she said as she walked past him.

Jeannine launched into a scolding of Mr. Sandoval that got everyone's attention. She finished by saying, "Can't you at least show me some respect by covering yourself up when I'm talking to you?"

Sandoval gave a palms-up shrug and said, "With what?"

Jeannine reached down her cleavage with one hand, held onto

her bra with the other, tugged hard, and came out with six inches of a pheasant feather.

"Here!" she shouted, handing the feather to Sandoval

He immediately held it in place, smiled and said, "It tickles."

While the crowd erupted in laughter, Shamansky's partner said, "I would have given him the Zorro hat."

Incensed by their laughter, Jeannine spun on her heel and took two steps toward the door when headdress cam picked up one of the old golfers pinching her butt.

"That's it! I quit! I'm never serving any of you another drink for the rest of my life!"

Vinnie got back on the microphone. "Don't you men feel ashamed of yourselves after that dressing down from Jeannine?"

She stopped and looked at Vinnie as if at least one of them heeded her words.

Vinnie said, "I think you all deserve a second round of spankings before the fun begins."

At that point Jeannine and Cory exited the hall. The last thing I saw before answering a call from Mrs. Vincigura was Shamansky's partner leaving the van and heading toward his car.

"Mrs. Vincigura I don't know what to say. We thought it was going to be a heist related to the poker game," I said.

"Don't you worry about that one little bit, Jason. You're talking to one very satisfied customer. That video, which I've copied by the way, is my ticket to a seat on the club's board of directors. I fully expect to be named the first female board member in the history of the club before the end of the month. Don't bother refunding any of my retainer, just be ready to testify if Vinnie ever starts to forget that I've got him by the gonads."

Shamansky picked up on the first ring. "Thanks for a lovely evening, Jason. You sure know how to show a guy a good time."

"Do you think there's a chance Vinnie and Hubert might still try to walk away with the money?" I asked.

"I think we know what tonight was about. But I plan on hanging around till it breaks up, just in case."

"Your buddy didn't look too happy when he left the van. I hope this doesn't blow back on you."

"I'll remind him before roll call that he left the stakeout of a highly volatile situation without authorization from a superior officer, and if he wants to keep an official reprimand out of his jacket he'll forget the whole thing."

"Thanks, Shamansky. How are Jeannine and Cory doing?"

"Cory has been talking a blue streak, and I do mean blue streak, ever since he got back to the van. Jeannine couldn't listen to him, so she's pacing back and forth on the sidewalk away from the hall. I called her a cab."

"I owe you one," I said.

"Have Cory print me a copy of the video and we'll call it even," he said.

"I'd hate to think of you wearing out the track where Jeannine extracts that feather."

"Actually, I spotted a very defendant-friendly judge in there wearing nothing but a skimpy mask and a unique tattoo. I suspect that the conviction rate on my cases will be taking a turn for the better."

Chapter 28

We all got started late on Thursday morning. Dad kept an eye on Nello Lapaglia until 1:00 AM because Navorocki set his alarm clock to 11:00 AM instead of PM. Patrick was at band practice until after midnight, and I didn't get to sleep until around 2:00 AM as clues and considerations whirled in my head. The image of Cory in my sister's gown didn't help either.

The morning paper ran an Entertainment Section headline article about the reunion show that would be taking place tomorrow night. The vast majority of the article covered the band's history. The recent murders weren't mentioned until the final four paragraphs on the continuation page. They also ran several photos, including one with Buzzy as lead singer.

We ate breakfast at Patrick's house at 10:30. Jeannine called just as we were about to work out the details for a look-see at the office of the Conservator's of Justice. I fully expected to be conducting a therapy session over the next hour, but she was all business.

"I couldn't sleep last night, so I came into the office. Your Scranton case helped to take my mind off of that horrible orgy."

"I'm really sorry you had to see that . . ."

"Let's not talk about it. I have some important information for you. Your bass playing attorney, Edward Pohanick, defended two of Select Sentinel's employees who were arrested on aggravated assault charges two years ago."

I took notes while she gave me their names and the particulars on the arrest, trial, and acquittal. As soon as we concluded the call I conveyed the info to Team Duffy.

"Why do you think there are so many nasty lawyer jokes?" asked Dad.

Patrick picked up the Entertainment Section of the paper and stared at Eddie's picture. "I can't believe I considered this guy one of my closest friends since junior high. He was an usher at my wedding."

I walked around the dining room table to console my uncle, but he bolted for the coat rack.

"Where are you going?" Dad asked.

"To get some answers from that sonofabitch."

"Don't jump the gun, Patrick. I'm sure you spooked him plenty last night. A lot of evidence was taken from Bongo and Louie's houses. If you roll into his office half-cocked with more accusations, that evidence might get destroyed," said Dad.

Patrick slumped into a living room chair, wearing his winter jacket. "What would you two say to a little Irish coffee this morning?"

"I'd say we need to be functioning at 100% if I'm going to let myself into the Conservators of Justice headquarters, and you're going to schmooze an office manager," I said.

Patrick unzipped his jacket. "OK, let's put a plan together."

Karen Felder worked as the office manager at Valley Vista Executive Suites since it opened eight years ago. For seven of those years she was certain that she worked for the greatest boss in the world. Last year he turned 50, immediately went into midlife crisis mode, and decided an affair with his attractive office manager would confirm that he hadn't lost his sex appeal. When Karen rejected the advances of her married boss he began looking for reasons to get rid of her. The downturn in the economy matched the downturn in her building's occupancy rate, and Karen found herself constantly fretting over her waning numbers. Last month she was forced to fire her receptionist and serve in both roles.

Patrick came through on getting me a winter uniform from

a former employee of North American Fast Freight. He also scored a hand truck and a broken handheld computer prominently displaying the corporate logo.

"You must be Miss Felder," I said, rolling my hand truck to the reception counter. "Trent Giles sent me over to find a few packages in his office and ship them out. He gave me a key. Which way is his office?"

"I'm afraid you won't be able to go in there without written authorization from Mr. Giles," Karen said.

"He not only gave me authorization, he gave me his key."

I produced a Schlage key that matched what Dad saw when he took the tour with Patrick.

"I'll give him a call," Karen said, and reached for her phone book.

I looked at my watch. "He's been on a flight to Jamaica for about a half hour now. He told my boss it was imperative that I make this delivery today. Giles Import/Export is a new client for us. The boss said that Mr. Giles knows a lot of small businesses that do shipping and his goodwill could make the difference in avoiding further layoffs at our Scranton branch."

Karen was giving me a sympathetic look when Patrick walked into the lobby. Her expression changed from sympathy to joy. Patrick took up a position behind me, waiting for us to conclude our business.

"Your tenant really needs your help on this one, ma'am," I said.

Karen pointed with her left hand. "It's down the hall and around the corner."

"Thank you very much."

I pushed my hand truck in the direction indicated and heard Karen ask, "Didn't I see your picture in the Entertainment Section of the paper today?"

"I decided to come out of retirement to find out if the pretty women would notice. I'm glad to see it's working," Patrick said.

"I loved the Luna Parkers," she replied.

Lock picking is a skill I learned from my Houdini wannabe math tutor at UCSD. I opened Giles Import/Export first, in case the receptionist decided to come looking for me. Dad watched the lobby from his rental parked in front of the building, and was set to call me if Patrick's charm wore thin.

The Conservators of Justice office had a ship shape look and feel. I turned on their computer and spent three minutes trying a variety of passwords that I identified as keywords from their website. Nothing worked, so I moved on to side-by-side two drawer file cabinets. A scan of the file tab labels revealed nothing of particular interest.

I pulled out a thick file labeled "Notes" and scanned the barely readable handwriting of the organization's secretary. Most of the info related to scheduled events, fundraisers, shooting contests, and how to handle members who were behind in their dues. I was about to put it away when I thumbed the final 50 pages and caught a glimpse of the word "Sentinel."

The page revealed that a representative of Select Sentinel would be presenting a fundraising check at the next board meeting, which was scheduled for six months ago. I went back to the file cabinets and was looking at label headings when my phone rang.

"They're about to get into the elevator on the second floor. You better get out of there," Dad said.

I pulled out a file labeled "Photos." They were arranged by dates, neatly printed in the upper right hand corner. I slid the photo of the meeting out of the file, and heard the elevator doors open in the lobby.

The photo showed Nello Lapaglia handing a golf tournament-sized check to a bald man with a ruddy complexion. I heard the distinct sound of high heels on tile heading my way.

I was about to tuck the photo back in the file when the signature caught my eye. Although closer to the chicken scratch of the secretary than the Palmer Method perfection of the photographer, there was no doubt that the check was signed by Rose Amanesco.

I heard Patrick's voice echo down the hall. "Karen, can I ask you one more question?"

The Doppler Effect told me that the receptionist changed course. A minute later I wheeled three large empty boxes past the two of them standing in front of the reception counter.

"Thanks again, ma'am," I said.

An hour later the three of us piled into Flannery's car which was parked across the street from a church that Lapaglia was helping to renovate. I handed him a fresh cup of coffee and told him about what I had learned without going into the details on how I came by the information.

"This confirms something that I suspected," he said.

"What's that?" asked Patrick.

"One of our older detectives told Navorocki that Rose's father, who is semi-retired from his development corporation, recently got shuffled off to Florida after running his mouth at a Chamber of Commerce cocktail party in Luzerne County."

"What did he say?" Dad asked.

"Nothing relating to our case. But he drank too much and mentioned a couple of properties he was trying to buy. Developers never reveal that kind of information unless they're trying to dupe someone, and that would never happen in a very public forum."

"How old is he?" asked Dad.

"Mid-eighties."

"It sounds to me like he's lost his fastball," Dad said. "Rose is probably running things now, but doesn't want the public to know."

"How does this relate to our case?" Flannery asked.

"I'll bet Louie found out about it from one of his company's sales reps. That kind of juicy gossip item would have been on the Internet before the party was over," said Patrick.

"Maybe Louie had something in his safe that gave Rose control if her father became incompetent," Flannery said.

"I don't see Louie hanging on to something like that after the divorce," said Patrick.

"You said he got totally screwed in the settlement," said Dad. "This could have been his opportunity to give her a taste of her own medicine."

"I can't imagine someone giving Bongo any type of important document, or Rose ever thinking Louie'd do so," I said. "Maybe he might give it to you, Patrick, but not Bongo."

"Flannery, did you ever get a look at Louie's MSA?" Dad asked.

"I gave it to our best man in White Collar Crimes. He said it looked like an NFL wide receiver trying to play basketball with an NBA All-Star. Eddie came across looking like a good lawyer who was simply out of his league," said Flannery.

We sat in silence for a few minutes.

"Let's do this," I said. "That stockholders meeting that I heard about the day I went nose-to-nose with Lapaglia is scheduled for tomorrow. Why don't you talk to your White Collar Crimes contact and figure out if you can sweat one of Select Sentinel's goons if any intimidation goes down at the meeting. Maybe bring the whole crew in and see if any of them is looking at a third strike."

"I'll see what I can do," he said.

My phone rang on our way back to Patrick's car.

"Mr. Duffy, this is Cyril from the Radisson. I'm calling to let you know that two packages just arrived from San Diego marked *Extremely Urgent*. Is it possible for you and your father to return to the hotel immediately?"

"We'll be right there."

Twenty minutes later we walked into the lobby and saw Kelly and Mom sitting on a couch.

"Surprise!" they yelled.

"What the hell are you two doing here?" Dad asked.

Mom's face dropped. "We wanted to be part of the Scranton side of the family coming together, and to see Jason and Patrick play in the show tomorrow night."

"Were you paying attention when I told you about the three of us getting shot at a few nights ago?" Dad asked.

"Clearly this was a mistake," she replied.

"You're darn tootin' it was," Dad said.

"Hold on a minute," I said. "Let's give them a proper welcome before starting the lecture."

Before Dad could reply Kelly fell into my arms and I laid a kiss on her that could have adorned the cover of a hot bodice ripper.

"Geez, Louise," Dad said. "Don't you know you're in a public place?"

We heard whooping and clapping at the entrance to the lobby. Patrick was all smiles as he hugged Mom.

"You're a sight for sore old sleep-deprived eyes, Molly."

"Don't try giving her one of Jason's R-rated kisses or you'll be sleeping right here in the lobby," Dad said.

Patrick settled for a hug, and I introduced him to Kelly.

Dad tapped Patrick on the shoulder. "Why don't you entertain the ladies for a couple of minutes while I have a word with my son?"

We walked into a hallway leading to the lounge. The happy hour crowd was just arriving, affording us limited privacy.

"We have to get them back on a plane home right now," Dad said.

Over the next ten minutes I got Dad to realize that flights out of Scranton were very limited and nothing was going to happen tonight. Also, that we might have security issues of our own in San Diego if we ran them off before the reunion show. Finally, I made a couple of concessions regarding safety precautions and, at Dad's insistence, I agreed to get Kelly and I our own room, even though we had separate bedrooms in our suite.

The five of us went to a nice Italian bistro called Sibio's before

Patrick and I headed over to Russell's for our dress rehearsal. My uncle played the role of Guest of Honor at dinner, thanking Kelly and Mom profusely for the surprise visit.

I expected Patrick to be exchanging barbs with Eddie all evening. Instead he gave me several loopy smiles, riding the pink cloud of a family undivided. Eddie did what he could under the circumstances. He shut up and played his best.

Russell had recruited Dylan Conway to take over for him on the sound board, and spent the afternoon teaching him a notebook full of sound settings for various songs. They also worked out the logistics for his tribute to Louie and Bongo. Dylan did a decent job at the dress rehearsal, only interrupting the flow on two occasions.

Patrick and I passed on the post-practice cannabis confab. As per my instructions, he didn't tell our band mates about Kelly and Mom. I'm sure he was glad to let Eddie think *he* was the reason for our early departure.

When I walked into my new room at the Radisson, Kelly was dressed in a full length night gown.

"I was hoping you packed that sexy nurses outfit for tonight."

"I was hoping your *pain in the ass* phase was over," she replied.

"Who's dog sitting Colonel Hogan for us?"

"Jeannine said she'd be happy to see the German Shepherd brothers spend quality time together. Hoover started playing with Colonel Hogan the minute we walked in the door."

"Did she seem a little shell shocked when you saw her?" I asked.

"If you mean: Do I think her ill-advised tour of the sausage factory will scar her for life? I think she'll get over it."

"Too bad she didn't bring Hoover into that banquet hall. One loud growl and you would have seen more wieners put away than at the annual Nathans Hot Dog Eating Championship."

"I missed you," she said.

"Imagine what it would have been like in 10 degree weather with only Dad's snoring or Patrick's gurgling bong to keep you company at night. Except for the danger I'm really glad you're here."

"Well, you won't have to worry about keeping warm tonight," she said.

"I'm not so sure. That night gown looks like it could have been made by the Trojan Corporation."

"Maybe you better put your detective hat on and check it out. I'm pretty sure I saw a label somewhere on the inside."

"I may have to send in my inspector from the sausage factory. He already has his hat on."

"Shut up and kiss me, you fool."

Chapter 29

Before opening my eyes on Friday morning a smile spread across my face. Kelly's scent had roused me from dreamland in a way that made me realize how much I missed her. As I gently stroked her chestnut hair, Dad's warning about the dangers of the case brought me back to the moment. While I was starting my day at 7:00 AM EST, Kelly was experiencing 4:00 AM PST and sound asleep. I zipped through my morning routine and finished by writing her a note.

Dad was in the coffee shop reading the morning paper. A third page story focused on all of the tragedy leading up to the reunion show, including the two close encounters of the lethal kind that Patrick and I experienced in the past week.

Dad tapped the headline after he set the paper down on our table. "This is exactly why I don't want the women here. It's a long way from being over, and I have a bad feeling about that concert tonight."

"Patrick didn't say a word at last night's dress rehearsal about them being in town, and he was remarkably restrained with Eddie."

Dad looked at his watch. "Flannery should be here any minute. Do you plan on going with us to the stockholder's meeting?"

"The sound check starts at 1:30, and I have a few things to do beforehand. Give me a call if Flannery makes any arrests, and we can meet up at the stationhouse if you get anywhere sweating the Select Sentry rabble-rousers," I said.

I headed off to Patrick's house before Flannery arrived. My thoughts kept returning to Buzzy West. The newspaper article tracked the band's misfortunes back to Megan's death shortly before the first scheduled reunion show. But I was sure that Buzzy's death played a significant role in all of the tragedy that followed.

Patrick slumped in his favorite living room chair, still wearing pajamas and a robe. The newspaper article sat on the coffee table in front of him. His stash box looked undisturbed and my nose told me that no weed had been ignited as yet.

"You have the rest of your life to ruminate, if that's what you choose to do with it. But today we have a lot of work to do before the sound check, so I suggest you put that article away and start giving me a hand."

Patrick carried the paper into his bedroom and emerged five minutes later dressed for the sound check. I sat at the dining room table looking at his bulletin board. My uncle took a seat across from me and also looked at the board.

"The newspaper said that the tragedy started with Megan, but we both know that's not true. From where I sit, it all traces back to Buzzy," I said. "There's a reason Bongo's body ended up where Buzzy died. It's no coincidence that Bongo was killed the night he gave me a detailed account of Buzzy's role in the band. It's also no coincidence that we came under attack twice after that night."

"So, what do you want to do about it?"

"Did Buzzy have any close friends that we might be able to talk with this morning?"

Patrick stood up and walked to the living room window. "Outside of the band, his two best friends were also his two best customers. Both of them are dead."

"Anything suspicious?" I asked.

"Both were one car accidents while driving under the influence. No big surprise there. But I do recall that he had a little sister that he was close to. She was an absolute mess at the funeral. Last I heard, she got married and moved to Tobyhanna."

"Is that far from here?"

"Twenty minutes, tops. And, I know somebody from her class who probably has her contact information."

A half hour later we were on the road. We learned that Mindy Wallenbeck married a man with a decent union job at the Tobyhanna Army Depot, and has been a housewife for the past 35 years. We opted not to call ahead. She lived in a nice corner house on the edge of town with a two-year-old Ford Explorer in the driveway.

A vague look of recognition registered on her broad face when she saw Patrick. He told her about being a former band mate of her brother, and that some new facts had come to light that suggested foul play may have factored into his death. We were shown into her living room.

Mindy insisted on a brief trip down memory lane, seeking validation that her brother was a very talented singer who would have made it big had it not been for his unfortunate demise. Patrick credited her brother with attracting many of the band's first fans, and rapport was established.

She told us that Buzzy sheltered her from the druggies who would show up at the house at all hours of the night. They would toss pebbles at his second floor window, and he'd climb down the latticework and conduct business in their detached garage on the back alley.

Mindy was two years younger than Buzzy and he forbade her from using drugs. He told all of the local dealers that if they sold to her he would put them out of business. At first she was angry, but later relented when he promised to let her in on all other aspects of his life except the drug business.

"Did you suspect anyone when he was killed?" Patrick asked.

"I did, but you're not going to like it."

"Was it a member of the band?"

Mindy nodded. "Louie Amanesco showed up at our house at 1:00 AM the night before Buzzy died. They woke me up arguing in the garage. When he came back inside he told me one of the band guys thought he was having an affair with his girlfriend. My brother swore to me that it wasn't true."

"Did he say anything else about it?" I asked.

"That was the last time I saw him alive."

"Are you sure it was Louie?" Patrick asked.

"I could see the front half of the Amanesco Construction pickup that he drove. Besides, I recognized his voice from when Louie would talk in between songs at your shows. Like I said, they were so loud that they woke me up. I have no doubt that it was Louie arguing with my brother."

Patrick was silent for the first five minutes of the ride home.

"Just because Louie called Buzzy on the carpet for a guy code violation certainly doesn't mean he killed him," I said.

"I know that. I was just trying to remember if anything specific happened just prior to Buzzy's death that prompted Louie to have that argument the night before he died."

When we exited Patrick's car he shook his head. "Late middle age is a bitch, Jason."

I passed on the opportunity to make a comment about how his pot use could be affecting his memory. Patrick was having a difficult day as it was, and didn't need me adding to his troubles an hour before the sound check.

"Why don't we see if your mother and Kelly want to have lunch?"

"Don't you think it's a little late to be going out for lunch?" I asked.

"If they like Texas wieners we can take them to Coney Island. It's just a block from the hotel."

Mom and Kelly were happy to have something to do before the show. Dad made Mom vow to not leave the hotel unescorted, so we picked them up and were seated at the luncheonette in a matter of minutes.

"Patrick, thank you so much for getting us such wonderful seats to the show and passes to the backstage party on such short notice," Mom said.

"Did Dylan personally deliver them to the hotel?" he asked.

"I don't know. A bellboy brought them up to the room."

"You're going to love the concert venue. The Scranton Cultural Center doubles as a Masonic Temple. The architecture is amazing. The backstage party will actually be on the second floor, in three adjoining rooms that look like staging for a Nick & Nora Charles film."

"That sounds fascinating, Patrick."

"Just don't accept any invitations to take a tour," I said. "We still have a killer wandering around and I'm certain he'll be in the building. He might even have a backstage pass."

The four of us focused on our exceptionally flavorful Texas wieners for the next few minutes.

"Are we sitting with any friendlies?" Kelly asked.

"I'm sure Dylan got you into the *wives and girlfriends* section," Patrick said. "I'll introduce you at the backstage party."

I looked at my watch. "We had better get over there for the sound check."

I walked the girls back to Dad's suite while Patrick retrieved the car. It was about 20 degrees out, but the wind made it feel more like zero.

"Kelly, send me a text when Dad gets back. Tell him I'll give him a call as soon as I can."

"Be careful, Jason. I wish your father was going to be at the sound check," she said.

Patrick was right on target about the Cultural Center. The architecture was unlike anything in San Diego. It was located right next door to the main branch of the public library, which was equally impressive with its French Gothic design.

The sound check reminded me of the adage: *Too many cooks spoil the broth*. Eli had been the sound man for the band before taking over as the lead singer. As such, he felt he had seniority on all sound matters. Russell felt that he earned the mantle of sound expert by virtue of the fact that it's been his job for the past

40 years. And, Dylan was a sound man before taking over the record store business from his uncle 15 years ago. He was also the official sound man for the night, and responsible for making the concert happen in the first place.

The main point of contention involved how to adjust for a gently inclined main floor, steeply pitched balcony, and a ceiling that could accommodate its own rain cloud. The three of them kept moving from position to position, asking us to test mics and instruments while a union tech made adjustments to the board.

Eli shouted from the balcony for Patrick to test mic #1, and he let out an amplified belch. "Too much chili pepper on my lunch. I'm going to run out to my car and get a bottle of Tums out of my glove box."

I thought it would be a good time to have a private chat with Eddie, since we were the only two left on the stage. I set my guitar in its stand, but before I could walk over, Eddie was on his phone.

"Are you excited about tonight?" Kristen Pohanick stood four feet below me in a long black coat.

"I can't wait," I replied. "Do you know if there are any vending machines in this place? I need something to drink."

"Follow me."

Before I could get down from the stage, Kristen removed the coat to reveal a blue and black print mini-dress. I saw her make sure Eddie was preoccupied before tossing her coat onto a chair in the front row of theater seats. She was in the lobby by the time I caught up.

"This place is amazing," I said.

Kristen pressed the elevator button. "You ain't seen nuthin' yet. There's another theater on the 4th floor, plus a huge ballroom, meeting rooms, and probably lots of rooms that only the Masons can go into."

"It looks like some kind of Gothic architecture, but I can't quite put my finger on it," I said as the elevator car rose.

"It's actually a Neo-Gothic and Romanesque pastiche."

"I'm impressed," I said, exiting the elevator.

"At my vast knowledge or my outfit?"

"How did you come by that little tidbit?" I asked.

"My mother has been dragging me along to cultural events and committee meetings since I was a little girl. Here we are."

The vending machine was recessed into an old phone booth alcove. I pumped quarters in and selected a 20-ounce water. "How long have your parents been together?"

"They were high school sweethearts. Cupid nailed the both of them in 9th grade. Do you believe in love at first sight?"

I spent the five minutes it took returning to the stage to tell Kristen about how I met Kelly. Her suggestive outfits and flirting told me she was trying to inspire a love at first site moment with a reasonable suitor. I did my best to let her know that love has many ways of revealing itself, and that it rarely happens in the storybook manner that most people imagine.

The only thing that had changed by the time we returned was that Patrick was back in the theater. Eddie was still on the phone, the brothers Shapiro were still debating with Dylan and each other, and Kristen was starting to act like one of my former patients who would never leave at the appointed time. An incoming text from Kelly, telling me that Dad had returned, provided a way out. I excused myself, walked backstage, and gave him a call.

"What happened at the meeting?" I asked.

"A couple of Neanderthals heckled the speakers while four other plants did their best to get the stockholders to applaud the disruptions."

"Was Lapaglia in attendance?"

"He used a layer of minion insulation for this project. All of the Select Sentinel men wore communication gear. Lapaglia was in an electrical contractor's van at the end of the block."

I heard drums and surmised that Russell had returned to the stage. "Was Flannery able to bring them in for questioning?"

"Last night the DA's office gave him a list of every possible infraction that would allow us to haul them in. But it looked like Lapaglia had the same list, and his boys did a good job of staying barely legal. Do you think Eddie Pohanick earned a consulting fee recently?" Dad asked.

Patrick called me to the stage over the PA system.

"I wouldn't be surprised," I replied. "Dad, can you get Mom and Kelly to the backstage party by five o'clock?"

"Are you nuts? There's a killer who's sure to be there tonight. I don't even like the idea of them being in the audience while the show is going on."

"I need you at the party, and I don't like the idea of having them show up on their own. Remember what happened to The Society Page Slasher's last victim?" Dad didn't reply. "I'm being called to the stage. What do you say? Can you handle being their bodyguard?"

"Goodbye," he said, and hung up.

Chapter 30

Kelly called at 5:00 PM to say Dad just parked his rental, and would I meet them in the lobby with the backstage passes. She definitely looked the part of rocker girlfriend in her backless cocktail dress, causing me to thrust my chest like Mick Jagger. Mom wore a blue jeans dress that Patrick was bound to love and Dad would detest. Dad wore black slacks, and a gray sports jacket. His only concession to cutting loose was a maroon shirt I had never seen before.

"Nice shirt, Dad."

"It's a gift from your mother. I'm letting my freak flag fly."

Mom's eyes rolled so far north I thought they might do a 360.

"Stick with me, Freewheelin' Franklin, and you just might reach Nirvana tonight," she said.

It was Dad's turn for eyeball aerobics. The elevator opened at the 2nd floor, and two mastodons checked our backstage passes. The bar was straight ahead of us in a general lobby area, identified by a plaque as Margaret Briggs Hall. To the left was The Ladies Parlor, a room filled with circular tables that would accommodate parties of eight. To the right was the Governor Robert Casey Library. A buffet table extended out of the library into an anteroom with adjacent coat room. There were less than a dozen guests at that point.

"Let's hit the coatroom first," I said. Kelly and I led the way.

"Isn't this building fascinating, Jim?" Mom asked.

"Don't get too distracted, Molly. There are a couple of killers running around town, and one of them is bound to be here tonight.

At least you didn't dress like Zsa Zsa Gabor, so the Society Page Slasher will probably leave you alone."

Kelly nudged me and smiled. We reached the end of the buffet table in the library. In front of us was a picturesque fireplace flanked by two beige loveseats facing each other. Becky Shapiro sat alone. I made introductions and Kelly sat down next to her. Mom and Dad sat opposite them. I offered to get drinks and Dad accompanied me to the bar.

"I hope you have some kind of plan in mind," Dad said.

"I need you to keep your distance from Mom and Kelly. I'm sure the perp knows that both of us are working the case, but not even the band members know about our better halves. Keep an eye on them from a distance."

"That'll be a little awkward with this small a crowd."

I placed our orders with the bartender. "There were over 75 backstage passes issued. It should start filling up soon. I like that the women are close to the buffet table. I'll circulate around the party."

"Won't I stand out all by myself?" Dad asked.

"The way you're dressed everyone will assume you're part of the Cultural Center staff, making sure the party doesn't get out of hand."

"I don't see how this is going to help us catch the perp."

"I'm convinced that the misinterpreted song lyrics played a key role in the murders." I stopped talking when the bartender returned with our drinks. "Getting back to the lyrics, the recorded version mentions *the ten of us*. I'm sure Becky Shapiro is considered one of the ten, so watch for anyone paying too much attention to her."

"What happens once the concert starts?" he asked.

"Mom and Kelly will be seated near Becky. Get them to their seats then check in with Flannery at the back of the theater. He'll coordinate duty assignments, and I'm sure he'll put you close to them."

I handed Becky her double vodka martini and Kelly her wine

216

spritzer. "I promised the band I'd keep the press entertained until they make their way up here from the dressing room. I'll stop back later."

Dad said, "I was told I need to look like a Cultural Center rep, so excuse me while I guard the chicken wings."

I spent the next half hour at a round table in The Ladies Parlor. It featured a mezzanine view of an empty ballroom, but I didn't get much of a chance to take in the sights. Reporters from all of the media outlets crowded around the table to ask questions about everything from my role in the investigation of the deceased band members to the murder attempts on Patrick and myself. A few also brought up The Concert Killer case since it received national coverage. I excused myself when an incoming text gave me an opportunity for a break.

Kelly texted: *Becky is tanked. 3 double vodka martinis since yours.*

I replied: *Find out what's wrong.*

I called Patrick and asked why I was doing a solo with the press. He explained that a lot of accusations were flying around the dressing room about Eddie's selling out Louie in favor of his business relationship with Rose. But, that the fence mending process had just started, and they'd all appreciate if I'd keep holding down the fort with the press.

I returned to the table and told the media that the band was having a private memorial tribute to Louie and Bongo, and they would have to keep talking with me for a little while longer. I gave them a ten minute version of the shootout in Patrick's backyard, and they were so enthralled that not a single one left for refills on the free food and drink. Before I could answer any questions my phone rang – Dad. Again I walked to the mezzanine rail. A pink curtain shielded me from the press.

"What's up?"

"Nello Lapaglia just went through the buffet line. When he got to the end he spotted Eddie Pohanick's wife sitting next to your mother, and said hello. "

"Where is Flannery?" I asked.

"Navorocki saw the Select Sentinel crew from this morning going into the theater, and Flannery went down to check out where they're seated before the place fills up. I think we should get your mother and Kelly out of here."

"Becky Shapiro is bombed, and Kelly is trying to find out why. We only have 40 minutes until showtime, and I'm sure the band will make an appearance at the party. As soon as you see them, escort the girls to their seats and stay in the theater."

Patrick tapped me on the shoulder. "Thanks for keeping the wolves at bay. Oops, I didn't see that you were on the phone."

"They're here. Tell Kelly to call me," I said, and hung up.

To Patrick I said, "I see you guys smoked the peace pipe before breaking camp."

"Time for me to play Meet the Press with the boys. Why don't you hit the bar or the buffet line? We'll see you back in the dressing room in 20 minutes," he said.

I needed a quiet place to talk with Kelly and didn't feel like getting a secondhand high in the dressing room. I took a set of stairs next to the library entrance, thinking they would lead to the vending machine on the 4th floor. Instead, I came out in a room on 3rd floor surrounded by a wall of leaded glass. I reached into my pocket for change while I had a decent amount of street light filtering through the window, and dropped a quarter. The coin made almost no sound when it landed on what appeared to be another wooden floor. A wall plaque told me I was in Craftsman Hall, which I exited and took the main staircase up to 4th floor. When I reached the landing I heard footsteps below me and thought it was probably a backstage party couple looking for a little privacy.

Halfway down the hallway I came upon the phone booth alcove that held the vending machine. Before I could try my luck with a dollar bill my phone rang.

"I'll bet you're that hot chick who's wearing the sexy backless mini," I said.

"I should have my head examined for wearing this thing. I'm freezing."

"I'll have one of Flannery's men bring the coats to your seat."

"Don't worry about it. Becky lent me her sweater."

"What did she have to say?" I asked.

"I asked her what was wrong three different times. The first two she just shook her head and kept drinking. But after her seventh double she got weepy and said, 'Everybody thought it was Buzzy but it wasn't.' Does that make sense to you?" Kelly asked.

"Yes, it does. Did she say anything else, like who it was instead of Buzzy?"

"Her husband discovered that she was loaded at that point and made a phone call. Two minutes later a man in a chauffer's uniform walked her out."

"Thanks, Kelly. Ya done good. If you or Mom needs to use the restroom during the show call Dad first and stay together."

"Will do. Should I throw my bra onstage to show that the old guys have still got it?"

"I didn't bring a defibrillator, so that would be a no. Besides, I can't imagine that anyone makes a bra small enough to fit under that skimpy dress of yours."

"Stay safe too, and you just might find out back at the hotel after the show."

"The groupie and the guitarist – I can't wait."

"As long as it doesn't involve a red rubber donut, I'm in."

Chapter 31

The instant Kelly hung up, my phone exploded in my hand. I dove to my right, scrambled behind the entrance to Shopland Hall, and peeked around the corner. The gunman from Patrick's backyard was waiting to see if I was going to return fire. The Glock I borrowed from Russell was wrapped in a hand towel inside my guitar case.

I remembered Kristen telling me that Shopland Hall was a 600 seat theatre. I entered the door on the right and took a quick reading. Night lights gave the large room a spooky quality. It had the layout of an old gymnasium that doubled as a theatre. At the far end was a stage with a row of chairs spanning its entire width. Their height reminded me of the back row of a chess set, minus the queen, with a king-sized seat in the middle, medium ones on either side, and smaller chairs on the wings. On each side of the hall were three rows of church pews facing each other. On the floor were removable eight-seater tables like the one I occupied in the Ladies Lounge. These were covered in new blue-pattern plastic tablecloths, illuminated from behind by a padlocked drink cooler against the back wall.

Except for the stage area, the room was ringed by a balcony. I spotted a set of stairs to my right and got almost to the top when I heard the door to Shopland Hall open. The shooter must have decided I wasn't armed or I would have returned fire by now. I eased my way to the top of the stairs, thanking the Masons for the solid construction.

The balcony had only two night lights per side, so I edged my way to the facing board that ringed the perimeter and peeked over the rail. The gunman walked down the center of the room toward the stage. His head swiveled from side to side and occasionally up at the balcony.

The windows told me I had an exterior wall to my back. Thinking that the Masons may have added an exit on the opposite side, I tried to edge my way across the middle balcony. There was almost no illumination in this section, and I kicked a metal folding chair that was lying flat on the floor. In an instant, silenced bullets were flying through the paneling that surrounded the balcony.

I crawled as quickly as possible to the second row of the right balcony and headed toward the stage. Hearing footsteps on the stairs, I stood up and broke into a sprint. I reached the far end of the balcony just as a burst of bullets caused plaster explosions on the wall in front of me.

Without slowing down, I pushed off the balcony rail with my left foot, and vaulted into the stage curtain. I dropped about half of the distance to the stage before managing to grasp it with both hands. An instant later a spray of bullets caused the curtain to rip, and I managed to land on my feet long enough to dive behind the stage lighting controls in the right wing.

The gunman tried shooting through the wall, but only managed to chip the plaster. When I heard him running back toward the stairs I hunched as low as I could and ran behind the chess row of chairs on the stage. Ducking behind the stage left curtain I spotted a set of stairs and beat feet faster than any Stairmaster workout in my life. I ignored the door to the next landing, figuring the gunman would make it his first stop, and popped out the second exit.

I found myself on the balcony of the Grand Ballroom, across the building from The Ladies Lounge, where I could see Patrick talking with the press. I speed-walked over there, with one eye on the door behind me.

"What were you doing on the other side of the ballroom? You can take the tour tomorrow. Let's go, we've got a show to do."

When we reached the dressing room The Luna Parkers were standing in front of the door with anxious expressions.

"Where were you two? We're about to get announced," said Eli.

"I'll tell you after the show," I said.

Eddie put his phone back in his pocket. "Dylan is on his way to the mic. Let's run out there with some enthusiasm."

A minute later we were in front of a full house that was obviously thrilled to see a favorite band from years past. The plan was to run on stage, strap on the guitars, and launch into the Cream version of Crossroads and four more classic rock songs before taking a breather. But Eli put his hands down to his sides with his fingers spread, telling us to wait. After a minute of soaking in the adulation he spun around and leaped into the air. When he touched down, Patrick started the famous opening riff and we were off.

Dylan did a wonderful job of arranging a first class light show with a video screen that consisted of photos from yesteryear, psychedelic color mixes, and live shots to keep the people in the upper balcony connected to the action. There was also a collage of photos and a very old video of Luna Park. The video was so old that I expected to see Charlie Chaplin walk through the park entrance.

Throughout my career as a musician I always functioned in the dual role of singer and rhythm guitarist, with the exception of my last gig on the Concert Killer case. Not having to multitask provided me with an unusual perspective during the show. I found myself looking at faces in the audience when the lighting would permit. I also found myself thinking about the case. An hour into the show, two pieces of information that I received since arriving at the venue aligned with a theory I had been considering for a couple of days.

The euphoria of my *Eureka* moment was dampened by a sharp look from Patrick, which told me I missed a chord change. While the audience applauded, I made my way over to Patrick.

"Would Buzzy refer to you as a band mate or one of the band guys?" I asked.

"We were mates, Jason. Get back in the moment. We can talk about this stuff later."

Over the next 45 minutes I did my best to avoid errors while I fleshed out my theory and plotted a course of action. Our big finish was The Luna Parkers #2 hit, and drew thunderous applause. We walked off stage to cries of "More" and "Encore" and *Parkers Luna Sea.*

Someone had laid out towels, iced beer, and water on a table in the middle of the dressing room. I was concerned that my band mates would immediately spark up for the encore song. But they were content to towel off and have a drink.

"I have a question about our encore song," I said.

"Fire away," replied Eddie.

"Who wrote the lyrics?"

"That would be me," Eli said, and took a slight bow.

"When you wrote, 'It took the tender's prune to bloom,' were you referring to your brother as the tender?" I asked.

Eli glanced at Russell who was shaking his head. "Russell has been our tender since the band formed. He booked our gigs, he landed our record contract, and he helped most of us financially long after the band broke up."

"I think he helped you in another way, too," I said. "He pruned a drug dealing singer who couldn't carry a tune, and enabled his highly talented, but very shy brother to take the band to the next level."

"Are you accusing me of killing Buzzy so that my brother could take over as singer?" Russell asked, rising to his feet.

"No. I'm accusing you of killing him because you thought he was having an affair with Becky. The opportunity for your brother to move up was just an added bonus."

Russell lunged for me, but Eddie and Patrick restrained him. "You son of a bitch!"

"Buzzy's sister told me about hearing Louie fighting with her brother the night before he was killed. Buzzy told her that Louie thought he was having an affair with the girlfriend of, quote, 'one of the band guys,' unquote. But Buzzy called his fellow musicians *band mates*, not one of the *band guys*. That's a term he used for everybody else affiliated with the band. Since you were still a small band, the only ones who fit into the *band guys* category were you and Eli. And we know that Eli didn't have a girlfriend," I said.

"Buzzy's sister is probably as reliable a source of information as her brother," Russell said.

"After she got drunk earlier tonight, Becky started talking about the affair at the backstage party. Her exact words were, 'Everybody thought it was Buzzy but it wasn't.' She's been living with the knowledge that you killed the wrong guy for almost 40 years. I don't think she can take it anymore, Russell," I said.

Russell's jaw dropped, and he looked at everyone in the room.

"Let me help you with the process of elimination," I said. "Eddie and Patrick have been in committed relationships since high school. Louie was the one who confronted Buzzy about the affair. And, during your band practice smoke breaks, Becky made it very clear to me that she never liked Bongo. I think there's a reason Eli never had a girlfriend all of these years. He's been carrying a torch for Becky."

Eli's face turned bright red. Nothing he could say or do would conceal his embarrassment. At first it appeared he was going to protest, but instead he sat down and wept into his towel.

Russell said, "The world is going to change for all of us after tonight. Even the condemned man gets a last cigarette. Let's go back out there and play *Parkers Luna Sea* one last time for the people who came out here to support us tonight."

Eli looked up from his towel. "Only if I can sing the original lyrics."

Russell nodded, and we sat in silence for two minutes until we heard Dylan start a chant for *Parkers Luna Sea*.

We skipped the triumphant jog back onto the stage. My band mates lost their youthful glow. By their response, the crowd interpreted this change in demeanor to mean they were all choked up over Dylan's tribute to their fallen friends.

Patrick took a step toward my mic, as if he was going to make his first comment of the night. Instead, he opted to launch into the song, allowing the original lyrics to speak for themselves.

After the bombshell I dropped in the dressing room I expected the Luna Parkers to go through the motions on what would probably be their final song as a band. To my surprise, we played the most stirring rendition of their hit that I had ever heard, including the original cut. Patrick and Eddie were all over the stage. At one point Patrick jumped so high I swear he could have dunked a basketball.

The biggest shock for the audience happened when Eli sang the original lyrics. As soon as the words left his mouth he collapsed to the floor with one hand over his heart and the other stretched out toward his brother. The crowd thought he suffered a heart attack, and several fans rushed the stage. But he popped up a moment later, not missing a beat.

It turned out that Russell had a bigger surprise than Eli. After the song ended we all headed to the front of the stage for a group bow. Russell climbed down from his drum riser, jogged toward his appointed position on the right side of the stage, kept going into a stage dive, and landed in the arms of the Select Sentinel crew. Russell cut through an empty row and out an exit door to the alley that runs behind the Cultural Center.

I ran to the opposite side of the stage hoping to pursue him. But the crowd thought I was lining up for a stage dive of my own, and I could see that the crush of fans would make a chase futile. So I ran to Eddie's mic and said, "Colin Flannery, get Russell!"

Once again, the crowd erupted. They thought I was trying to get him back to the stage for a second encore. A woman in a bright red parka stuck her head out the exit door and yelled. She then looked back at me and shrugged.

"Jason," Navorocki called from the far left corner of the stage.

I ran to him and knelt down. "Russell's our perp. He knows we're on to him, and ran out that exit," I said, pointing across the swarm of fans. "The woman in the red parka saw which way he ran."

He immediately got on his radio. Eddie and Patrick had returned to the dressing room while Eli continued to chat with fans at the front of the stage. I briefly considered asking him to call his brother and try to talk him into surrendering. But my Psych training told me he was in the process of blocking out something he couldn't face, and substituting it with fan adulation.

I needed a phone, so I ran to the dressing room and borrowed Patrick's. He was in the middle of a low intensity argument with Eddie. I called Flannery.

"What did I miss?" he asked.

"I'll tell you in a minute. Did the lady in the red parka tell Navorocki which way Russell went?"

"She said he was headed toward Mulberry Street. What's going on?"

I gave him the three minute version. He told me he was going to Select Sentinel, and was sending Navorocki to stake out Russell's car dealership. He also said he was trying to reach his captain to redirect the task force into a manhunt for Russell.

When I hung up I heard Patrick scolding Eddie.

I interrupted. "Can I borrow the Prius?"

Patrick handed me the keys and said, "I need to call your father."

I handed him the phone, grabbed my guitar case that held the Glock Russell had lent me, and ran out the stage door. Rose was in the middle of all of this, and her house was my best guess as to where Russell would head. Also, Mulberry Street was the fastest way to get to Clarks Summit according to Patrick's GPS.

It didn't take long before I realized that Dad would say I was going off half-cocked. My Arctic jacket was still in the cloak room on the 2nd floor and my phone was in a hundred pieces on the 4th floor. I took the Clarks Summit exit off of the Scranton Expressway and stopped at a red light in the town of Chinchilla. Reaching in the back seat, I opened my guitar case and was relieved to find the Glock still wrapped in the towel. I placed it on my front seat and drove another mile before hitting another red light. I picked up the gun and tried chambering a round, but it didn't work. A quick inspection told me the magazine had been removed. It appeared that Russell had been doing more than smoking his brains out while I was at the backstage party entertaining the press.

Chapter 32

I made a left onto Rose's street and turned off my headlights before reaching the point where it sloped downward toward her house at the bottom of the hill. I coasted to where I could barely see it, and parked at the curb. Four early 20th century lampposts lit the driveway and entrance. Two vehicles were parked in front of the four-car garage. One belonged to Nello Lapaglia, the other I didn't recognize.

I needed to find out what was going on inside of the house. With no jacket, no, hat, and no gloves, a tour around the perimeter was out of the question. So I opted to use my knowledge of psychology and gift of gab as my weapons, and rang the front doorbell.

Russell answered the door holding a .357 Magnum. "Isn't this a pleasant surprise? I was just talking about you."

He led me to the rear living room where Rose sat on a white Eileen Gray chair that consisted of a chrome base, leather seat, and what appeared to be two large leather Tootsie Rolls bent into the shape of U-bolts, stacked one on top of the other. Silver duct tape bound her wrists and ankles. Lapaglia sat on the bottle green couch at a right angle to her. Also on the couch was the gunman who chased me through the Cultural Center earlier in the evening.

"Have a seat in the white chair, Duffy," said Russell, pointing to the matching chair opposite Rose. "I'm going to have Ziggy wrap you up. You look a little cold."

A roll of duct tape sat on top of the couch's built-in tray table arm. Ziggy, who was seated adjacent to me, began wrapping my wrists.

"I'd hate to take your seat, Russell. Why don't I just stand next to the door?"

"I don't think so. I won't tape your mouth if you can keep it closed long enough for us to finish our conversation with Rose."

I nodded. Ziggy placed the roll of duct tape on my head like a crown when he finished. I nodded again and it was in my lap.

Russell struck a pose in front of the fireplace, ten feet to my right. "So Rose, like I was saying, if you keep refusing to give me your password I'm going to start taking those ten little piggies of yours to market one at a time."

Rose snapped to an erect posture. "You wouldn't dare!"

Russell said, "You missed a magical night of music at the Cultural Center, Rose. Why not end it on a Beatles classic? Sing along if you feel like it, Jason. I'll be the conductor."

He removed an ornate sword from above the fireplace, tapped it on the coffee table, and assumed an orchestra conductor stance.

"Have you seen the little piggies, crawling in the dirt. And for all the little piggies, life is getting worse."

On the word *worse*, Russell drove the point of the sword into the big toe on Rose's left foot. Her scream was louder than the feedback Patrick generated on his Hendrix solo earlier in the evening.

"Did that little ditty jog your memory?" he asked.

"Go to hell! You're the fucking piggy, Russell!"

"You'll be glad to hear that the song has nine more verses just like that one. Let's try it again."

Russell tapped the sword on the coffee table.

"Wait! I don't care what you take out of my computer. The password is MontanaMissy. Capital M on Montana and Missy."

"Nello, go check it out."

He walked into an office on the other side of the dining room. Two minutes later he returned. "It didn't work."

Russell tapped his sword again.

"How did you spell Missy?" I asked.

Russell nodded.

"M-i-s-s-i-e," Nello replied.

"It's M-i-s-s-y," Rose said.

A minute later we heard Nello yell, "Bingo!"

"Keep an eye on them," Russell said to Ziggy, and walked into the office.

"How is the arm?" I asked Ziggy.

"Better than your dead phone. But the good news is that I expect the two of you to be joined together in eternal cyberspace within the hour."

Rose looked like she was going into shock. I wished that she had shown me how to open her Uzi-toting tray table on the off chance that I could talk the boys into a game of musical chairs upon Russell's return.

"How do you fit into this crew, Ziggy?" I asked. "Are you the Select Sentinel employee of the month?"

"I'm not telling you anything," he replied.

"Why not? If I'm on my way to eternal cyberspace, who am I going to tell?"

"He runs Russell's Wilkes-Barre car dealership," Rose said.

"Shut up, bitch, or I'll stomp on your foot." Ziggy slid across the leather couch toward Rose, raising his foot into a stomping position.

"I'll bet the security cameras in the Cultural Center got a pretty good shot of your face earlier in the evening. I'd say that makes you a big liability to Russell right now," I said.

"I've got a pretty good shot at your face right now, Duffy." Ziggy positioned his gun six inches in front of my nose.

"That's enough, Ziggy," Russell said from the dining room, walking toward us. "Give me the gun."

Ziggy handed the gun to Russell. "I was just scaring him."

"Ziggy's actually a very nice man. He'd never shoot anyone in the face at close range." Russell turned to Rose, held the gun six inches from her nose and pulled the trigger. Her head flew backwards, sliding the Tootsie Roll chair at least three feet. "But I would."

Nello ran into the living room. "What the hell!"

"Breaking up is hard to do, Nello," said Russell. "Her computer won't be revealing any secrets, and neither will Rose."

Russell brought the gun to bear on me. I knew he'd be pulling the trigger any second if I didn't give him a reason to keep me alive.

"Russell, before you do that, I've got to find out if Nello gets promoted to local drug kingpin, or if he joins his ex-girlfriend in the family plot."

"What do you know about the local drug business?" Russell asked.

"I know that you did more than take Buzzy's life, you also took his business. In fact, you used that business to bankroll your first dealership, and probably use the dealership to launder the drug money.

"But you'll have to retire to some secluded island after what went down tonight. The question is whether you entrust your operation to Nello, knowing that he's seen you commit murder and could be a major loose end if you don't make it out of the country, or if you get extradited at some point down the line," I said.

"Don't listen to him. He's just stalling to keep himself alive," Nello said.

"Do you know what my dad's been up to while we've been at band practice? He's been tailing Nello. Scranton PD made him a deputy, and he's been in a three man rotation doing a 24-hour surveillance. I could probably give you a better accounting of his whereabouts over the past week than he could," I said.

"That's bullshit. Nobody tailed me," he said.

"I even took a shift when you had your meeting at Carley's. Although, I was disappointed that you didn't actually attend the stockholder's meeting this morning. Sitting in a truck a half block away just isn't the same thing."

"No, it isn't," said Russell.

"Russell, do you really think a guy who can't figure out that he's being tailed constantly will make the right choices as your replacement? Did you see the look on his face when you shot his girlfriend and he yelled at you?" I asked.

Russell slowly walked around the couch to where Nello was standing. Ziggy looked uncomfortable not being able to see what was happening behind him, so he stood up and moved in front of the window to the backyard, where Russell had been standing. Since he no longer had his gun, Ziggy picked up the sword.

"Nello, Nello, Nello," Russell said. "Didn't you learn anything from our talks about keeping layers of insulation between yourself and everyone who gets his hands dirty?"

"This is all bullshit. He's just trying to start trouble to save his own skin."

I said, "Nello, did you tell Russell about our conversation in Carley's last weekend? That's how I found out about the stockholder's meeting. Nello actually caught me, and accused me of listening in. But then he just told you that he had no idea he was being tailed. Definitely not the level of consistency you want in a managerial candidate, Russell."

Nello tried making a run for the office door, but Russell fired before he completed his first step. The bullet hit him in the side of the head, and propelled him into a dining room chair.

"Russell lookout!" I yelled. "Captain Jack Sparrow is about to attack!"

Russell looked at Ziggy holding the sword and said, "What do you think you're doing with my conductor's baton?"

"Just getting your back in case Nello tried anything."

"Ziggy's worried that you'll realize he can't be of any use to you now that the cops have his face on the Cultural Center security video," I said.

"Shut up, Duffy. I should have killed you on Van Brunt Street," Ziggy said.

"Instead, you fell for the *chase the rock noise in the wrong direction* trick. That's just the kind of skill set that Russell's looking for to help with his getaway. And, don't worry about that lead slug in your arm when you're walking through airport security. Tell them you ate a lot of paint chips as a kid. Once they get to know you I'm sure they'll buy it," I said.

Ziggy ran toward me with the sword cocked in the run-through position. Russell shot him in the neck, and he was mercifully quiet as he bled out.

"I saved the next one just for you, Duffy."

"How about a last cigarette for your soon-to-be ex-band mate?" I asked.

"You don't smoke."

"Then let's just call it a last request. I don't want to go off to the hereafter scratching my head. Would you answer a few questions for me?"

"Since you're playing the band mate card, and you seem to have some insights into my current situation, I'll grant your request. What would you like to know?"

"Why did you kill Aunt Megan?"

"She came up with the idea of talking about the misconstrued lyrics in *Parkers Luna Sea*. Megan told Eli that the paper was going to make a special insert out of the story. I couldn't let all of Scranton apply the same logic that you used to figure things out."

"So you set up one of her Vietnam War Vets to take the fall?" I asked.

"You'd be surprised how easy it is to match up classic vehicles when you own a few dealerships."

"What made you kill Louie when you did?"

"I've been using Select Sentinel to do product distribution for the past five years. They needed an infusion of clean cash from a reputable person with standing in the community. So I talked Nello into seducing Rose and getting her to invest."

"So, why kill Louie?"

"In spite of their constant fighting and bitter divorce, Louie still had feelings for Rose. He told me that he used to drive past Rose's house when he was feeling lonely, and noticed that her handyman had regular sleepovers. The band had a practice at Eddie's house just before Christmas, and went to the Bar Chord afterwards. Louie went into the restroom to take a piss and nearly gagged from the smell. It was probably Paulie; he eats those pickled eggs all day. Anyway, Louie opened the window to get some air, and saw me talking to Nello in the rear parking lot."

"Did he chase you down in the lot?"

"He came to my Scranton dealership the next day acting very cagey. He told me that he'd been thinking about the *tender's prune* and just figured out that the tender took the clippings home with him."

"That's a bit cryptic. How could you be sure he was on to you?" I asked.

"When Louie went back into the bar after missing me in the lot, he showed Bongo a picture of Nello that he took on his phone outside of Rose's place. Bongo said he met Nello at a party at his old dealer's house. Louie asked if Bongo had any pictures of his old dealer and they took a ride up to his trailer."

"And?"

"And the dealer in the picture is lying next to your right foot. I took Bongo out the night Louie came to my office, and he told me everything after I got him loaded." Russell looked at his watch. "So, I got the original lyrics to *Parkers Luna Sea* from Louie's safe, and took Bongo's picture collection."

"How did you get Bongo to drive to Nay Aug in the snowstorm?"

"I told him that our conversation about Buzzy at the Ranger Room made me cruise through the park on my way home. I said that I skidded off the road, got stuck, and would pay him $100 to pull me out with his truck. When he finished, I gave him a capsule that I described as the newest version of Ecstasy on the market, and if he'd try it out for me that night I'd give him 20 hits at the next band practice. Ziggy took care of the rest. Now it's time for *me* to take care of one last detail before retiring to Margaritaville."

"Russell, I can't die in an Eileen Gray chair. My dad is as Irish as Paddy's pig. I'd much rather my crime scene photos have a bottle green background. If you'd move me three hops to the left I'll be able to find the Irish section of heaven a lot sooner."

"This band mate thing is wearing thin, Duffy. Don't try anything or I'll pose you on the toilet."

Russell stuck the gun under my chin, lifted me out of the chair, and tossed me onto the couch. This gave me a straight on view of the window to the backyard. I discreetly nodded toward the window when I knew Russell was looking.

"I'm not buying that you're trying to signal someone outside," Russell said.

"I wasn't signaling. I was bowing my head to say a final prayer."

"Bullshit! I heard you carping about having to go to church with your father at band practice last Sunday."

He moved quickly to the wall to my left and slowly made his way toward the window. I put my duct taped hands on top of the tray and pushed down, hoping it would release Rose's Uzi. But nothing happened.

Russell flipped a switch and the backyard illuminated the winter wonderland. He angled his head to see around the pyramid pool cover. I pushed my hands against the side of the couch's arm and saw a silver button just below the seat cushion. I'd either be getting a fighting chance or reclined legs en route to the Pearly Gates. I knuckled the button.

The tray quietly flew open and the Uzi immediately popped up to my right, poised for action on a ball socket. I dropped my right shoulder, allowed my head to flop over to the far side of the gun stock for aiming purposes, and guided it toward Russell.

Looking out the window he said, "There's nobody here."

"Oh yeah?" In my best Tony Montana accent I said, "Say

hello to my little friend."

Russell got off a single shot from 35 feet before my little friend drove him through the window and onto the snow covered deck.

Chapter 33

I woke up just after 10:00 AM and noticed that Kelly's side of the bed was made. When I returned from the crime scene last night she took a sleepy-eyed stab at playing the groupie, like we had discussed moments before my phone was murdered. It was clear that neither of us was up for it at 4:00 AM.

I stretched to a standing position, and was on my way to the bathroom when I spotted a note on top of my wallet on the dresser. It said: *I borrowed Patrick's car to return Becky's sweater. He said it was OK and gave me directions last night. See you soon. Love, Kelly.*

After a quick shower and shave I called my parents' room. Dad answered.

"It didn't take long for you to get back to your rock star sleeping schedule."

"I didn't get out of Rose's house until 3:30. Did anybody fill you in on what went down?" I asked.

"Flannery called me at 8:30. What the hell were you doing walking into that place without backup or a gun?"

My brain was still in warm up mode. "All's well that ends well."

"If you consider four dead bodies *ending well* you might want to apply for a job at SWAT when we get home," he said.

"Did Flannery have anything to say that I don't already know?"

"He's in the process of getting a warrant for Russell's house and computer. He said we could ride along."

"Kelly's on her way over there right now to return Becky's

sweater."

"She's not back yet! We saw her leaving as we were walking out of the coffee shop at eight o'clock."

"I'll call you back," I said, and hung up.

Kelly's phone went to voice mail after six rings. Five minutes later Dad and I pulled out of the hotel parking lot. Saturday traffic was minimal, and Dad was able to cautiously run every red light. Neither of us talked as he focused on his driving, and I wondered if Kelly could have found Becky OD'd on the floor.

There were no signs of bodyguards as we pulled into Russell's driveway. Patrick's car was parked in front of a garage door. I rang the doorbell for two minutes before trying the door. It was locked.

I noticed a fresh set of footprints as we walked around the house, wading through snow drifts of up to two feet, trying to see into the windows. It was impossible until we reached the rear, where a set of double French doors led from a rear sitting room to the covered swimming pool behind us. There was no sign of anyone. I pounded on the back door and called Kelly's name to no avail.

After borrowing Dad's phone, I tried calling her again. I thought I could hear it ringing faintly inside the house. Dad's 64-year-old ears couldn't pick it up. While he was dialing Patrick to see if he had a key to the house, I grabbed a garden gnome poking out of the snow, and rammed its head through a pane of glass in one of the French doors.

"Geez, Jason. Do you really want to spend the next three to five years in Pennsylvania?"

I ignored him and let myself in. "Hit redial on Kelly's number."

Her purse was on a Louis XV foyer table. I ran through the first floor calling her name. When I returned to the rear sitting room Dad was finishing a call.

"Flannery's on his way. Navorocki will wait for the warrant."

"I'll take the basement, you take the second floor. There's a safe room on the far end of the gun room," I said.

The basement was quick and easy. Lots of open spaces in the ballroom and bar. A run through the party kitchen revealed no sign of a struggle. I took the elevator to the second floor, and continued calling out for Kelly. Dad waved me into the gun room.

"The safe room was open and vacant. But it looks like at least one rifle is missing from Russell's gun cabinet, and the space is between two automatic assault rifles."

"Hopefully, it's on loan to a Select Sentinel employee. Did you go through the other rooms?"

"They're clear. No sign of a struggle up here. Let's take a closer look downstairs."

In the elevator I told him about my theory that Becky may have OD'd and Kelly could have ridden in the ambulance.

"I'll call the area hospitals while you fine-tooth comb the first floor."

Ten minutes later Flannery arrived. Dad had struck out with the nearest hospitals and took a break to join our conversation. Flannery seemed unusually distant, which I mistook for sleep deprivation. He let me run through my account before speaking.

"Jason, why don't you sit down?"

"I'm fine. Tell me."

"There's something about the Society Page Slasher that we've been keeping out of the papers. He uses a serrated blade, and always carved an eye-shaped oval on a wall somewhere near his victims. I saw one next to the garage door on my way in. The task force should be here any minute."

My internal organs felt weightless. My mind raced, but no coherent thoughts formed. I swallowed hard. Dad put an arm around my shoulder and led me to a chair. A squadron of cops passed by. A few people offered to take me back to the hotel, but I declined. Eventually I wandered outside and stared at the carved eye, which was guarded by a uniformed officer. I pulled the hood up on my jacket, and kept my head down as I barreled past the press.

The cold weather snapped me out of my funk. I told myself that I was doing Kelly no good by acting like a zombie. One-by-one I sifted through every bit of information I could recall about the Society Page Slasher. It seemed very reasonable that Becky could have been a target. If the killer had access to a police scanner it's also possible that he was aware that Becky would be alone in the house.

I started crossing the street and spotted Patrick in Megan's microbus coming around the corner toward me. I pulled my hood down and he stopped.

"Get in here. I have an idea of where they might be," he said.

"Tell me!"

"Remember Annabelle Grainger – the victim who lived alone, two blocks from Russell's house?"

"That makes perfect sense. The house is vacant. If I abducted two women in broad daylight, I'd want to travel as short a distance as possible. What's the address?" I asked.

"It's on Wyoming Avenue. I don't remember the house number, but I drove past it and know where it's at."

"Take me there," I said.

Patrick put his hand on my shoulder. "Let's go get Flannery and the cavalry."

"If we tell Flannery it might take an hour to get a SWAT action approved. They can't just charge in without a warrant. Flannery's captain will want to find out if an heir might have moved in. Who knows how long the killer will keep Kelly alive?"

"It's too dangerous to go in there without backup."

"You're right, Patrick. Here's what we're going to do. You drop me off at the house. I'll circle it and see if I can spot them. You go to Russell's house and tell Flannery what I'm doing, and I'm sure they'll skip the approval process and come right over."

"That works for me, as long as you don't try pulling anything like you did last night. You're lucky we're not picking out a casket this morning. Here we are."

Patrick pulled to the curb three doors away from the victim's house. I noticed that the walk leading to the front entrance hadn't been shoveled since the last snowfall.

"Is there an alley that runs behind the house?" I asked.

"I think so."

"See you later."

Annabelle Grainger lived in a two story white Victorian house with green trim. Her front porch spanned the entire width of the house. All of the drapes were drawn except for one to the left of the front door, which was bordered in stained glass. I could see a set of stairs through the window.

I walked to the end of the block then turned right and proceeded up the hill until I reached the entrance to the alley. Rear garages and evergreen shrubs shielded my view of the back of the house until I reached a set of six steps leading into the backyard. Fresh tracks on the stairs hastened my heartbeat. All of the curtains on both floors of the house were closed.

I moved quietly through the snow, thanking God that it was neither crusty nor crunchy. A slow turn of the backdoor knob confirmed that it was locked, and an expensive deadbolt made me dismiss the possibility of using the lock picks in my wallet. The backdoor was actually on the left side, near the end of the driveway. An inspection of the cellar windows told me I wouldn't fit. However, just past the first cellar window, about a foot higher on the wall, was a hinged cast iron cover, secured by an old padlock. Since Scranton is in the heart of anthracite country, I assumed it was an old coal chute. Judging by the rust on the lock it hadn't been used for many years. The lock took two minutes to pick. I could have done it in one, but the rust slowed me down.

A hang drop down the chute and into the old coal bin (which still held about a foot of coal) left me looking like the chimneysweep in Mary Poppins. The basement was as dark as the final moments of twilight. There were no windows in the front

241

and back walls, and snow had drifted over the two windows on the far wall. I briefly considered searching for a tool that might serve as a weapon. But flashing on nearly getting killed after kicking the chair in the dark of Shopland Hall last night, I opted to head straight for the cellar steps.

Standing at the base of the stairs looking up, I considered the possibility that my coal chute entrance could have been heard, and that the Slasher could be standing on the other side of the cellar door. Eying the old wooden steps that hadn't been painted in many years, I elected to keep away from the center of the stairs to avoid squeaks. With great care, I put my weight on the first one.

"Yeowww!" screamed a brown and tan cat, as she leapt out from behind the stair.

I spun on my left heel and crouched behind a huge bag of peat moss. The cat arched her back, eyed me with suspicion, and trotted off to the darkness of the far wall. No movement was heard above me, so I made my way to the top of the stairs. At that point caution seemed pointless. If the Slasher carried a gun and was on the other side of the door, I was going to get capped no matter what I did.

Time was not on my side, so I opened the door and found myself in a small hall with a bathroom entrance on my left and a walk-in pantry on my right. I heard voices coming from the front of the house.

The pantry was just off of the kitchen. From my vantage point I could see through the kitchen and into the entrance foyer, all the way to the front door. Two steps into the kitchen revealed an entrance into a living room on the left, just beyond the kitchen. The wood laminate floor was new and quiet. My vantage point into the living room from a 45 degree angle revealed a sliver of Becky sitting on a blue upholstered chair with her hands folded in her lap. She faced the Slasher, who sat with his back to the wall in front of me. All I could see of him was a hand holding the barrel of an automatic weapon whose butt was resting on the floor. The room was done in a southwestern motif, with murals of Indians on the walls.

I leaned forward a bit to see more of the room and was instantly shocked. Kelly stood stark naked with her hands and feet tied behind her, around a two-foot wide totem pole that extended from floor to ceiling. My instincts told me to charge into the room and lunge for the gun. But the rational side of my brain told me that I'd never get to him in time, and that Kelly would be shot before my blood had a chance to stain the sand colored parquet floor.

I needed a weapon and thought it reasonable that Annabelle Grainger had some type of gun stashed nearby. The kitchen took up half of the width of the house and a bedroom took up the other half. Rather than run the risk of being heard opening drawers in the kitchen, I started in the bedroom looking in night tables and dresser drawers. It was obvious that this was Annabelle's bedroom. At the far end of the dresser was a walk-in closet that illuminated when the door opened. I hoped to find a rifle leaning against one of the walls, but there was none. Clothes hung from the three walls of the closet; dresses on the right, skirts and blouses on the left, and evening gowns nearly reaching the floor in the middle.

A footstep on laminate caused me to grab the closet door handle and close it as quickly and quietly as possible. I didn't have time to MacGyver a weapon out of a coat hanger, so I moved behind the evening gowns and crouched as low as I could go. Something against the rear wall poked me in the back as I attempted to squat lower.

Suddenly, the door opened. I felt a vacuum and saw the evening gowns in front of me billow forward. I heard a footfall followed by a loud unnatural squeak.

"Humf," said the Slasher.

A shorter version of the squeak occurred, and a red rubber mouse came to rest a few inches from my foot. The door closed and the lights went out.

I reached behind me to find out what was poking me in the back and felt a door lock. Just below the lock was a recessed handle. I pushed it an inch and realized it opened into the living room. An idea formed.

After closing the hidden panel, I waited until I heard a male voice in the living room. With toy mouse in hand, I opened the closet door and sidearmed the mouse through the bedroom, through the kitchen, and into a cabinet door below the sink, squeaking on impact. The noise got an immediate response.

I pulled the closet door and hidden panel closed behind me as I entered the living room with a finger to my lips. The women got the message. I ran behind the totem pole and started untying Kelly's hands.

"Act like you're still tied up," I whispered. "If he gets close enough, smack him in the balls."

Becky held her fists on top of her chest and trembled. I couldn't imagine why she wasn't tied up like Kelly. Before I could start on the rope that held Kelly's feet I saw the barrel of the gun in the doorway, and ducked behind the totem pole.

The Slasher didn't say a word as he strode into the room. The parquet floor told me he was heading straight for Kelly.

"It's that time," he said in a familiar voice.

My brain didn't have a chance to make the connection before I heard the unmistakable sound of a switchblade flying open.

I reached for the barrel of the rifle, heard him make a guttural sound, and knew that Kelly had connected with the low hanging fruit. He still had a firm grip on the gunstock. The knife hit the floor before I looked at the Slasher's face and saw Eli Shapiro with Charlie Manson's eyes flashing orbs of madness.

I clamped my right hand on the stock and a mighty tug-of-war ensued. I had age and conditioning on my side. He had the unnatural strength of a psychopath in full manic mode going for him.

Eli did a drop-step and yanked hard to his right. I sent a floor lamp with a Sitting Bull shade to the happy hunting ground. He tried to bring the stock up into my face as I leaned forward, but I bent my knees and pulled the weapon and Eli into a backward roll. All four hands remained on the rifle as we pulled ourselves up to a standing position. Becky picked up the knife and danced around us like a referee at a boxing match.

Eli let go with one hand and reached behind his back. I saw a pistol at the last instant and managed to hook my thumb around his wrist to keep it from pointing at me for the moment. But my thumb strength would be no match for Eli's adrenaline addled arm.

Becky tossed me the switchblade just as my thumb gave way. I snatched it out of the air and across Eli's throat in one motion, causing a Carotid artery spurt to drench me in blood. Eli let go of both weapons and fell onto his back as his hands tried to stop the exsanguination process.

Becky put a palm against the side of his face and Eli looked into her eyes. "Go join Russell, Louie, Bongo, and Buzzy. The rest of the band will be along in a few decades."

Eli closed his eyes and stopped fighting death.

She continued to kneel next to Eli while I untied Kelly's feet then gave her a hug.

"I'm so sorry, Kelly," I said.

"Where's my bra? I'm freezing."

"He put your clothes on the other side of the couch," Becky said.

As she was pulling her sweater over her head a battering ram smashed the front door open. Flannery, Navorocki, and Dad rushed into the living room as Kelly pulled up her red panties.

Dad did an immediate 180 degree pivot and said, "Jesus, Mary, and Joseph."

Chapter 34

Kelly was in a deep sleep when I woke up at 7:00 Sunday morning. Even though Eli died in the early afternoon, we didn't get out of the police station until 9:00 PM. After what Kelly had been through, I made it clear that I wanted to accompany her on a flight home this afternoon. The police took thorough statements on our involvement with the Shapiro family, and said they would get back to me on my departure request. Kelly got checked out at a local hospital while I answered 100 questions.

Before I got out of bed I wondered if Dad would be waking us up to go to church. It turned out that I was correct in assuming he'd be avoiding eye contact with Kelly for a while.

For the next five minutes I worried that Kelly might suffer from post traumatic stress. She told me when we moved in together that her wild upbringing prepared her for any dangers that might come from living with a PI. But I doubted that anything could have prepared her for yesterday's close call. I hoped that my experience as a counselor would serve me well if she showed signs of serious psychological damage. A set of fingernails inching their way up my thigh told me that she made it through the ordeal just fine.

"Aren't you the girl who sat in the fifth row wearing a mini-dress, cut so low that my guitar strings pointed at the ceiling all night?"

"I was hoping maybe you'd let me play with your guitar stand after the show. But you just ran off before we could hook up."

"Well I'm here now, and would love to play Stairway to Heaven for you."

"Then put some Led in your Zeppelin and show me what you've got."

Sometimes it's best to let therapy take its own course.

Mom called at 9:00 to say we were meeting Patrick and Flannery for breakfast at a restaurant called The Barrel on 307, not far from his house. The four of us arrived at 11:00 and, even though the rest of the restaurant was packed, we were shown to a rear dining room where Patrick and Flannery were the only occupants.

"Somebody's getting the rock star treatment today," I said.

"I'm a regular," Patrick replied.

Dad held up a newspaper that was covered in stories about the Shapiros, and our role in taking them down. "I'm sure they're very proud of you."

"We all are, Patrick," said Mom.

"I know I wouldn't be here if it wasn't for you," Kelly said, and gave him a hug.

"Let's just sit down and have a nice breakfast. The food here is amazing. Flannery can fill us in on what's happening after we order."

Our waitress was so excited she could barely write. As soon as she left we all looked at Flannery.

"There won't be a need for endless depositions since all of the perps are dead. So, the captain approved everyone flying back to San Diego today, on one condition. We need to find out from Kelly if Eli gave a reason why he became the Society Page Slasher."

Kelly looked at each one of us at the table before speaking. "It was clear to me that both Eli and Becky knew all along that Russell murdered the band members and Megan. Eli always believed that Becky loved him, but couldn't resist the allure of Russell's money. He started killing Society Page women to make Becky wish she was no longer a part of that crowd.

"Just before Jason arrived he told her that he believed she

247

was enamored with Russell's willingness to kill for her, and that he needed to prove his love in a similar fashion. Becky denied it. But Eli pointed out that her inaction after Buzzy, Megan, Louie, and Bongo spoke volumes to him about what it would take to finally win her love," Kelly said.

"So he thought he was going to win her over. Is that why he didn't tie her up?" asked Flannery.

"He also told her he'd slit my throat if she made any attempt to run."

"Did he explain why he made you strip before tying you to the totem pole?" Flannery asked.

"He said that the totem pole was Russell and I was Becky at 25. He told her that she was nothing more than a sex toy to Russell, but that she'd be his entire world if she gave herself over to him. He also said that the old Becky would die soon."

Dad looked very uncomfortable. He turned to Flannery and asked, "What's going to happen to Select Sentinel and the Conservators of Justice?"

"There's going to be a full investigation of both organizations, headed up by yours truly."

"Did you get a chance to look at Rose's computer yet?" I asked.

"It showed that Nello Lapaglia was recommended to head up Select Sentinel by Conservators of Justice Vice President, Ziggy Rolenski."

"Was that the guy who tried to shoot me?" Dad asked.

"One and the same. He was also the manager of Russell's Wilkes-Barre car lot, and top dog in his drug business. We brought the DEA in last night. They're executing warrants on ten properties today."

"Was there any sign of Becky being involved in the drug business?" Kelly asked.

"It's too early to say, but I don't think so. Russell was obsessive about maintaining layers of insulation between himself and the drug trade. I'd be surprised if he even laid eyes on a drug in years."

Patrick and I exchanged knowing looks.

"What?" Flannery asked.

"Our food's here," said Patrick.

It was every bit as delicious as advertised. Patrick received a call as we finished.

"It's Eddie. I'm going to take it outside." Five minutes later he returned. His efforts to suppress a smile were unsuccessful.

"Let it out, Patrick," Mom said, "you're going to shoot an aneurism if you keep trying to stifle the news."

"Eddie just told me that Rose named Louie as her sole beneficiary."

"Does that mean you'll end up with the six million dollars from the insurance company?" I asked.

"That's exactly what it means. I was Louie's sole beneficiary. Up until now it meant that I inherited a stack of bills and a house that may or may not cover them. I guess I don't have to worry about that anymore."

"I took a look at Louie's house with Flannery one day," said Dad. "Why don't you start by moving in there? Then you can plan your life of leisure."

"Are you kidding? I'm in enough hot water with Megan as it is. I could never move away from a lifetime of memories."

"You could afford a lifetime of cruises with six mil," said Dad.

"I'll probably end up giving most of it to Megan's favorite charities, over time."

Dad looked like he was about to start arguing when Mom jumped in. "I think that's wonderful, Patrick. Although I do hope that you save enough so that you can come out and visit your California family once in a while."

"You can bet on that one, Molly."

We said goodbye to Patrick and Flannery in the parking lot. We then returned to the hotel to pack. Ten minutes into the process Dad called and asked me to come to his suite to pick up a few of my things that I had left the day Kelly and Mom arrived.

Before I could pick up the bundle on my old bed he asked, "Do you think Patrick has a screw loose, talking about giving away all of that money?"

"I'm sure a lot of people might think so. But this case taught me that while the facts never change, perception of the facts can change dramatically. I checked out Patrick's case files one afternoon while he was napping. He's a damn good investigator. Yet for forty years Russell ran a huge drug business under his nose, while Eli yearned to rekindle his affair with Becky." I said.

"Maybe he's not as sharp as you think."

"Maybe another investigator that I respect thought his brother stabbed him in the back when, in fact, he was doing everything in his power to help him come home alive." Dad tried to butt in, but I wouldn't let him. "He risked his eternal relationship with his beloved Megan to save his brother's life, and hopefully avoided the second half of the Duffy-Pennamite War."

Dad's never been one to take criticism without a fight. When the defense isn't working it's time to counterattack.

"So, what's the Jason Duffy takeaway from all of this? Do you think that girlfriend of yours showed you enough to merit a ring?"

I still have scars on my back from being down this bullying road with Dad last summer. I picked up my bundle of clothes, walked to the door, turned and said, "In the sage words of Louie's Uncle Connie - fuckifiknow."

I felt like I won our little battle for about two minutes. But that question followed me all the way home to San Diego, like an obsessive-compulsive stalker.

ACKNOWLEDGEMENTS

I appreciate the assistance I received from the following people: Pat Brazill, R. Glenn Cooper, Craig Correll, Kimberly Escobar, Carol Gillern, Pat Gillern, Jason D. Helman, Marie Lumsden, Larry Moss, Maryann & Mike Nebraski, Lou Refice, Donna Riviello, Vince Shumski, and Robbie Walsh. Your contributions and expertise helped bring this novel to life.

OTHER ROCK & ROLL MYSTERY NOVELS
by RJ McDonnell

Rock & Roll Homicide:

Jason Duffy's first murder case could easily be his last. Hired by the widow of a slain rock star, he quickly learns about an unhealthy tie between the victim's recording company and the Russian Mafia. But his suspect list is not limited to the bent-noses of the Borscht Belt.

Midwest Book Review: "A brilliantly told tale of sex, drugs, rock & roll, and the Mob."

Beverly Ford, 20-year veteran Boston Herald crime beat writer: "As an avid reader, I've found McDonnell to be one of the most engaging, enjoyable, and funniest writers I've come across in a long, long time."

BookPleasures.com: "RJ McDonnell's enjoyable style is somewhere between Carl Hiaasen's in *Basket Case* and Michael Connelly's in *Chasing the Dime*."

Paper and ebook copies available through Amazon and www. rjmcdonnell.com.

Rock & Roll Rip-Off:

Premier Book Awards: 2010 Mystery/Thriller of the Year

Jason Duffy thought he had accepted a routine burglary case when a career studio musician hired him to recover a stolen memorabilia collection. But Jason quickly finds himself at the top of a hit list that has nothing to do with The Top 40 and everything to do with a table for one at the San Diego Coroner's Office.

Once again, Jason's staff of former outpatient mental health clients contributes a large measure of humor to this musical mystery novel. He reluctantly adds to his payroll a paranoid security expert who fancies himself as *King of the Improv*.

Compounding his troubles, Jason must deal with major girlfriend issues after his father meddles in his relationship with Kelly. Female readers are treated to a peek at the unique logic men apply to crises of the heart.

Paper and ebook copies available through Amazon and www. rjmcdonnell.com.

The Concert Killer:

A religious fanatic serial killer tries to shut down the concert industry. A group of independent concert promoters hire private investigator Jason Duffy and his staff of former outpatient mental health clients to catch him. The killer believes that God rewards His favorites with the most money, and keeps score of his victims on the back of a dollar bill. Jason uses his background as a counselor and club musician to battle his cleverest and most twisted adversary ever.

Besides offering readers a backstage pass to the music industry, *The Concert Killer* brings to light a potentially catastrophic danger that few have ever considered.

Paper and ebook copies available through Amazon and www. rjmcdonnell.com.

www.ingramcontent.com/pod-product-compliance
Lightning Source LLC
Chambersburg PA
CBHW070914180626
46817CB00003B/1052